THE HONEY SIEGE

GIL BUHET

Translated from the French
LE CHEVALIER PIERROT
by Geoffrey Sainsbury

PENGUIN BOOKS

Penguin Books Ltd, Harmondsworth, Middlesex
AUSTRALIA: Penguin Books Pty Ltd, 762 Whitehorse Road,
Mitcham, Victoria

—

Le Chevalier Pierrot first published 1952
This translation first published by Jonathan Cape 1953
Published in Penguin Books 1958

Made and printed in Great Britain
by Richard Clay & Company, Ltd,
Bungay, Suffolk

TO CLAUDE BONCOMPAIN

How well I remember that evening when, pacing up and down my room, you told me the story of the Honey Siege.

We were to have written it together. For reasons known only to us that was not to be, and at the first halt you gave me the signal to carry on alone.

Now the work is done, and I bring it to you with just that little twinge of trepidation which we used to feel as students when we laid our essays on the Master's desk.

G. B.

PART ONE

ONE

JUST as the alarm clock was about to ring, M. Grillon forestalled it.

Each morning began like that, with a victory of human punctuality over machinery.

Comforted by this thought, the schoolmaster dragged his thin, hairy legs from under the bedclothes and walked over to the window.

He threw it open to air the room, standing there for a minute to enjoy the freshness of the morning. Autumn was well advanced, but only by the calendar. October was going out in a blaze of sunshine. Outside, the light was so gay and so pure that it made everything look as brightly coloured as in the *Images d'Épinal*.

M. Déodat Grillon took off his nightshirt, rose on his toes, then bent his knees, breathing deeply. This he did ten times, counting out loud.

And each time, as he bent them, his knee-joints creaked.

The deep breathing was of course the important part. It said so in chapter two of the *Manual of Hygiene*. He wasn't a man to enjoin principles upon others which he did not observe himself. His precepts weren't always very original, like 'a place for everything and everything in its place', which happened to be one of his favourites. He carried that one out too, and when he went to shave he could have put his hand on his shaving-brush blindfold. A methodical man, pernickety even, as is so often the case with a man who lives alone.

Going downstairs to the classroom, the schoolmaster opened all the windows wide. His pupils must learn to breathe too. The hands of the clock above his desk were at ten minutes to seven, and he checked their accuracy by the watch in his waistcoat pocket. With a sweeping glance he satisfied himself that everything was in order, then, picking up a piece of chalk, he wrote up on the blackboard the problem that he had composed the previous night before going to sleep.

Work out the interior volume of a beehive with a conical top whose external diameter is 1·25 metres and whose height is 60 centimetres at the circumference and 1 metre in the middle, the walls being 32 millimetres thick.

Writing on the blackboard is an art in itself. He looked approvingly at his upstrokes and downstrokes, clapped his hands to remove the chalk, then retraced his steps up the well-polished, beeswaxed stairs.

'Georget,' he called.

He tapped four times on the door, being eventually answered by a yawn from within.

'Georget ... Come on, Sonny; it's time to get up,' he said in the gentle voice that, since the death of his wife, he had adopted for speaking to his son.

'Thanks, Dad.'

'Slept well?'

'Yes, Dad. And you?'

There was nothing spontaneous about this dialogue. Each day had to begin with it. M. Grillon stood for a while on the landing, listening to the sound of the boy's bare feet on the tiled floor, the creak of the shutters as they were thrown open, the splashing of water. Reassured, he went down to get the breakfast ready. Here, too, each detail was a matter of routine, even of ritual. Yesterday's milk was kept in the cool cupboard under the sink, an enamel coffee-pot stood proudly in the middle of the dresser, while on the second shelf were two bowls, the sugar-basin, and the table napkins. Above them was a long row of pots of honey. From a drawer M. Grillon took a knife and a couple of tablespoons. Finally he lit the gas with his lighter – a souvenir of the trenches, made from a brass cartridge case.

It was never otherwise. Each movement was woven into a pattern that was rarely departed from. To preserve his peace of mind he had, since his wife's death, become a slave to habit. Yet he hated it, hated the barren existence to which it condemned him, a closed circle from which there was no escape. Not even during the holidays. For he was rather like a monk who, though he had lost his faith, was unable to break away from the mode of life he had once and for all adopted.

If there was no room for the passions in such a life, there was at least room for a hobby. M. Déodat kept bees, and they brought light into his day and took his mind off himself. It might almost be said that he loved them. At any rate the sight of them busily at work, guided only by their instinct, was enough to persuade him that the world was an orderly and harmonious creation – and so was his own life.

The air was cool and keen, but so tempting was the early sunshine that he actually deviated from October custom to the extent of opening the kitchen window. Yes, it might have been a real spring morning. M. Grillon's garden, already brown with fallen leaves, was a large rectangle traversed by a single path which led to the beehives. The latter were all turned to face the same way, chosen with the utmost care. The north was too cold, the south too warm, sometimes tempting bees out to their death when the air was still chilly. The west exposed them to driving rain and to the rays of the setting sun.

So Déodat Grillon's bees faced east, and they were surrounded by plants intended to make the garden a little paradise for them – sainfoin, verbena, snapdragon, jasmine, saponaria, and phlox. The hedge was of white thorn, and the wall was covered with wistaria. A clump of Japanese lilacs offered their treacly mauve flowers for well-nigh half the year. The trees were limes and acacias, but M. Grillon kept their branches low so that swarms could easily be captured. Finally he had arranged a supply of running water which trickled gently over some brushwood near the hives, so that the bees could drink.

Watching them, he was often tempted to philosophize.

'What an object lesson to man!' was one of his most frequent observations.

But the siren of the quarry interrupted his reverie. It was answered by another, nearer – that of the distillery. It was seven o'clock.

M. Grillon was in the act of spreading a thick layer of honey on a second piece of bread when he heard a buzz. After a moment's hesitation, a bee flew in and alighted on his knife.

He sat still, gazing in astonishment. It was a fine worker bee, almost black, with grey down on its thorax. It set to work busily, gorging itself with honey.

'There's one that's been taken in by the weather,' thought M. Grillon. 'Thinks the spring's come round again, no doubt.'

Looking very busy and self-important, the bee flew back into the garden, and it was not till M. Grillon was spreading the fourth piece of bread – there were always two for him and two for Georget – that it came back again, accompanied by five or six others whom it had obviously gone off to fetch.

This time Déodat Grillon was so surprised that he forgot all about the spirit-lamp, and the milk, seizing the opportunity, boiled over, spreading over the oilcloth and soaking the slices of bread. It even dripped complacently over the edge of the table on to the school-master's slippers.

The bees left, only to reappear shortly afterwards in still larger numbers. Having discovered the pot of honey, they seemed determined to recapture its contents to the last drop.

M. Grillon could hardly believe his eyes.

He had lagged the hives so that they should provide warm winter quarters. Only two days previously he had stocked them up with winter food carefully weighed out – five kilos of honey to each and five litres of a special syrup he made himself, following a recipe he had read somewhere, consisting of grape-juice, pears, dried figs, and aromatic plants; it was much better, he maintained, than the ordinary sugar with which so many bee-keepers fed their hives in winter.

'My dear creatures, have you taken leave of your senses? We're within a week of All Saints' Day. Think what you're doing. The morning air will be the death of you.'

But the bees' only response was to buzz more busily than ever as they hovered in a velvety halo round the pot or attacked the sodden slices of bread-and-honey lying in the spilt milk.

Something must be wrong. Déodat felt sure of it. He was assailed by an unreasoning anxiety such as comes to mothers when their children are threatened by mishap. Leaving the kitchen, he strode down the garden path.

Ranavalo came out of her kennel, yawned, stretched herself, then gambolled round Déodat to bid him welcome. A bitch with a yellow-ish coat, a cross between a cocker spaniel and a *bleu d'Auvergne*. When she ran she seemed all feet and ears.

To her astonishment, M. Grillon didn't stop to pat her, but merely growled:

'Lie down, Ralo ...'

Disconcerted, she crept back into the kennel, from which she studied her master with woeful eyes – they were naturally pathetic – as much as to say:

'What have I done wrong this time?'

But the schoolmaster took no notice. With long strides, he made straight for the hives.

It would be untrue to say that Georget Grillon was not fond of his father, but there are limits to the affection that can be felt for a father who is also one's schoolmaster, a just schoolmaster, but a somewhat sad one, and so anxious to show no favouritism that he was inclined to be stricter with his son than with any of the others.

'Grillon,' he would say, 'the next time I catch you talking to your neighbour, I'll put you outside. Do you hear me?'

And Georget would answer pitifully:

'*Oui, Monsieur.*'

Speaking to his schoolfellows, he called his father by the nickname they all used, Piquet. It wasn't inapt, for M. Grillon was certainly rather a stick, but it never even occurred to Georget that he was being disrespectful.

At home their lives were lived on two different levels.

M. Grillon had his books, his pupils' exercises to correct, his studies in the science of apiculture. His thoughts often wandered into the past, and if he nursed any day-dreams they were not the kind of thing you could discuss with a child. He certainly loved his son, but awkwardly, without knowing how to show it, and the boy suffered from being boxed up with a man who was melancholy and preoccupied. Any real family feeling was obtained from his schoolmates. Full of life and eagerness, his thoughts were all focused on the future.

Since his mother's death there had been no gaiety in the house. The midday meal was taken at the Auberge Daranluz, where they sat facing each other ceremoniously, looking much more like master and pupil than father and son, while at the tables round them sat quarry-men and cork-cutters. Supper they took at home. It consisted of tinned foods and soups made from packets. Between his lessons and his homework, Georget did the shopping or washed up the dishes. Sometimes he even had to sweep out the classroom, when Maria, the servant at the inn, was too busy to come and do it.

From his mother he had inherited a round face with chubby cheeks and a nose which 'bayed to the moon'. He was short but agile. With a tall father as an example, his shortness was his despair. Any resemblance between the man of fifty and the boy of thirteen was confined to a taste for high-sounding phrases. They both, when they got going, liked the sound of their own voices.

That morning, when Georget opened the kitchen door, he found the room swarming with bees. His habit of gesticulating had earned him many a sting, and he was thoroughly mistrustful of these creatures which his father knew so well how to manage. Quickly he shut the door again and, not knowing what to do with himself, went down to the classroom. Once again Maria had failed to turn up. Stoically, Georget fetched the broom and started to do her work for her. Anyhow, it was better than nothing. He hated doing nothing. Besides, the girl was rather a pal of his and it would save her a scolding at lunch-time. For at the Auberge Daranluz it was she who waited on them. She was a foundling, owned by nobody, but more or less at everybody's beck and call.

Passing in front of the blackboard, he saw the problem which had been set for the class.

'Here's a bit of luck,' he thought. 'I can swot that up before-hand.'

He had no thought of stealing a march on the others. In any case it wouldn't have been any good. He was never top of the class, not even in recitation. His father was too anxious to prove his impartiality.

Snatching up his arithmetic book, Georget soon found the right formula and scribbled it on a bit of blotting-paper, which he stuffed into his pocket, delighted to think of the service which he would presently be able to render to the community.

Hungry, he went up to the loft for some apples.

Déodat always approached a hive from behind, so as not to alarm his little friends. The hives were screened from the bustle of the world by some gooseberry and black-currant bushes, and the whole width of the garden stretched between them and the school yard, which echoed with shrill voices during the morning break.

Five of the hives were plunged in the stillness of hibernation. The sixth, a big one of twenty frames, of which the schoolmaster was justly proud, was the scene of extraordinary agitation.

The entrance was black with worker bees which hurried in and out as busily as when the season was at its height, while a small swarm flew frantically round and round over the roof.

'They've gone crazy,' muttered the schoolmaster, with a worried look on his face. 'They've gone completely crazy.'

It was obvious that the bees were suffering from something, but he was at a loss to know what. This uncalled-for hum of wings was quite unlike that which preceded swarming and which he liked to call *le chant du départ*. It was more like a hymn of revolt. His ear was attuned to their language; he couldn't be mistaken. He stood there, hesitating, reluctant to open the hive with a slight northerly breeze blowing.

Besides, he never violated the privacy of his little friends without first putting them in a good temper with a ration of syrup, like bribing children with sweets. Not until that was done could he disturb them without wearing either mask or gloves or stupefying them with smoke, only whispering to them with reassuring words and moving with a cautious gravity that made him look like some priest performing a sacrament.

Time was running out, however. He would never be able to give his attention to his class with such a load on his mind. When he went to open the hive, he found the hooks had not been replaced. Such negligence could never be imputed to him. The horrible suspicion dawned on him. Had someone been at the hive during the night?

Déodat Grillon looked round him, bewildered, as though the thief might still be there, lurking behind the gooseberry bushes. Then, looking down, he saw footmarks in the soil in front of the hive. They were short and narrow, left by small, bare feet. Farther off, traces of sabots crossed the cabbage-patch.

Fearing the worst, he opened the hive with trembling hands. What he saw made him groan with pain and indignation. The hive had been ransacked. A clumsy hand had wrenched the combs out of their frames and even upset the bowl of syrup, leaving nothing for the bees but famine.

Suddenly, as though the bees considered M. Grillon responsible for their plight, they went for him, stinging him furiously on the hands and face. He took to flight, pursued by an angry horde. His fingers swelled. The palm of his right hand became hard as wood. His face was burning. But the physical pain was as nothing compared to his mental distress. What a dirty trick! What sacrilege!

Breakfast was forgotten. He made straight for the classroom.

'The wretches!' he cried. 'To do a thing like that to them! To do a thing like that to me!'

And for the first time in his life M. Déodat Grillon vowed vengeance on his pupils.

An apple is much more likely to create appetite than to assuage it, particularly on an empty stomach. Racked by hunger, Georget returned to the kitchen, to find the table in an unholy mess, the spirit lamp still burning.

Seized by anxiety, he ran out into the garden, looking for his father. He didn't like to shout for him. Having often nursed the idea of running away himself, he occasionally dreamt that his father had abandoned him. Had he simply gone off into the unknown? But why should he? And whom would he go with?

He caught sight of him standing by the beehives, and the panic subsided. He regained his breath and his composure, though with them a slight feeling of disillusionment. Childhood fears dramatic events, even as it longs for them.

The year before, he had wandered into his father's room and, finding that the key of the bureau had been accidentally left in the lock, he had peeped inside and discovered a bundle of old letters which had passed between the young schoolmaster and his fiancée.

Dédé chéri ... ma toute petite ... these and other expressions danced before the boy's eyes. Like old and faded photographs the letters none the less conjured up the vision of a young and beautiful girl – his mother – and the shock they gave him was all the stronger for being mixed with a sense of guilt over his prying into someone's secrets. Who has not dreamed of a young and lovely mother whose singing fills the house, the touch of whose gentle hand leaves a delicious coolness on your forehead? *His* memories were quite different. Mme Grillon sitting in the green armchair, counting out the drops of her medicine, which clouded the surface of the glass of water. Mme Grillon coughing, with a handkerchief to her mouth. God, how she coughed! As though she would never stop. In the end, out of breath and with bloodshot eyes, she would nevertheless try to smile at her little boy.

One morning the child had been led to the bed on which she was lying. Her lips were colourless. Her hands, round which a rosary was entwined, would never move again. Nevertheless the face, stern as it was, seemed to be alive. Then ... No, nothing but the flickering of the two candles and the dancing shadows ...

At the moment Georget hadn't been overcome with grief. 'Like that, she won't cough any more,' he had thought.

But when he stumbled on the letters a strange feeling swept him off his feet. Shutting the bureau, he fled, from the house, from the garden, from the village. It must have been on a school holiday. It was a lovely day. He walked on, not caring where he went. The important thing was to keep walking, as it helped him to think of his mother. He felt he was going towards her, that she was waiting for him over the brow of the hill at Perdigane, that he would find her looking just the same as in that little shiny photograph he had found among the letters, and she would have '*Mon Dédé chéri*' on her lips.

From hill-top to hill-top he pursued his dream. And he made a resolve. On his return he would give his father a hug and say something nice to him, such as:

'Dad, I love you ...'

Only ... could you say a thing like that to an old stick?

He didn't say it. When he got home, Piquet, who had been worrying over the boy's long absence, scolded him roundly. All the good intentions, all the tenderness which had blossomed during his walk was suddenly blighted. Instead, he gave his father a sulky, obstinate look, the sort of look which positively invited a slap.

But M. Grillon never hit him, nor for that matter any of his pupils. It was one of his principles. So for three days those two lived painfully and silently in the big house, avoiding each other as far as possible, neither of them able to find the word which would break the spell. It was then that the boy came to realize what it meant to lose one's mother. And a vague jealousy grew within him, an unthinking grievance against this man who had known his mother in her loveliness yet never spoke to him of her. How could he have guessed that Piquet, too, might have shed his melancholy by talking of the old days, of his youth and that of the person they both missed so sorely?

But there it is. Parents are always afraid of speaking simply and openly to their children. Whether from shyness or delicacy, they have to bottle it all up, Déodat Grillon more than most.

Two years had passed since those unforgettable days, and Georget was now convinced his father had forgotten his dead wife.

He had proof of it, yes, an absolute proof.

Formerly it had been a bell which had summoned the children into the classroom, but, thinking that it smacked of the dark ages, the schoolmaster had condemned it to silence. He simply clapped his hands. The big ones started school at half past eight, the little ones at nine.

Georget loitered about in the playground where each morning he awaited his pals, impatient to resume 'the game'. As usual, the first to arrive was Gustave Grosbelhomme, holding his little birdlike head on one side. A beige Balaclava helmet, crowned with a pom–pom, came down almost to his eyes. A black cape reached to his feet which were in snow–boots that his mother, the herbalist of Casteilcorbon, had bought cheap. In fact, the boy was dressed almost entirely in bargains, and so abundantly that he looked as though he was peddling carpets and was weighed down by his wares.

Georget went to meet him, trying to remember this week's pass-word. He needn't have bothered, for Gustave – Tatave for short – got straight down to business.

'Abra?' he challenged.

To which Georget gravely replied:

'Cadabra.'

And the two boys crossed their fingers, then shook hands, saying together:

'Blood and Freedom!'

With this rite performed with proper reverence, Tatave came at once to the subject that was on his mind. It was the same each day. He came a quarter of an hour early to be sure of getting the school-master's son alone and being able to discuss their common pre-occupation.

'Well?' he asked. 'Nothing to report? They didn't see each other?'

'I don't know,' answered Georget, 'but I'd be very surprised if they did. My father didn't go out yesterday except just to cross the road to the convent.'

'To the convent? To see the nuns? What on earth's he got to do with them? He never goes to church.'

'Oh, it's just to do a good turn to the Mother Superior. Every month she gets in a stew over the dispensary accounts and he goes and straightens them out.'

Gustave Grosbelhomme smiled bitterly.

'Funny idea ... But I don't believe you – I'm sure they must have met.'

'They couldn't have. He just nipped across and came back a few minutes later with an account book.'

'Look here. My mother went out at six exactly, leaving me to see to the shop ... Get it?'

18

'Yes. But I don't see …'

'I felt sure something was up, so I sneaked out after her. I saw her go into the church. "Good," I thought. "That's where she always meets him." '

'Exactly.'

'So I turned back home and didn't think any more about it. But I can see the whole thing now. We've been done in the eye once again.'

'How do you mean?'

'Use your brains. After the service she slipped out through the little door leading to the cloisters. The dispensary's just there. It'd seem quite natural as she gets some of her herbs from them.'

'Are you sure?'

'Absolutely. As a matter of fact she came back with a packet. So you see …'

'Yes,' said Georget, 'I do now. Pretty smart!'

'Not bad. Each coming different ways and meeting as if by accident. Among the nuns. But grown-ups are like that – always out to diddle you somehow.'

With that observation Tatave shook his head like an old man bowed down with years of disillusionment. Then, through the slit in his cape, he thrust a thin and none too clean hand which seized the lapel of Georget's jacket.

'But I don't want them to go on meeting in secret like this. Nor do you, do you? Then why can't you say so? Tell Piquet. Couldn't you?'

'I might … At least … not exactly … In fact I don't see there's anything we can do about it.'

'There's any amount we could do. There's only two of them. Two against two. We've got as good a chance as them. Besides, we know. We're one up on them there. They haven't the least idea we've got wind of it.'

The hand was drawn back under the cape.

Georget turned the situation over in his mind. At bottom, he wasn't so violently opposed as was his friend to the idea of this woman, Mme Fabienne Grosbelhomme, becoming the mistress of his father's house. She wasn't a bad sort. A fair, plump little woman, constantly laughing, and lively in her movements, who was always ready to give him a sweet or a stick of liquorice. And there were many practical points in its favour. It's not at all a bad thing to have a woman in the house.

She sweeps, she cooks, she washes up. Above all, she darns socks. It's a horrid feeling when your toe sticks through a hole.

Yes, there were advantages. And as for her son, he was already a closer friend than any brother.

Nevertheless Georges Grillon had from the first stood by his friend and espoused the cause. This thing was not to be! It wasn't the sort of thing you argued about. It was a matter of feeling.

Then there was that old photo of his mother. You couldn't get over a thing like that.

'Besides,' he said to banish any qualms, 'if they meet in secret, that settles it. If you don't want people to know, it's because it's wrong.'

Gustave pursed his lips and once more shook his head deprecatingly.

No sooner had he sensed that there was something on foot between his mother and Piquet than, gnawed by a vague jealousy, he had set to work patiently to make Georget his ally. He had succeeded.

'Of course it's wrong,' he said. 'It's wrong to forget people. Do you forget your mother? Of course not, any more than I forget my father. And it's for us to stick up for them.'

'I suppose it's not the same thing when you're old. If they do get married – what should we do then?'

'We'd clear out,' said Tatave, who had given a lot of thought to that question. 'We'd leave them to each other and go off on our own.'

To run away! Georget's dream was instantly revived. To sleep out in the open under a haystack. To wander together along the roads which led out into the great world where every minute would bring a new experience, if not an adventure.

'Yes. That's what we'd do,' he declared firmly. 'Blood and Freedom!'

Then his tone changed as he heard Victorin whistle in the distance.

'Here, look at this,' he said quickly. 'It's for the sum on the blackboard. $v = \pi r^2 h$.'

Tatave threw his cape back over his shoulders, adjusted his spectacles like an elderly clerk, and laid his satchel on his knees. Then from somewhere under his cape he produced a large fountain-pen filled with red ink. Having unscrewed the cap, he thought better of it, replaced it, and stowed the pen away again in the same mysterious pocket it had come from. Finally, after rummaging in another, he took out a tiny indelible pencil.

'It's the volume of a cylinder,' explained Georget.

Rolling up his sleeve, Tatave licked his arm, then wrote the formula down on it.

'Georget!' called the schoolmaster from a window.

That was something out of the ordinary.

'Coming,' answered the boy.

Then, turning to his friend,

'Believe it or not, we've had no breakfast this morning. I can't imagine why.'

Tatave sniffed. The least mystery always made his nostrils dilate.

'Quick!' said Georget. 'Here's the rest: $v = b + \dfrac{h}{3}$. Pass it on to the other smugglers when they get here. It's a hive, you see. The last bit's the top. All you've got to do is to allow for the thickness of the sides.'

And he dashed off to join his father.

Tatave licked his arm again. With an air of self-importance, he went to meet the son of the mayor of Casteilcorbon, Victorin Muche, a tall, strongly built fellow, commonly referred to as the hefty lout, who, despite his sixteen years, was still in the 'elementary' owing to a quite remarkable incapacity for learning, whatever the subject might be.

'Spit in your hand,' ordered Tatave after the ceremonial greetings were over.

Obediently this outsize dunce did as he was told, and Tatave with his indelible pencil wrote the two formulae on the palm of his friend's hand, having first spread out the wet with his finger.

M. Déodat Grillon was sitting with a bowl of vinegar in front of him, dabbing his face with a wad of cotton wool.

'Come here,' he said.

That was the usual prelude to a sermon, whether in class or at home.

Lowering his eyes, as an outward sign of submission, Georget made a quick inward survey without being able to find anything more serious on his conscience than the little matter of the volume of a bee-hive. He advanced cautiously, keeping the kitchen table between him and his father – an unnecessary precaution, since the latter never hit him, but an instinctive one.

M. Grillon opened his mouth, then closed it again, and swallowed.

He did this several times, groping for words to express his sorrow and indignation. Unable to find any that were adequate, he merely said in the end:

'Drink your coffee.'

It was almost cold, but Georget hastened to obey, meanwhile making various observations. First of all, the bees had left the kitchen. His father had put the pot of honey outside on the window-sill so that the bees could help themselves. They buzzed round it and flew back and forth between it and the hive they were restocking. Another thing Georget noticed was his father's face, which, in spite of his bathing it with vinegar, was swelling with every minute. One eye was half closed, giving the effect of a wink, which contrasted absurdly with the doleful expression of the other.

'You see,' said the victim finally. 'They've stung me.'

Georget tried in vain to find something suitably commiserating to say, but only succeeded in swallowing the last mouthful of coffee the wrong way.

'They had every right to,' went on M. Grillon. 'They received a cruel injury at the hand of man. Someone came treacherously in the night and robbed them of their winter provender, condemning them to die of starvation. It's only logical they should hit back.'

He rose to his feet, his wad in his hand.

'It's outrageous behaviour towards these trusting creatures who do so much for us. Justice demands exemplary punishment for the perpetrators, even if they are children, and everything points to their being children. Even if they are your playmates ... your friends ... What's more: you have no right to shield them. It's too grave a matter for that.'

He raised his hand, three fingers of which were swollen up like sausages, and went on ponderously:

'Georges Grillon, those innocent creatures cry aloud for justice. They demand retribution. Haven't you anything to say to me? There's still time to put things to rights before I report the matter to the *gendarmerie*.'

Georget was used to these solemn objurgations. All the same, he was impressed, and he would have liked to find something to answer. Still, he couldn't very well trump up a charge just to satisfy his father and his bees. After an awkward silence he ventured:

'It might have been gypsies ... or a tramp ...'

But the schoolmaster had already envisaged those possibilities.

'There are no caravans anywhere near Casteilcorbon, at the moment. As for tramps, they wouldn't have known how to open the gate.'

The gate had a special fastening that required some initiation.

'Whoever it was, they didn't climb over the wall. They simply came through the gate, crossed the school yard, and entered the garden through the hedge, leaving footprints all over the cabbage patch.'

M. Grillon raised one of the swollen fingers to add:

'Besides, Ranavalo didn't bark. That doesn't leave much room for doubt, does it?'

Georget was thoroughly uncomfortable. But he kept silent, and with good reason, since he knew nothing whatever about the theft.

The schoolmaster waited several seconds, but still his son didn't speak, and he could only interpret the boy's silence in one way – the way any grown-up would. He lowered his voice and said very quietly in an injured tone:

'Very well then, fold up your napkin. You can go and join them.'

In the school yard the new arrivals exchanged their secret signs and passwords. The 'game' had been going on since term began in October. It had been invented by Francisco Guartorella, a nice-looking boy of fifteen, very intelligent but nevertheless backward in his studies for the reason that he only came to school one year in two. His father, a former smuggler from Catalonia, had the strangest tales to tell when his tongue was loosened by liquor, which happened only too often. As a result, his son, called Cisco for short, had his head full of dreams: dreams of secret hide-outs and passes through the mountains, dramatic encounters with customs officers, and pistol-shots in the dead of night.

Like his father he extolled the solidarity of those who practised this dangerous occupation. And, fired by his stories, which were infinitely more interesting than any M. Grillon had to tell, the boys had founded a secret organization. Its object was to smuggle provisions out of the family larders and transport them to a hidden store without being found out by the parents, who of course represented the customs. If there was a shop to raid instead of a larder, so much the better. Half a barrel of salted herrings had disappeared from the *épicerie*. Many indeed were the parents who were puzzled by some loss or other: M.

Daranluz, the innkeeper, over his dwindling stock of potatoes, the mayor over a missing ham, Mme Grosbelhomme over a carton of jujubes, and M. Martelot, the blacksmith, who at a pinch served as motor mechanic, over a bag of tools. For food wasn't the only thing considered worth smuggling. As for Georget, he hadn't yet found the courage to steal anything from home, unless you counted an old telescope that was in any case more or less his own property. Nor had Cisco brought along any loot so far. That was understandable, for both his parents drank more than they ate, and the home was much too poor to provide any booty. But after all he had given them all the idea. Wasn't that contribution enough?

But after a month of organization, secret meetings, and fruitful raids, the enthusiasm of the smugglers was beginning to wane. Fresh objectives were lacking. Reality lagged too far behind imagination. Cisco went on talking of alcohol, silk stockings, and gold ingots which the real 'outlaws' smuggled across the frontier on the other side of that mountain crest which on clear days rose up behind the foothills of Casteilcorbon. With a wide sweep of his hand, he would refer to it as 'our frontier'. It was too far away, however, for legs that were thirteen to sixteen years old.

In other words, the game was getting stale.

Victorin had even been bold enough to say openly that it was silly to 'win' things for no purpose.

'If we ate the stuff, there'd be some sense in it. But simply to hoard it ...'

Georget reached the group, puffed up with self-importance as the bearer of sensational news.

'All hands on deck!' he ordered, for they drew on the vocabulary of pirates too.

His face was really grave and it was obvious to everybody that something serious was afoot. Besides Victorin, Tatave, and Cisco, there was a blue-eyed boy, with tow-coloured hair. This was Riquet, the blacksmith's son, who belied the sulky expression on his face by being the nicest boy in the world, always ready to fall in with anything.

They all gathered round, but Georget hesitated. Their leader wasn't there yet.

He dealt with the practical question first, asking:

'Has Tatave given you the dope?'

He was answered by friendly grunts.

'The thing is we've got to work out the volume of a beehive inside. All you've got to do is to subtract the thickness to get the inside measurements. After that it's just a cylinder and a cone. You work them out separately from the formulas, add them together, and there you are. It's potty. And talking about beehives, there's something else.'

He couldn't wait any longer for the leader.

'My father's been stung by his bees. That's why he hasn't called us in.'

A smirk from Cisco.

'Be decent to him,' pleaded Georget. 'He's in an awful mess. His face is all swollen up and bright red, like that clown in the circus two Sundays ago.'

All the same he couldn't help grinning himself.

Victorin flinched at the mention of the circus. Ever since, his nights had been troubled by the visions of the equestrienne in pink silk tights.

'That's not all,' went on Georget. 'There's trouble brewing.'

'Come on then. C ... c ... cough it up,' said Riquet Martelot, who suffered from a stammer.

Tatave had turned suddenly grave. Was his friend going to let out their common secret? He was soon reassured.

Georget looked round for the missing boy, but as there was no sign of him he took the plunge.

'It's like this: my father – I mean Piquet – thinks we raided the hives last night.'

'What? Honey?' exclaimed Riquet, with greedy eyes. 'Wouldn't have been a bad idea!'

But Cisco smiled rather contemptuously.

'For once you've had a shot at getting something for us and made a hash of it.'

'It wasn't me,' Georget protested. 'I swear it wasn't. It was during the night. Someone broke into the garden, went for the biggest hive, and swiped everything. Pretty good cheek!'

As far as that was concerned, he was on his father's side.

'I should think it was!' said Victorin.

'And Piquet's got into his head it was one of us that did it. What's more, he thinks I know.'

He shrugged his shoulders and looked round, hoping to find a trace of guilt reflected in one of the faces. But he could see nothing.

'If anybody's in on it, he'd better look out. There's no doubt about it – Piquet's on the war path.'

There was a slightly anxious silence. Then Victorin said dejectedly: 'It had to happen.'

'What had?' asked Tatave. 'You mean you took it?'

Victorin was as tall as a man. To look at him, Tatave had to bend his head over one shoulder and lift into the air his long, yet upturned nose in such a way as to reveal its contents to all the world.

The tall boy was up in arms at once.

'I just said it had to happen. That's all. Is that any reason to …'

'Come off it!' cut in Cisco. 'If we're going to start quarrelling over it … The thing is to decide what to do.'

'Exac … exactly,' stammered Riquet. 'Wh … what are we going to do?'

The five boys were taken aback by this unexpected charge. They had a whole hoard of booty in their possession, but that didn't justify this accusation. It was uncomfortable. Mysterious too, for Georget couldn't altogether shake off the feeling that his father might be right. And it hurt his pride to think that his fellow smugglers might have organized a raid on his father's hives without letting him into the secret. Didn't they trust him? Did they think he'd blab?

Victorin was a prey to rather similar misgivings, though for different reasons. He was older than the others and hailed from a different sort of family. His father was not only mayor of the village but the head of one of the most prosperous distilleries of the district, Distillerie Muche et Cie, and his mother, a beautiful woman, dressed like a lady. All this combined to create something of a barrier between him and the others. Sometimes he was proud of being different, but more often felt guilty about it. And it didn't make it better when the other smugglers sneered:

'You really ought to be a policeman … You ought to be on the side of the law …'

That was a cruel snub.

'If only Pierrot was here,' sighed Cisco, who avoided responsibility.

Indeed, the band of Blood and Freedom were all too conscious of their weakness in the absence of their little chief. Through all their minds ran the same thought:

'Yes. If only Pierrot was here.'

'Ah! There he is,' exclaimed Riquet. 'He's c … coming.'

From the school they could see a curved sweep of road and the beginning of the Avenue Neuve, at the corner of which was the entrance of the Auberge Daranluz. Bareheaded, his dark hair flying in the wind, Pierre Daranluz, captain of the band, came running as fast as his short legs could carry him. Round his waist was a leather belt from which hung an old cartridge pouch. Unfortunately he reached the others too late. M. Déodat Grillon was already in the doorway clapping his hands.

Panting for breath, Pierrot fell in with the others. There was no time to tell him what was afoot. All Georget could do was to slip into his hand the little bit of blotting-paper on which he had scribbled the two formulae essential for the morning's work.

TWO

Pierrot had entered his fourteenth year in the middle of August. Thirteen! Parents are only too apt to speak of it as the awkward age. Having got used to simple notions about their children, they are unprepared for this eagerness to break bonds, to assert an independent personality, to discover life.

Thirteen! An age of bewilderment which readily becomes tinged with bitterness and revolt.

But Pierre Daranluz had kept that spontaneous charm which children generally lose with their dimples. As a matter of fact he had kept one in each cheek, which appeared every time he laughed, and that was often.

An innate sense of justice was the dominant trait of his character. He was fervid and inclined to be dictatorial, and there was something irresistible about him which knocked obstacles down like ninepins.

At the age of five he had said to Fébo, the old man-servant at the inn:

'When I'm big and you're little, I'll make whistles for you, like you do now.'

And he added:

'Then you'll get big again and I'll give you an inn with people in it to do what you tell them.'

In those two sentences he readjusted the order of things, which seemed to him disgracefully unfair as it was.

All the same, that didn't prevent him wanting always to be the first. And he always was. In class his intelligence and concentration took him easily to the top. In games the fact that it was he who invented the rules more than made up for any physical shortcomings. At home it was the same. In fact, wherever he was, if he had an idea in his head – and God knows his head was teeming with them – he always managed to get them accepted by young and old, by visitors to the Auberge Daranluz, and even by the beasts of the field.

If he was late today, it was because Maria, the maid, was laid up in bed, and it was he who had taken her place. He had drawn water from the well, fed the hens, swept the floors, and run to the baker's for the bread – all this with a grin on his face and with yesterday's lessons going through his head. He was still reciting them inwardly when he sat down at his desk.

When he looked up, he almost burst out laughing at the schoolmaster's swollen and discoloured face. But there was on it a look of such bitter sadness that the boy was touched, and his smile died on his lips.

For he was fond of M. Grillon. He respected his great learning, which was stimulating without being overpowering.

Each morning, before starting on the lesson, M. Grillon blew his nose with a seriousness which made it quite impressive, one might almost say majestic. His pupils knew the procedure, knew that this was their last chance to glance at the passage they had been given to learn by heart.

It began with the production of a large check handkerchief, carefully folded in the original creases. Piquet would walk up and down shaking it out as though to air it before use, but really waiting for inspiration. The first detonation – and that is hardly too strong a word for it – was prefaced by various grunts and sniffs and followed by others of the same force, these discharges sounding something like a volley of musketry.

When it was over he would look complacently at the result of his efforts, and from this data draw various physiological conclusions. Then, wiping his moustache, he would return to his platform, lay the handkerchief on his desk, and fold it up once more in the same creases as before.

The morning's work could now begin.

'The arithmetic exercise is put off till tomorrow,' said Piquet.

Expecting a faint sigh of relief, he was surprised to hear a murmur of disappointment. He couldn't understand it.

'As you see, I had prepared a problem for you,' he went on. 'And, as you see, I now rub it out.'

He had unfolded the duster with a deliberation which recalled the handkerchief. Gravely and carefully he wiped the blackboard clean. It was solemn. It was impressive. There could be no question about it now: something was up.

'Instead of that, I'm going to tell you a story.'

A story! Surprise was written on every face.

Admittedly, M. Grillon was at any moment apt to go off at a tangent into some flight of oratory. But that could hardly be called a story. Only on his birthday was he inclined to relax and launch out into some reminiscences of his boyhood so arranged as to form an edifying tale of persistence and its reward.

The boys exchanged glances.

Georget was the only one to have an inkling of what was coming, gathered from what his father had said to him earlier. He was uncomfortable, acutely uncomfortable, and to ease the strain he tried to focus all his attention on a delicate operation: that of picking off a scab on his wrist without making the scratch bleed.

Victorin Muche yawned, crossed and uncrossed his hands under his long, lymphatic face, and sank gradually and peacefully into the state of wool-gathering which was his normal one during working hours.

Tatave opened a shiny black exercise book which was secured by an elastic band and which contained what he called his private notes. He hesitated between two fountain-pens, then decided on a propelling pencil.

'It's a true story …'

Riquet found a puzzle in his pocket. It consisted of some interlocking metal rings which had to be separated, though that was apparently impossible.

Cisco took out a pocket mirror and examined his parting. Restricted to the shabbiest of clothes, his vanity was focused on his hair, which he took a lot of trouble over, and a brass ring he wore on his ring-finger. Propping the little mirror under cover of his dictionary, he was able to contemplate himself at his leisure without being found out.

As for Pierrot, he gently pulled his cartridge pouch round to the front and opened it, and something soft and warm crept into his hand.

Thus each of the boys had some secondary occupation to follow as he listened to the story, that is if Victorin's wool-gathering can be called an occupation.

'We have recently been studying in our history lessons,' began M. Grillon, 'the unhappy results of the oppression of the weak by the strong … Grosbelhomme, I'd be glad if you stopped chewing … I showed you the revolt of the slaves in ancient Rome. I showed you …'

And the schoolmaster depicted once again the blighting hand of selfishness, cruelty, and despotism down to the day when the Great Revolution of 1789 proved to the world that a people can choose its own masters and planted in the breast of every Frenchman the notions of liberty, equality, and fraternity.

Pierrot was already seething. Nothing pleased him more than to hear the master in this vein, pleading with eloquent and passionate republicanism the cause of the underdog against oppression.

'I have given you various examples. No doubt you can give me others taken from the history of France. Muche, let us hear one from you.'

At the sound of his name Victorin started as though he had been hit on the head. He had been considering how he would go about asking his mother for four hundred and sixty francs, which sum he had lost to the mason, Guartorella, Cisco's father, in the process of learning the three-card trick.

'Well, Muche? What about it?'

Opening his mouth, Victorin produced a nondescript sound which showed so clearly that he hadn't the faintest idea what was being discussed that M. Grillon gave it up. In any case he hated the mayor's son. Already three hands had been raised, which helped him to overlook the default without losing face.

'All right ... Grosbelhomme?'

'There was the revolt of the Bagaudes.'

'Good! And you, Daranluz?'

'The Pastoureaux. In 1251. When Saint Louis was away on a crusade. They were put down by Blanche of Castille.'

'Excellent. But you'd do better to call the King Louis IX instead of Saint Louis. Guartorella?'

Cisco had his example, too, and, satisfied with these three answers, M. Grillon deigned to smile. It was the first time he had done so and it merely made his distorted features look more grotesque.

'Any others?'

No offer. M. Grillon was on the point of giving some more examples himself when he suddenly changed his tone to rap out:

'Martelot, when you've finished fiddling with those rings, you'll be kind enough to put them back in your pocket.'

Riquet blushed to the roots of his colourless hair.

Then, with real feeling in his voice, Déodat Grillon went on:

'Another revolt has broken out this very morning in a small republic which resembles ours in many of its manners and customs. If you wish you can help me to see that the oppressors of these unhappy creatures are brought to account.'

He had led up to this point so skilfully that no one except Georget saw what he was getting at. Cisco, whose imagination was easily fired, already saw himself taking part in the liberation of Andorra, in which little protectorate he had an old cousin.

'It happens,' went on M. Grillon, 'that the people in question are model citizens, each one ready to sacrifice his life for the sake of the community, people with whom no others can vie in industry and self-denial. Not content with satisfying their own needs, they each year hand over the major part of the fruits of their labour to others who are incapable of producing the marvellous provender of which they alone have the secret. What they do keep for themselves is just sufficient for their barest needs ... And then last night – not far from here – some tyrant, belonging to the very race for whom these creatures do so much, some tyrant, I say, came stealthily and robbed them of their small reserve of food, without which they must perish. Coldly and cynically, with calculated cruelty, he ransacked the store, leaving these patient benefactors to die ...

'Boys, what do you think of that? ... Are you going to allow such injustice to go unpunished?'

There was something really pathetic about the appeal. M. Grillon had never spoken so gravely or with such obvious sincerity, and his swollen face was no longer comic now, but touching.

The boys sat very still. They were troubled. They were beginning to understand what he was getting at. Only Pierrot, who had come too late to be briefed, could listen with a sympathy unalloyed with misgiving. He was a generous boy, always ready to respond to an appeal. Was the schoolmaster preaching a crusade against injustice? All right. He would be the first to rally to the cause. For a moment he forgot to stroke the little furry creature which trembled in his hand.

The master had never had greater prestige in his eyes. The distorted features were forgotten. Even Tatave was impressed by the phraseology. At any rate it was worthy of a mention in his note-book and he wrote:

'Thursday 27 October. Morning class. Injustice. Do we stand idly by?'

Little by little Déodat Grillon worked round to his favourite theme, the highly organized social life of bees and the miniature factories in which they worked, the unquestioning devotion to the community and the prodigious industry which goaded them on to produce far beyond their needs – to the great benefit of man.

'And just think of it – their year's work over, just when they settle down to enjoy the repose they have so richly earned and eat the food they have so laboriously stored, without scruple, without pity, some abject human comes to trample on their rights and rob them of their modest board.'

And plenty more in the same vein. M. Grillon spread himself. Then, leaving generalities, he reconstructed the crime detail by detail. After that he paused. Dead silence. Then very gently he went on:

'I can only suppose that whoever committed this grave offence was unaware of the seriousness of what he was doing. A childish, thoughtless act perhaps, undertaken in a spirit of adventure, without a thought for the misery that must result from it. It was in that mood perhaps that Nero of old set fire – or so they say – to the poorest quarters of Rome, thinking no doubt … Grosbelhomme, I've already spoken to you once about chewing. Whatever it is you have in your mouth you'll oblige me by spitting it out … Now, where was I? Nero? Never mind about him. What I was coming to was this – perhaps the real object of this raid was to wreak vengeance on me. In that case the perpetrator can be proud of his success. And I'm not speaking of the stings themselves. He succeeded in something much more painful – in making my little friends into bitter enemies. When I went near them they rounded on me.'

That remark got under Pierrot's skin. He had been rather disappointed with the outcome of the story. Anticlimax. He had expected something much more exciting. And it turned out to be only bees!

'If the culprit is in this room,' said M. Grillon suddenly, 'I ask him simply to stand up. His frank admission will redeem his offence, which I am only too glad to put down to thoughtlessness.'

The suspicion weighed heavily on them. But no one stirred.

The master waited for what seemed like an eternity.

Pierrot found it almost unbearable. He was very sensitive to an appeal to honour. In fact he almost wished he had committed the crime himself so that he could stand up and bring this aching suspense to an end.

M. Grillon was speaking again, once more in generalities. He made comparisons between the conditions of bees and that part of our human society called the working class, plunging into an involved lecture on political philosophy and upholding the right to strike. Getting into rather a muddle, he came down to earth abruptly with:

'Since I am convinced that one of you is guilty – and indeed I have proof of it – I can only conclude by your silence that the whole class ranges itself on the side of the malefactor. In that case you make yourselves all collectively responsible and I must punish you collectively. It is my firm intention to do so unless the guilty person is promptly disclosed.'

It was ten past nine. The second-form boys outside – a dozen little boys delighted by the unexpected delay in starting school – were rushing about wildly, playing some childish game.

'I will give you till the end of break to think it over ... And now,' he concluded curtly, 'open your arithmetic books at page 144 and work out problem No. 563.'

Pierrot was indignant.

The master's prestige evaporated. Was this the man who spoke of honour and justice in such moving terms? To punish a whole class for the guilt of one! To blackmail boys into sneaking on their schoolfellow!

Pierrot's attitude underwent an abrupt change. It was M. Grillon himself whom he now saw in the role of oppressor. All right. Let him punish the class. Pierrot hadn't the faintest notion who had robbed the hive, and, if he had, nothing would induce him now to give the chap away.

Sitting in the front row, he wanted to make a sign to his fellow smugglers. He couldn't turn round. So, slipping the white mouse back into the cartridge pouch, he raised his hand behind his head and crossed his fingers, which, in their own private language, meant:

'Hold tight and keep your mouths shut, Blood and Freedom!'

The school yard was flanked by an old tower, once part of the fortifications of Casteilcorbon. The rest of what had once been the castle and its outer walls had been effaced by the village which had grown up higgledy-piggledy on its site, using the stones of medieval grandeur to make foundations for the common dwellings of modern man.

But modernity had not yet succeeded in encroaching on the keep, which still stood proudly on a jutting rock, as proudly as in the days of the Barons, rising disdainfully 100 feet into the air and dwarfing the low tiled roofs around.

It seemed contemptuous of its surroundings, and it had a right to be, for it had nothing in common with these houses whose chimneys smoked. On the eastern side was a wall of rock as steep as any cliff, on the other a moat spanned by a drawbridge which no longer worked. The moat was still used. The village women did their washing there, and geese paddled about at the foot of the historic walls.

As for the building itself, its slowly turning shadow provided a useful sun-dial. If the villagers constantly glanced at it, they only rarely raised their eyes to the crenellations at the top, the haunt of rooks, and they were at a loss to understand why so many tourists stopped in front of it to take a snapshot. They generally referred to it as the *Bastide* and transformed its vaulted rooms into warehouses. The baker kept his reserves of flour there, the Fire Brigade its hand-pump and hoses, the local band its instruments. But whatever they might say or think, its presence none the less gave Casteilcorbon, particularly from far off, the aspect of a citadel.

Besides the keep, four towers remained. Originally they had stood at the four corners of the wall, but they were now lost in the cluster of lanes that made up the little town, which in character was really no more than an overgrown village. The one by the school was the best preserved, but it was a very rickety structure. On the street side, the entrance to it was blocked, at any rate to sensible people, by a wooden gate, but still more by a thick growth of nettles and junipers. Inside, the stairs were already crumbling. The lower steps had gone altogether, so that they began in mid-air. On the eastern side, the wall was bulging dangerously. Shaky though it might be, however, this tower had an irresistible attraction for M. Grillon's pupils. First of all because it was forbidden to them. That alone made it quite a thrill to climb up to the second platform. Secondly, this circular room made a perfect hiding-place for their secret hoard of 'contraband'. Who would think of looking there for the various items missing from their homes?

On the western side, that is to say in the school yard itself, was a small opening under a pointed arch. This was precious, as it enabled the boys to crawl in without creaking the hinges of the front gate. It was quite a squeeze to get in, but practicable nevertheless. Once inside, they had to clamber up through a huge chimney. No question of the stairs – they were really too dangerous.

Victorin, Georget, and Riquet, being practically-minded, regarded the tower as a convenient headquarters, since it was inaccessible to grown-ups. For Cisco, Tatave, and Pierrot it had something more: a romance which gave a genuine lustre to their exploits.

As soon as break began, ignoring the little ones who immediately started romping in the yard, they gathered in the shadow of the old tower. They were all anxiously waiting for Pierrot's opinion. It was Victorin, however, who broke the silence.

'Pretty rotten,' he said, exposing his long teeth like a donkey munching frozen carrots.

That summed up the situation perfectly, though it hardly shed any light.

'As a matter of fact,' said Cisco, 'it's really quite simple …'

'Shut up,' said Gustave.

They all turned to their young chief, who, however, was silent.

Riquet began to fiddle with his metal rings, making an irritating noise. Mascha, the white mouse, poked its head out of the cartridge case and, as everything seemed peaceful, ventured up its master's chest and snuggled against his neck. There it began to nibble at its forepaws like a boy biting his nails. It, too, seemed to be reflecting on the situation.

Pierrot felt strongly about it all. The trouble was that his feelings were varied and conflicting.

He was indignant at the theft of the honey, indignant that a raid had been organized by his friends and brought off successfully without his knowledge, indignant at the idea of collective punishment. Most of all, he considered it outrageous that Piquet should have incited them to sneak on each other.

Too many things to be indignant about. Difficult to get them sorted out.

But at last he made up his mind.

'As for sneaks, we know what to do with them. Secondly, the chap that did it is a skunk. We'll find him out. And we'll deal with him. Piquet'll never know who it is. If he thinks he can put the squeeze on us … he'll see how far it gets him. He can punish till he's blue in the face … Abracadabra!'

'Abracadabra!' came the answer.

They all looked up, relieved that the thinking had been done for them.

'How are we going to find out who did it?' asked Tatave. 'Shall we set up a Court of Inquiry?'

'That's the idea,' answered Pierrot. 'And as there's still a quarter of an hour of break, we might as well start straight off.'

It was to be done properly, and Gustave Grosbelhomme was made clerk of the court. Opening his note-book he began to sketch out the procedure under various headings: *Suspicions. Witnesses. Evidence* ...

'What about confrontations?' asked Riquet. 'They always have confrontations.'

Down it went: *Confrontations*. The last heading was *Conclusions*.

'I think,' put in Cisco meditatively (he was apt to look meditative) – 'I think we ought to start with who didn't do it.'

It was part of Pierrot's talent for leadership that he always knew the right role for each boy. He agreed at once.

'Quite right, Cisco. We're all under suspicion until we're cleared. Even Piquet. He may walk in his sleep for all we know. Fire away, Cisco. You ask the questions.'

The idea of M. Grillon having robbed his own bees put everyone into a lighter mood. Francisco Guartorella accepted the task proudly. His age, his physical strength, and his intelligence would have given him a good claim to leadership of the gang, yet never for a moment had he entertained the idea. Though quick-witted and resourceful, he lacked stamina and preferred making suggestions to being responsible for their being carried out.

'Right you are; and we'll begin with Smuggler Grillon. Grillon, you were certainly close to the scene of the crime last night. What do you know of this business?'

Georget winced. To be suspected by his own friends was something he hadn't bargained for. It was going too far. And the cruel thing was that the mere fact of being suspected made him look guilty. It's sufficient to walk between two policemen to acquire in the eyes of the passers-by the features of a murderer.

'I swear I don't know anything,' he answered, hanging his head.

'Come on! You know a lot. First of all, why has Piquet made a dead set at us?'

'Because of the footprints. And because the dog didn't bark.'

'There you are! You see – you've plenty to tell us. Let's have it.'

His tongue once loosened, Georget went into endless detail. It was rather a rigmarole.

'I hope you're taking all this down,' said Cisco sententiously to Gustave.

The latter, who had been struggling to keep pace, stopped writing at once, just out of cussedness.

'Can't you see,' went on Georget, 'that if I'd wanted to pinch some honey, I'd only to take a pot out of the cupboard when he wasn't looking? It would never have been noticed.'

'Then wh ... why haven't you ever d ... done it?' asked Riquet, who couldn't understand how such a temptation could be resisted.

Georget let that question pass.

'Besides,' he added, 'you know very well I'm scared stiff of bees.'

That sounded convincing, and another suspect was put through the mill.

Each had a water-tight alibi. Pierrot hadn't left the inn. Victorin had never been allowed out in the evenings since the day he – but we'd better leave that alone. Everyone knew that Tatave was pretty securely tied to his mother's apron-strings. The night before, they had been sitting up late making up small packets of lime-blossom.

Riquet was already to all intents apprenticed to his father. Poor boy! Every minute that wasn't spent in school nor strictly necessary for his homework had to be devoted to the blacksmith's trade. Besides, he was out of the running anyhow. He was much too meek and mild and much too unimaginative to have conceived anything so audacious as the previous night's raid. That didn't save him from being questioned, however, nor from cutting a pitiable figure, stammering painfully.

'Well, that's the lot,' Cisco announced, dismissing him.

'Oh, no, it's not,' snapped Tatave.

'Who do you mean?'

'You yourself.'

'Quite true. Well, as a matter of fact I was out all last night. But it's a deadly secret. Swear you won't tell a soul. Particularly you, Victorin. If your father knew ...'

They all took the prescribed form of oath, spitting on the ground and holding up their hands.

'Right. Well, we went out after dark, my father and I. We cut straight up through the pine-wood to the Perdigane Hill, where we set a lot of snares. Then we went and ransacked old Féroulet's hut. After all, no one's taken any interest in it since he died. When we went back to the snares, we found four rabbits and a little fox.'

'A little fox? Was it alive?'

Pierrot was passionately fond of animals.

'I should think it was! Look what it did to me when I caught hold of it.'

He pulled up his sleeve to show a set of little tooth-marks just above his wrist. Then he added rather haughtily:

'You see, we'd more serious business than pinching Piquet's honey.'

'What about the fox? Did you kill it?'

'Of course I did. At least, my father did. When he takes the skin to the Town Hall he'll get a reward.'

He winked at Victorin Muche before adding:

'Naturally he won't hand it in here, but somewhere else. Your father might ask too many questions. See?'

Victorin 'saw' only too well. He was always being made to feel ashamed of his father's exalted station.

'Pity you killed it,' observed Pierrot regretfully. 'If you'd given it to me I'd have tamed it.'

Gently he put Mascha back in the cartridge pouch.

When school started again M. Grillon's face seemed more swollen than ever. Throughout the break he had kept an eye on the little group, expecting at any minute one of them to come over to him and confess his guilt. He couldn't believe it would be otherwise.

But as they sat down at their desks the boys assumed a reserved, hostile manner, like envoys visiting enemy headquarters to announce the refusal of an armistice.

It was obvious they were not going to tell him what he wanted, and he decided it was high time to pass from vague threats to precise ones.

'Messieurs ...' he began sternly.

Normally he preferred to address them as '*mes enfants*', but the moment for tenderness had passed.

'Messieurs, next Tuesday and Wednesday are All Saints' Day and All Souls' Day respectively. It had been my intention to give you an additional holiday the day before, that is on Monday, 31 October.

With the extra day thrown in you would get four clear days. That *had* been my intention. And it still is, provided I have been informed by the evening of Saturday the 29th of the name of the person who broke into my grounds last night and robbed one of my hives. I might add that the guilty one would be given the same holidays as the others in recognition of his frankness. If, on the other hand, I should fail to receive that information, not only will you have the full day's work on Monday, but I will find extra work for you to do on the other days as well. Is that clearly understood? I'll open the school specially for it.'

To make it clearer still he added in a casual tone:

'You would for instance have ample time to copy out the whole of your algebra note-books.'

There it was. They knew exactly what to expect, yet the six smugglers made no response. As a matter of fact their reactions were very different. Victorin Muche could hardly bring himself to take the threat seriously. All that fuss over a bit of honey! The schoolmaster would have to explain it to the parents of six families. Besides, was it likely he'd spoil his own holiday for the satisfaction of getting his own back? He lacked the imagination to see that, if M. Grillon had chosen that form of punishment, it was precisely because it hit him too, thus proving the purity of his motives.

For Tatave, the punishment was really no punishment at all. He didn't like being at home, where his mother positively smothered him with attentions of all sorts. Sitting in the classroom doing extra work, sitting sullenly shoulder to shoulder with the other members of the gang – that would be something new, and, yes, rather attractive. And then Pierrot had declared that whatever the punishment was they simply wouldn't do it. 'Piquet can try it on if he likes,' he had said. 'He'll see how far he gets!'

And Tatave had unswerving confidence in his chief.

Henri Martelot was very upset. He racked his brains to find a way out, and, generous as he was by nature, even toyed with the idea of confessing to the crime himself. It would save the holiday for the others, and even for himself, for that matter, since Piquet had promised an amnesty. But Piquet might very well go and complain to his father, and the thought of what the latter might do was sufficient to deter the boy from such self-sacrifice.

From the first mention of a four-day holiday, Francisco Guartorella had made his plans for spending it. Casteilcorbon was only some thirty kilometres from the sea as the crow flies. You could just see it from the top of the keep on a clear day – a dark grey streak under the pale blue sky. What's more, Cisco had an uncle there, a fisherman, who was always ready to take him out to sea. There was nothing the boy loved better, particularly when they fished off the coast of that Catalonia his father was always talking about and which his uncle Tio Ricardo was to introduce him to later. Mentally Cisco was already on the road when he heard the promised holiday cancelled, or at all events jeopardized. He, too, racked his brains for a solution. The only one he could find was the same as Riquet's, except that he would have them draw lots for who should confess. With any luck ...

What Georget Grillon felt more than anything else was a sort of shame, something rather like what Victorin felt when his pals teased him about his father. Inevitably a certain amount of odium must fall on his head, since he had the misfortune to be the son of an 'oppressor'. All the more firmly did he resolve to identify himself with the others and uphold the common cause.

'If only Ranavalo had barked,' he thought wistfully.

As for Pierrot, the flame of righteous indignation burnt in his heart. With each minute that passed he became more convinced that none of his smugglers had had a hand in the outrage. Naturally impetuous, he jumped from one idea to another. But though many of them were contradictory, one remained fixed in his mind. M. Grillon, having incited them to rise up against oppression, had now assumed the oppressor's role himself, and he, Pierrot, would take up the cudgels against injustice with the enthusiasm of a crusader.

Nothing else counted.

He was the chief. He would rise to the occasion. He had never felt more called upon to lead. Blood and Freedom!

The last half-hour of school was drawing to a close.

M. Grillon's face had stopped swelling. From time to time he felt his chin, his cheeks, his forehead, thinking ruefully that when the boys left he must avoid showing himself at the entrance. Mme Grosbelhomme might be there. She often came, nominally to fetch her boy, but also to give the schoolmaster a smile that was more eloquent than any words.

'Wh ... what is a b ... blood oath?' asked Riquet.

It was Francisco Guartorella who had been reading about it in *The True Story of the Three Barons of Casteilcorbon*, a somewhat shabby volume purchased from one of the village shops. The three barons in question had been besieged in their fortress by the Comte de Roussillon, whose niece they had kidnapped. They had mixed their blood and drunk it, swearing to shed it to the last drop rather than surrender the maiden with whom they were all three in love.

'Does it hurt?' asked Victorin.

He wasn't very brave about pain, nor was he particularly responsive to the glamour of legendary customs. He thought the game was going a bit too far.

Summoned by their leader, the smugglers had assembled that same Thursday afternoon in their tower, or, to give it its proper name, the Tour de la Reine. Taking every possible precaution, they had sneaked in one by one when the coast was clear and scrambled up to the second platform. Georget was there too.

A council of war. As a matter of fact it was the first time the whole gang had met in their hide-out. As a rule it was just one member who went there at night with whatever booty had been collected, generally Cisco, who was freer than the others.

The place smelt like a cellar. That was because of the potatoes, pilfered from the inn, which were piled up against the wall. But there were much worse smells than that. A piece of ham was going rancid. As for the salted herrings, they positively stank. While over all floated a medicinal aroma given off by Tatave's contributions from the herbalist's. There were several cardboard boxes and a mysterious soap-box fitted with chains and padlocks. That was Riquet's handiwork, and his own idea. It was the treasure chest, and on this occasion it served as a sort of throne for their chief.

It was difficult to see. The loopholes provided excellent look-outs, but owing to the thickness of the walls they allowed little light to enter.

To do justice to the occasion, Pierrot gave orders for the road-mender's lamp to be lit: a storm lantern with red glass on two sides and plain on the other two, which was one of the gang's latest 'acquisitions'. That was Riquet's job, he being the engineer. He did as he was told and placed the lamp in the middle of the floor, thus dividing the tower into four sectors, lit up alternately by yellow and red rays.

The effect was truly impressive.

'From now on,' declared Pierrot to the squatting circle, 'we're not smugglers any more.'

With a sweep of his hand he put away such childish diversions.

'We've got something else to do now, something more important. *One for all: all for one!* Our honour is at stake. Will those who want to be my Knights please rise?'

Riquet was on his feet at once. Pierrot had made an appeal: that was enough. Georget followed suit, then Cisco and Tatave. Lastly Victorin, carried with the tide, stood up too.

'Good!' said Pierrot, inspecting them contentedly. 'You are my Companions,' he went on grandiloquently. 'Together we will see that justice prevails.'

'Justice?' asked Victorin. 'What do you mean?'

Taken aback, Pierrot frowned. Cisco came quickly to his rescue.

'What's the good of explaining it to him?' he asked contemptuously. 'When you're the son of a mayor, you can't understand a simple thing like that.'

Victorin looked at the floor.

'Justice,' put in Georget, 'means not to take things lying down. Silly ass! Didn't you hear what Piquet threatened us with this morning? Justice means standing up for the downtrodden – widows and orphans and all that.'

'Oh! I see.'

Victorin thought it over. Widows and orphans. There was Maria, the servant at the inn. She was an orphan. As for widows, there was Tatave's mother and old Mme Broc who kept the grocer's shop. That's where they'd snaffled the salted herrings. Was that standing up for widows? It was all very complicated.

'In pictures,' went on Georget, 'justice is always shown as a lady with scales and blindfolded. That's so that she shan't see what she's weighing so that there's no favouritism. She's …'

But Pierrot Daranluz thought this had gone far enough.

'That'll do. Justice means being just. We all know what that means. We've only got to look around us. There are rotten things being done to people all the time. Take us, for instance: we're being punished for what we didn't do, and it's time we dug our toes in.'

He paused, then went on:

'Since we're all agreed, I appoint you five my Knights. Our companion-in-arms, Gustave Grosbelhomme, will draw up an oath for us

43

to swear. For we must have an oath. We must swear to be loyal to each other all our lives, in bad times and good, in sickness and health, and all that sort of thing, and to stand up for justice.'

Tatave put his spectacles straight and started to write.

It was a momentous occasion.

While the oath was being drafted, Pierrot got out his knife and in big letters scratched on the floor:

THE BLOOD OATH WAS TAKEN THIS THURSDAY 27 OCTOBER ...

THREE

In spite of its name, the Auberge Daranluz was dark. From its beams, black with generations of smoke from the wood fire, hung strange, flat, golden-brown sausages something like the *chorizo* the Spaniards are so fond of. Between them were festoons of red peppers.

'I'd much sooner see them hanging there than put them in my stew-pot,' the mistress of the house used to say. 'But there you are! With all these Spaniolos coming to the place, I can't help myself. The more pepper you give them, the more they seem to want.'

Mme Daranluz prided herself on her French cuisine. Her Christian name, Josephine, had been abbreviated to Fine, and she was generally spoken of as Mme Fine.

She was scraping carrots. Her hands were as nimble as her tongue. Every other second there was a 'plop' as another carrot dropped into the basin of water, and each time the two black griffons lying in front of the hearth pricked their ears. They were only pretending to sleep while they waited for that most blissful of all treats to dogs, cats, and men – a crackling fir-cone fire at the end of an autumn day.

'These "regulars" are all very well,' thought Pierrot's mother, referring to her *pensionnaires*, 'and admittedly they bring in steady money. But oh, the work they give! Besides, they fill the place up and keep tourists away.'

When Benoît, her husband, had first suggested it – and it wasn't such a bad idea – she had never believed she could cope with so many. Day after day, without so much as a breather ...

'Viette! Take your hands out of that basin. You've got a cold as it is.'

'They're my fish,' protested the little girl. 'My red fish. I was only counting them.'

She was five and was apt to be bored when her brother wasn't there to keep her amused with his inexhaustible fund of games.

'They're not your fish, they're Mummy's carrots. You leave them alone.'

Viette knew very well they were fish. Pierrot had said so. He had invented a game the day before for the special purpose of getting her to eat up her soup. And if Pierrot said so ... But then grown-ups never could understand things like that. Least of all Mme Fine ...

'There's the siren at the quarry sounding already,' mused the latter. 'And how the days are drawing in! To have all those men in the place from half past five – how on earth can I ever get through my work? All the same, they drink more in winter to pass the time away, and that's so much more money. There's always something to be thankful for, I suppose.

'Viette! If you put your fingers in the water again you'll get your bottom smacked.'

A couple of cork-cutters came in. They were never apart. A couple of loafers! It was true that in the cork-works it got dark earlier than at the quarry. Still, that was only an excuse.

'Evening, Mme Fine. Here's something for you.'

'*Buenas tardes.*'

They each carried a big faggot of kindling.

'*Bonsoir*, Sébastien; *buenas*, Domingo. Put them down over there, will you? Pierrot can put them away later. Thanks. Sit down. I'll just finish these carrots, and then I'll bring you something. That'll be on the house.'

'Oh, it wasn't for that we brought it,' said Sébastien. 'There's plenty of it and it's no trouble at all. We can bring you a bit every evening this winter, can't we, Domingo?'

'*Si. Mucho fuego para la tarde, bueno.*'

Domingo could understand everything that was said to him in French, but he couldn't string two words together himself.

Boulou and Barbette, the two dogs, sniffed at the forest smell the men brought with them. The latter had no idea what a wealth they carried in their fustian jackets – whiffs of rabbit, vole, and squirrel, perhaps even of fox.

Benoît Daranluz was the next to arrive with four others. He was foreman at the quarry, and he wasn't daunted by the burden of two jobs at once. While the others flopped into chairs and sprawled with their elbows on the table, he put on his blue apron, patted his wife on the forehead as he passed, and went straight to his place behind the bar, where he immediately started rinsing glasses.

He would never have been seen kissing Fine in public. You could love your wife and see eye to eye with her in everything without making an exhibition of yourself.

'It's pitch dark in here,' was all he said by way of greeting.

Fine smiled at him.

46

'Yes. The dark falls so sudden you hardly notice it. As a matter of fact I was waiting for Pierrot to come and light the lamp and the fire. He's late this evening. Viette, fetch me a box of matches from the kitchen. And tell Maria she can start laying the tables.'

The little one trotted off proudly. A moment later she could be heard saying:

'Maya ... Lay the tables ...'

Two more workmen. Sawyers white with fine sawdust. They walked straight up to the bar.

'I'll tell you this – the *curé*'s an ass,' went on the shorter of the two, continuing the discussion they'd been having on the way.

'You can stop that, Miguel,' interrupted Mme Daranluz sternly. 'When we talk about people here, it's to speak good of them. If Pierrot was here he'd have something to say to you.'

'Where is Pierrot?' asked Benoît, pouring out two *anisettes*.

Twice the dogs had pricked their ears at the boy's name. Viette came back with the matches and handed them to her father.

He struck a match, lit his pipe, then the lamp. Instantly it seemed like night outside. The little girl stood in front of her father with her hands behind her back.

'You didn't say thank you,' she said reprovingly. 'And when people don't say thank you they're put in the corner.'

Her head didn't come up to her father's apron-strings.

'The little shrew!' thought Mme Fine, but all she did was to ex-change a glance with her husband, one of those tender glances which express adoration better than any amount of words.

She was from Ustou, a mountain village in the Alet Valley where the Pyrenean race was at its purest. But she wouldn't speak the dialect and she hankered after one of those cafés in the big towns in which the *patronne* sits at the cash desk while others run to and fro.

'In my village in the old days,' she used to relate, 'everyone was occupied breeding and training bears. Every daughter got a bear as a dowry when she was ready for marriage. My mother would never part with hers. She was called Martine – the bear, I mean – and she lived like a prince, well fed, with no work to do right down to the day she died. Sometimes I used to go to sleep snuggled up against her in her hut.'

Pierrot loved hearing stories of this bear, and Viette would listen, entranced. That wasn't the child's real name. She had been christened

Marie-Vivienne, but that was altogether too much of a mouthful for a little tot, and it had long ago been forgotten.

It is possible that Benoît Daranluz had been doing a bit of smuggling himself when he found Fine in that out-of-the-way village. But he would never have admitted it, unlike others who boasted of being smugglers. He had settled down in his native Roussillon, buying the inn at Casteilcorbon. He had become deputy mayor, a most respectable, law-abiding, tax-paying citizen, and a model husband and father.

A fine-looking man was M. Benoît. As good-tempered and hardworking as his wife, who, as mother, cook, and *patronne* of the café, was on the go from morning to night. The only help she had was from old Fébo, who at seventy-two or more wasn't all that good, and this insufferable girl, Maria, who couldn't be entrusted with anything more responsible than washing up and laying the table. And even at those jobs …

'She's a lazy, good-for-nothing creature, untruthful into the bargain,' Mme Fine would say. 'Since we took her in she's broken her weight of plates and glasses.'

The door opened again. Was it Pierrot this time? No, only the old man.

'*Ve alli*, Fébo!' called out Domingo.

The old man-servant had been seeing to the horse. You could smell it – and without lifting up your muzzle like Boulou and Barbette. His were all the odd jobs about the place, and he could turn his hand to most things provided he wasn't ordered about. When that happened he made a point of disobeying.

'I'm seventy-two,' was his favourite answer when anybody spoke to him.

As a matter of fact he didn't really know, but the number seventy-two seemed to have taken his fancy. He had been seventy-two ever since he came to work for M. Daranluz, and that was quite a long time ago.

'Company …' he muttered by way of greeting.

His beard sprouted irregularly and you could see his yellow cheeks through it. No one had ever told him that his name was that of the sun-god, Phoebus. A pity. He would have been delighted.

'Company!' he repeated a little louder, glancing round to see if anybody looked like standing him a drink.

No one did, and he plodded across the room with that jerky, mechanical gait which belongs to the very old. His trousers were of such thick material that they looked like stove-pipes, buckling like metal with the bending of his knees.

'See anything of Pierrot?' asked Mme Fine.

She swept the peelings off the table into her apron. She still had two chickens to pluck and draw and was wondering how she was going to manage. But Fébo, who liked to have his hands busy, had already picked up one of them and, with deft movements, started pulling out the feathers, with all the more alacrity since no one had asked him to.

'Pierrot,' he said. 'Yes, I've seen him. Just now. With his *amigos*.'

Fébo was the sort of man who has always seen everything. With that, he was quite a gossip. Only his speech was made up of so many dialects that, though highly picturesque, it was often quite unintelligible. Not for those who were used to him, of course, like Viette. She could understand him perfectly.

'*Son tré fastidiosos, les pobré! Sé lé accouse, l'instioutor, dé haber robado sa miel. Todos!*'

Ah! So the schoolmaster was accusing the boys of stealing his honey, was he? The theft was already known at the inn, for M. Grillon had been there as usual with Georget for the midday meal. It was Viette who had asked him, and not altogether innocently:

'Why have you put on another face today?'

At Fébo's words, Mme Fine bristled.

'My boy accused of stealing!'

Really! That schoolmaster was going too far! No wonder Pierrot hadn't opened his mouth all through dinner, just sitting there glowering at the other corner of the table where M. Grillon sat.

If the boy had done anything wrong she'd soon find out. She'd only to ask him. He was frankness itself. Never hid a thing – no, not even when he'd taken potatoes from the cellar for some game or other he played with his schoolfellows.

'Evening, Mme Fine ... Is the soup ready?'

Mon Dieu! Four more of her 'regulars' – fortunately, the last – workmen from the *Distillerie Muche*, where they always worked overtime. The table wasn't laid. And Pierrot hadn't come home. And Maria ...

'Maria! ... Ma ... ri ... a ...'

'*Oui, Madame,*' came a voice from the next room.

'Are you deaf, or *won't* you hear?'

'Coming, Madame.'

'What about the tables?'

'*Oui, Madame*. I'm just going to do them.'

What a girl! It couldn't go on much longer like this. More trouble than she was worth. They'd have to get rid of her.

Two or three times a day Mme Fine made this resolution, and had been doing so for the last six months. The only thing was – where was she to go? No use thinking of the Public Assistance. They wouldn't lift a finger.

And there it was! Mistress Daranluz was much too soft-hearted to put Maria out into the street. Besides, the girl had really not been looking well that day.

'Viette! Take your hands out of that water and go and fetch Maria.'

The little girl skipped off, light as a wagtail.

'Maya … Maya … Quick … Mummy says …'

But the maid didn't appear.

'The little minx!' muttered Mme Fine, sending up a cloud of down from the white chicken. 'I know what's at the back of her mind. If she waits for Pierrot to come in, he'll do half the work for her.'

Her hands never stopped for a second. You could hear her right across the room – cra-cra-cra-cra – as though she was tearing linen.

'*Basto!*' cried one of the men playing *malilla*, as he flung down an ace of clubs on to the green baize square which advertised Muche's products.

And suddenly, long before there was any clatter of wooden soles in the street, Boulou and Barbette sprang to their feet, wagging their tails, their spines quivering with welcome. Viette made a dash for the door. Benoît put down his pipe, a smile on his lips. Mme Fine assumed a severe expression, which, however, she would be quite unable to maintain for more than ten seconds.

The lines disappeared from Fébo's forehead, and at last Maria appeared, carrying a huge pile of plates. The clock struck seven.

'*Bonjour, Papa! Bonjour, Maman! Bonjour tout le monde!*'

It was Pierrot with his cartridge pouch.

He kissed his parents, shook hands with his friends with a gravity that was amusing, swept Viette off her feet, and put her down on

50

Boulou's back. Boulou was frantically holding up a paw. Pierrot took it.

'That's right. Now the other …'

The inn had recovered its soul. In a twinkling Pierrot had adjusted the wick of the lamp, lit the fire, and put the faggots away, while all the time giving Barbette a lecture on good manners, for she hadn't yet learnt to shake a paw.

Viette trotted after him everywhere, holding up her arms and clamouring to be picked up by him. Maria slouched from one table to another, walking with a slight limp. She dealt the plates out carelessly; they clattered on the marble tops.

She interrupted the game of *malilla*. As she passed, Domingo patted her leg. Then he exclaimed:

'Stockings! You've got stockings on! What on earth's got hold of you today?'

'Keep your hands off.'

She tried to hit him and nearly dropped the pile of plates. As a rule she wasn't so particular. But when Pierrot was there …

She was fourteen, though you'd have taken her for sixteen any day. That's why the men were so ready to make a pass at her. At first sight what you saw was a red mouth and two dark eyes that looked at you boldly. On closer inspection other details were noticeable. Her neck wasn't very clean and her hair was dishevelled. She had big hands and feet. Her dress was torn, and her finger-nails bitten to the quick.

She often snuffled, like Tatave, having no handkerchief. She wasn't allowed to blow her nose like Fébo, who simply leant forward, closed one nostril with his thumb, and blew through the other. Very simple. From some points of view, hygienic. But Mme Fine didn't hold with it. Leastways not for girls. So Maria snuffled all day long.

Pierrot, on his knees, was blowing the fire. The flames spurted up between the fir-cones, which began crackling at once. When he stood up, he found Maria gazing at him, fascinated by the glow of firelight on his strong, well-drawn features. He ran to her and snatched half the pile of plates.

'Come on,' he said. 'We'll do it together.'

The Auberge Daranluz was at the junction of three streets, the Allée des Trois Tourelles, the Avenue Neuve, and the Grande Rue Noble, so that, for those who found it difficult to pass a café without having a drink, it wasn't so easy to avoid the temptation. The Allée encircled the fortress at the heart of Casteilcorbon. All that had been necessary was to fill in the ditch which had run round the outer walls and plant trees on either hand and there was the charming promenade of which the villagers were justly proud.

There had originally been a tower at each of the four corners of the outer wall, but, since one of them had practically disappeared, the name of the street referred only to three. What was left of the fourth tower was in the yard of the inn. It housed pigs, rabbits, pigeons, and, in the one part fit for human habitation, Maria.

Of the other streets which converged at the Auberge Daranluz, the Avenue Neuve was broad and of recent construction. After a short stretch, it changed its character, becoming a country road leading south-east towards the sea. The Rue Noble was always rather a joke to strangers. It was the shortest and narrowest street in the place and would more suitably have been called a lane.

Poor little Grande Rue Noble! It had once been the only approach to Casteilcorbon, leading to the drawbridge. But its old houses had gone, some of them to make way for that ugly block of a Town Hall, over whose gateway flew the French flag. A clearance had to be made too for the Place de la République, after which only a few yards was left of the old and noble street. Admittedly it started again on the other side of the Place, though under a different name, the Impasse des Suisses. What it had to do with the Swiss no one could say except M. le Curé, who had a learned theory of his own about it.

It was along the Impasse that Tatave hurried home, for in it was the back door of the *herboristerie*. Mme Grosbelhomme heard him coming, snuffling as usual, and her bosom swelled with reproaches. She was like a hen with only one chicken, inclined to smother it with maternal anxiety, affection, and fussiness.

'Why are you so late? Where have you been?'

'With Pierrot.'

That was a clever answer. The innkeeper's son enjoyed a great reputation. Everyone thought him perfect. There are people like that, whose very name is reassuring, just as there are others who immediately inspire misgivings.

'What about your homework?'

'We did it all together. I've only got to copy it out.'

'Take off your galoshes and put your overall on.'

'Yes, Mum.'

'Aren't you going to kiss me?'

'Of course, Mum.'

Tatave came up to her and lifted up his face unenthusiastically.

'You might at least blow your nose first. *Mon Dieu!* When are you going to grow out of that disgusting habit? Snuffling all day long at your age! ... But your hands are icy. My poor lamb! Come along and get warm. I've put your slippers by the stove.'

The kitchen was beautifully clean. But it was cluttered, for it did duty also as a laboratory in which Mme Fabienne prepared certain mysterious concoctions which she sold to peasants. For besides giving advice to the villagers on moral questions she was also consulted on all matters of health. She acted as midwife and was not far from usurping the functions of doctor. Her shop was much better stocked than the convent dispensary, and the peasants and workmen would far rather bring their aches and pains to this smiling, amiable widow than to the Reverend Mother, for all the latter's diplomas, which entitled her to make up proper prescriptions. Crusty, and above all deaf, she was more fitted to look after people's souls than their bodies. For when she did grudgingly hand over a bottle of lotion or a box of pills, she made it quite clear that the medicine had no healing properties whatever unless it was by the Will of God. Prayer would in any case be far more efficacious. She was quite consistent.

With Mme Fabienne Grosbelhomme it was just the opposite. She believed ardently in her medicaments. Better still, she knew how to impart her faith to her customers.

'Tatave. Your cod-liver oil.'

'The bottle's finished.'

'Then go and get another from the shop. You know – in the cupboard where I keep the stuff from the convent.'

For, thanks to an understanding with the Reverend Mother, the herbalist managed to keep a certain amount of drugs she was not strictly entitled to deal in.

Her son shrugged his shoulders. Discreetly. In the shop, his first concern was to reach for the bottle of iodine. He rolled up his sleeve and applied the antiseptic to a cut in his upper arm which was still bleeding.

'Pierrot didn't do it by halves,' he said to himself. 'All the same, he might have put the point of his knife in the flame of the lamp to sterilize it.'

But then Tatave had been brought up in a more or less medical household. He knew all about such matters. He blew on his arm and, as soon as it was dry, painted on another coat. Then he took a sealed bottle into the kitchen and opened it with his own knife, for the pleasure of using that marvellous instrument, whose eight blades were so stiff that it was necessary to use another knife to open them.

Under his mother's watchful eye, he poured out the exact dose into a graduated glass. The smell of the stuff nearly turned him up.

'Ugh!' he exclaimed, making a grimace which had become almost a matter of ritual.

'Come on, Tatave. Be a man,' urged his mother encouragingly.

Glass in hand, the 'man' went over to the sink. That was only prudent, in case he was sick.

'How considerate he is!' thought Mme Fabienne.

'Ugh!' exclaimed Tatave again, as though struggling against a violent aversion.

In the little mirror over the tap he watched his mother attentively, and at the first favourable moment the cod-liver oil went down the waste-pipe.

'Ugh!'

He played the part to perfection.

'Bravo! You see, it's soon over.'

'Can I have a peppermint to take away the taste?'

'Of course, *mon chéri*.'

Tatave thought he'd earned two. Mme Grosbelhomme looked on approvingly as he got his books out and sat down at the table. She was thinking that, with the assistance of the cod-liver oil, he would one day be able to live up to his somewhat imposing surname, a name she'd had some difficulty in getting used to in the early days of her marriage.

Tatave was dying to tell his mother of the dramatic developments of the day, of the schoolmaster's suspicions and his infamous decision to impose a collective punishment. But after a moment's reflection he gave up the idea. To mention M. Grillon's name under his own roof was distasteful to him, knowing that if he did so his mother's face would at once light up. No, it was better to keep quiet about it. She would find out sooner or later, and her comments on the subject would enable him to guess whether M. Déodat had once again succeeded in arranging a clandestine meeting with her.

Still snuffling, he took out his private note-book and spread it over his maths exercise book, which was exactly the same size. Choosing the fountain-pen with red ink, he wrote:

LES CHEVALIERS DE CASTEILCORBON
Chronique historique
par
Le Sieur Gustave de Grosbel

Switching to green ink he wrote on the next page:

Chapter I
In Life and Death

And finally in ordinary black ink (they sold ink in the shop, so he was particularly well supplied with that commodity) he began his narrative.

Nourished on tales of chivalry and romance, he made a pretty good job of it, and the day's events took on a very different aspect – and a much more imposing one – when all the names had been suitably transposed and ennobled. Pierrot appeared as the Chevalier Pierre d'Aranluz, Georget as the Sire Georges de Grillon. The others were Henri de Martel, Francisco de Guartorella (a noble Spaniard who had come to France in search of adventure), and Victorin as the *écuyer* of Herculean strength.

... With that Pierre d'Aranluz raised his iron-gloved hand to heaven crying:

'Friends, brothers in arms, destiny itself has spoken from your lips. We are bound now in life and in death, to struggle against injustice. I demand the blood oath.'

Whipping out his dagger, he plunged it into a vein, and the rich vermilion blood spurted out into the golden goblet. With one accord the cavaliers followed suit, till the blood overflowed the precious cup. One by one they raised the goblet to their lips and ...

'Have you got a lot more of that stuff to copy out?' asked Mme Grosbelhomme commiseratingly.

Fearing more exhaustive inquiries, Tatave slipped the manuscript under his grammar.

'There's still quite a bit,' he sighed. 'I'm going as fast as I can.'

55

'As soon as you've done we'll have supper. Afterwards I want you to prepare some suppositories for me.'

'Who are they for?' asked Tatave, always inquisitive.

'Mme Muche. It's this powder you've got to put inside. Three decigrammes in each. Two dozen, she wants, and she's calling for them tomorrow morning.'

It was a job he loved. For one thing, there was the very delicate balance to use. And then soldering up the capsules with a spirit lamp. Lastly the capsules were made of cocoa-butter, and any broken ones were slipped into his mouth. Delicious things, those capsules.

Dropping the tale of romance, he hastily did his homework, then, while his mother got the supper ready, he took down the scales and got out the capsules.

'How obliging he is!' mused Mme Grosbelhomme. 'Always ready to do things for me.'

Yet when she fetched him in to supper she said to him tartly:

'Tatave! Once and for all, will you blow your nose? And pull your socks up.'

The mayor's house seemed to be perpetually guarded by the bronze soldier of the war memorial. Erected when the Council decided to sacrifice the old quarter to construct the Place de la République, the house was a pretentious affair with a flight of steps leading up to the front door, in which were panes of yellow, blue, and red glass. In every flourish it proclaimed that this was indeed the habitation of M. Guillaume Muche, mayor of Casteilcorbon and the richest and most important distiller in the neighbourhood.

Generally Victorin derived a certain solace from the contemplation of his home, which went a long way to compensate for his manifold intellectual shortcomings. But there were times nevertheless when he couldn't help feeling ashamed of it.

On one occasion M. Grillon had said:

'Poverty, particularly when it is hidden, raises always a presumption of honesty. How few, on the other hand, are those who have amassed wealth while observing strict standards of honesty and fair play. Yet they glory in it.'

Slow-witted though he might be, Victorin had understood that, all the more so since every boy in the class had swung round to look at him. He had turned scarlet as abruptly as a shrimp dropped into boiling water.

Another time, Cisco had said to him in a tone of genuine pity:

'Poor chap! You know, you positively stink of money. And your parents too. Made it a bit too quickly, I suppose.'

The others had sniffed, as though he really did give off a bad smell. It was Georget who had come to his rescue.

'Fortunately you're a good chap in spite of it. So it's all right really.'

And Pierrot had added:

'After all, it's not his fault, is it?'

It certainly wasn't, any more than it was his fault not being very quick in the uptake. As for his father, it wasn't really fair to blame him either – a big, florid man, more enterprising than his neighbours. He had always been sure of success, and succeed he always did. He distilled lavender from the Pyrenees, mimosa, bergamot, fruit – particularly plums – orange peel, and all sorts of waste products from the jam factories of Limoux, Toulouse, and Agen. He would have distilled pebbles or horse-droppings if there'd been anything to be got out of them. In short, a man who had worked his way up from the bottom and in building his own fortune had brought an air of prosperity to Casteilcorbon, though without ever giving his workers much more than was necessary to keep body and soul together.

Le gros Muche, he was called. A man who ground the face of the poor. A sort of dictator in shirt-sleeves, by turns violent, cordial, and pompous, sometimes crafty, sometimes straightforward, according to the needs of the moment.

A large garden lay between his home and the business premises, the offices, warehouse, and distillery proper. He had only to cross it to get to his work, which was no doubt why he seldom bothered to put a jacket on.

That Thursday evening Victorin crept into the house on tiptoe, hoping his father would still be busy with his correspondence. He was out of luck, however. There was the huge mass of a man blocking the way.

'Where have you been?'

'Where have I been? ... I've been ... [he swallowed] ... I've been ... er ... with Pierrot.'

M. Muche grunted. In his eyes the Daranluz family stood next to his own in Casteilcorbon. Moreover, as deputy mayor, the innkeeper was his right-hand man in all matters concerning the municipality.

'Come here ... It's all right. I'm not going to eat you. There's no need to cringe. Were you alone with Pierrot?'

'Yes ... I mean no. There were ... there were the other chaps.'

'I thought so. Always hanging about with those good-for-nothings. It's not the thing. Not for a Victorin Muche. At your age! Ganging up with a crowd of guttersnipes!'

'But ... they're my schoolfellows. I sit in class with them, and I can't very well help ...'

'Listen to me. Admittedly they're your schoolfellows, but whose fault is that? If you hadn't been thrown out of three secondary schools, and even out of the Lycée at Perpignan, because you could neither work nor behave yourself, you wouldn't now at the age of seventeen be rubbing shoulders with the sons of my workmen.'

'Guillaume,' said Mme Muche, appearing in the hall, 'you know you mustn't get excited. It's bad for your heart. Please, Guillaume ...'

She joined her hands in supplication.

M. Muche's second wife must have been still under thirty. The first wife had died after two years of marriage, spent in a state of perpetual terror, in giving birth to this lump of a Victorin whom she might just as well have kept to herself.

The present Mme Muche was the dream of pretty well every man in Casteilcorbon.

'A magnificent balcony she has, to be sure,' said Sébastien the cork-cutter, referring to her bosom. And in saying that, he just about summed up the general opinion – that is, among the males, of course.

By the other camp she was regarded critically, though no one could help envying her her hats or her queenly bearing. Despite the latter, Mme Muche remained a very shy person. She was a worrying, over-scrupulous woman, and an ardent church-goer.

Victorin took advantage of her weakness to squeeze money out of her.

'And now to come to another matter,' roared his father, 'what did you do with the thousand francs you wormed out of "Little Mother"?'

He gripped his son by the arm at the exact place that was still sore from the blood oath. He shook the boy roughly.

'Oooh!' cried Victorin.

He was on the verge of tears. So 'Little Mother' had betrayed him. A dirty trick. She quailed beneath the accusing glance he gave her. As a matter of fact the last thing she was capable of was a dirty trick, and she spent her life trying to appease the anger of her irascible man.

'My Guillaume is choleric by temperament,' she used to say to her friends, thinking she was employing a rather distinguished expression.

Unfortunately her Guillaume had suddenly demanded her account book that day, before she'd had time to cook it.

'You're going to tell me here and now what you did with those thousand francs,' shouted the mayor, shaking his son more violently than ever. 'And I'd be very interested to know what a brat like you can find to spend a thousand francs on in a place like this. Come on, answer, or I'll ...'

'Guillaume,' pleaded Mme Muche, 'think of your heart.'

Muche stopped. She was quite right: he must think of his heart. But at the sight of Victorin standing before him, his indignation welled up again.

'Are you going to answer me, wretch? Or must I drag it out of you?'

The wretch took a deep breath.

'It was ... it was because of the honey.'

With that he plunged helter-skelter into a long, rambling explanation.

'You see, Piquet's honey was stolen last night. And he accuses us of having taken it, and if we don't own up by Saturday he'll keep us in all through the holidays, d'you see? Four whole days copying out our algebra. But we can't own up because we didn't take the honey. We couldn't, could we? So I thought ... I thought that, if we paid for the honey ... that would put everything straight, d'you see? Because the others don't want to be kept in. They want ... As a matter of fact they've got some funny ideas ... But the thing is they've none of them any money, and I thought that by paying Piquet ...'

'M. Grillon, please! I forbid you to call him Piquet. He may be a useless bit of work, but that doesn't entitle you to speak disrespectfully of him.'

Victorin hung his head penitently and went on with his laborious explanation, staring at his shoes.

'I thought if we did that, M. Grillon would call it quits. That is, if we paid for the damage. Otherwise, it's going to be a pretty rotten show. And because of the others I thought it was up to me to ...'

Guillaume Muche was getting redder and redder in the face. He couldn't make head or tail of this honey business.

'Well,' he said at last, 'how much did you give him?'

'Me? ... But ... I haven't given him anything yet.'

'Then the thousand francs – where are they? Show me the note. I want to see it at once.'

'Guillaume, dear,' put in Mme Muche, who was trembling more than Victorin, 'do be careful. Think of ...'

'Where's that thousand-franc note?' roared the mayor.

'The thing is,' stammered Victorin, hopelessly feeling in his pockets. 'The thing is ...'

M. Grillon pushed his armchair between the kitchen stove and the wireless set in readiness for later on. He always finished the evening sitting there, but before that there was work to do, and as soon as Georget had cleared the table after supper he settled down to correct the boys' exercises in red ink. Then, when the cuckoo had come out through his little door and made his peculiar call nine times, Déodat turned towards his son with the invariable words:

'Georget, my boy, it's bedtime.'

He got up himself, lit his second pipe, wound up the gold chronometer watch which was the only legacy he had from his father, and sat down in the armchair to listen to the news.

'Listen, Dad ...'

This was something out of the ordinary. Instead of going up to his room, Georget stood gravely in front of his father.

'Well? What is it?'

'I only wanted to say that you're ... you're ... What I mean is it wasn't any of us who did it ...'

The schoolmaster sighed. Since the morning they had carefully avoided any allusion to the pillaged hive. The only thing to recall it was Déodat's face, which was still a little swollen.

'It wasn't us, Dad. I swear it wasn't.'

M. Grillon shook his head.

'There are certain words which it is legitimate to use in denial of one's own guilt, but not of other people's.'

Quite naturally he had slipped into a didactic tone.

'If you said to me: "I swear I didn't do it myself," that touches me, and I'm ready to take your word. But when you swear that others didn't, your words lose all their persuasiveness. After all, you can only be sure of yourself, if indeed we can be sure of anything in this life. I therefore forbid you to swear on behalf of others. An oath is a sacred thing.'

'Exactly. That's why I feel so sure,' thought Georget, feeling the wound on his arm. But of course he couldn't speak about that.

'Really, Dad,' he repeated, 'I'm quite sure. Whoever it was, it wasn't anyone in our class. You must believe me, you really must. Try looking somewhere else for the thief, and until you find something definite please call off that punishment. It's not fair. Aren't you listening?'

Yes, M. Grillon was listening all right. He was also wondering. He could see that the boy's plea was charged with emotion and he realized that something quite extraordinary must have happened that evening to urge Georget to overcome his natural shyness.

'Did the other boys ask you to come and speak to me about it?' he inquired gently.

'Heavens, no!' (What strange ideas grown-ups get into their heads!)

'Come on. Tell me all about it. What makes you so certain your friends are innocent? I'm only too ready to listen. All I want is to be just.'

'It's like this,' began Georget eagerly. 'We held an inquiry. Everybody had to say exactly what he was doing last night. And there wasn't one that could have got here to swipe that honey. So you see ...'

M. Déodat smiled rather sadly. He was touched by the boy's eagerness to defend his schoolfellows.

'I'm very glad to hear you speak like that, Sonny. It's a long time since you've spoken to me so frankly. Moreover, it's quite right that you should want to stand up for your comrades. It shows your heart's in the right place and that you have a natural instinct for social solidarity. But, having said that much, it's my duty to warn you that there should be a limit to your credence in other people's assertions, even those of your friends.'

Once again Georget's hand went to his wound. There was something else behind that than 'other people's assertions'.

'If, later on,' M. Déodat went on, 'you are honoured as I have been by being called upon to serve on the jury at the assizes, you will learn to be chary of accepting statements made in the witness-box, even those alibis which seem absolutely water-tight, but which are only too often the means by which guilty people escape responsibility for their acts. Wherever there is a crime there is always a guilty person, but very rarely anybody to come forward and admit it. Nothing is more difficult than to extract the truth.'

'Exactly. So you're ready to forgive what happened?'

'That's not what I said,' retorted M. Grillon, a little irritated at having failed to make himself understood. 'Taking everything into consideration, I am forced to conclude that the culprit is someone familiar with this place. You know yourself what a rage Ranavalo gets into when a stranger so much as touches the gate. All the more if it happens at night. And I'm convinced that, if I compared all your footprints with those that were left, I would discover the thief.'

'Then that's what you ought to do.'

'No. I can't bring myself to stoop to police methods of that sort. I prefer a spontaneous confession – at least a more or less spontaneous one – which is in keeping with human dignity. I've made it easy for the culprit by promising not to deal severely with him. I'll go further. You can tell your friends that if he comes to me in private no one will ever know his name. Could anyone be more indulgent than that?'

'In that case,' said Georget firmly, 'I may as well tell you I took the honey myself. I did it for … for fun … to see if I dared.'

The schoolmaster shrugged his shoulders.

'Come on. Don't be silly. Self-sacrifice is a very noble thing, but there's a limit to everything. I know very well you didn't take the honey, for one thing because you can help yourself to as much as you want here at home. Besides, you're much too scared of the bees. And lastly you don't wear clogs.'

'Are you really sure I didn't do it, Papa?'

'Absolutely.'

'Yet you're going to punish me along with the others.'

'Look here, my boy. I've had about enough of this. Go to bed.'

Georget had made an intense effort to dissuade his father and was now at the end of his tether. He made one last fling, however, dissolving in tears as he did so.

'All right,' he stammered, 'I'll ... I'll go ... But think it over. It'd be unfair to punish ... everybody ... If you do ... look out.'

Ill-chosen words. M. Grillon drew himself up to his full height and looked down on his son.

'Get out, you insolent boy. Go to bed at once. To start lecturing me on how I should behave! Unheard of! It would serve you right if I ...'

Georget fled in terror.

The schoolmaster's pipe had gone out and the news was finished. Instead of sitting down again, he strode up and down the kitchen. Unfair! The word burnt into his soul. He who regarded himself as a model of equity.

My Georget! Who could have thought it? Lecturing me, and even finishing up with a threat. All right! We'll see who's master here.

No sooner was he back at the smithy than Riquet received a slap on the face, a good sound one, one of old man Martelot's best. The boy's left cheek went red. Tomorrow there would be a bruise. He had a sensitive skin.

The pain of it darted through his head like the sparks that fly from a bar of white-hot iron under the blows of the hammer. But the boy was nimble and quick enough to dodge the kick which, as he knew well, would accompany the blow. A matter of habit.

M. Martelot's toe fetched up against the anvil instead of on his son's bottom, and the pain this caused him didn't help matters at all.

'I'll teach you to come loafing home at this hour of the night.'

Since the middle of the afternoon the smith had been watching for the boy's return, as he wanted his help in fitting the metal tyre to a wheel. It couldn't be done single-handed. The tyre had to be heated, and ever since he had been strong enough for the job, Riquet had been put on to the huge forge bellows that were fixed to the roof and worked by a sort of bell-pull.

He at once dashed to the rope and started blowing. The greater part of his leisure time was spent that way, staring at the anvil. Who indeed could take his eyes from forge-work? Certainly not this boy, who gazed fascinated at the white-hot metal while his father twisted it, flattened it, bent it, straightened it – in fact juggled with it in every possible way.

Riquet longed to ply that wonderful trade himself.

One day he would be smith, wheelwright, locksmith, mechanic, and everything else remotely connected with metals, like his father, to whom all manner of articles came for repair, and who never said no to a job. But for the moment he was on the bellows. Oh, those eternal bellows! That wasn't amusing at all.

'Good for you,' his father would say, with a grin on the days when he was in a good temper. 'Teaches you the trade. The more you go pulling on that rope, the less puffing and blowing you'll have to do before you die.'

Encouraging, that! But the days were rare when M. Martelot was in a good temper. A hard-bitten man from the north, who never spared himself nor was inclined to spare others. Later on, Riquet was going to become like him when white hairs began to invade his tow-coloured mop and when the pink of his young cheeks had been turned into a florid complexion made up of tiny red and purple lines. They had the same washed-out blue eyes with red lids, the same slow movements, the same practical intelligence and capacity for concentration, the same taste for finding a way round a technical difficulty. Neither of them could rise beyond the level of that patient endeavour which brings satisfaction but no joy.

Yes, the blacksmith and his son were of the same race all right. It was their situations that were different. The man cursed, grumbled, and gave orders. The boy trembled and blew the bellows. Sometimes the rhythmic movement became so monotonous that he dozed. But, on the brink of unconsciousness, two things never dimmed – the fear of blows and the need to keep pulling on the rope.

'Blow, boy. Blow. I'll teach you to yawn.'

This evening each movement irritated the open wound on his arm. A queer idea that – to cut yourself deliberately. There was something about that procedure which transcended Riquet's practical mind. But he possessed in the highest degree the sense of solidarity and obedience. Pierrot was to him an altogether exceptional being whose decisions were not to be questioned. What did it matter if he'd had a clout from his father? It was at the chief's command that he had neglected the forge that afternoon, and whatever followed from it must be accepted.

'Blow, boy. Blow. What's the matter with you tonight?'

Later on Riquet, with shoulders as broad as his father's, would start wandering over the face of France. He was obsessed by the desire to leave this house in which he had received so many blows. Like his father, who had come from the far north to settle down in Casteil-corbon, he would fetch up in some other corner, where his colourless hair and strange accent would astonish everybody. There he would work hard, talk little, grumble a good deal, and beat his son to 'teach him the trade'. Perhaps, in his own way, he would be happy.

Not yet, however! And Riquet, as he pulled on the rope, compared his lot with his friend Tatave's. The latter had never really known his father.

'Lucky beggar,' thought Riquet. 'I shouldn't miss mine.'

Without a sign of effort, the smith lifted the hoop out of the furnace. The metal, that had looked blue in the flames, now glowed a dull red. Rushing to his aid, Riquet snatched up some tongs and held the hoop in its jaws while his father adjusted the curvature. Each hammer-blow jolted the boy's arms. Then, together, they placed the hoop on the wheel, which promptly began to smoke. Two bucketfuls of cold water were quickly flung over it. A hiss of steam, a wet, metallic smell. There was nothing more to do now but put the wheel back on the carriole.

'So much for that,' grunted M. Martelot, wiping his great thick hands on his leather apron. 'And now, what've you been up to all the afternoon?'

'I was with P ... Pierrot ... We were d ... doing our homework.'

'Well, why ever didn't you say so before?'

Encouraged by that, Riquet, who had been on the verge of tears, now embarked on the story of M. Grillon's accusation.

The smith didn't grasp it very well. He wasn't quick to understand anything he couldn't touch with his hands.

'Let's go and have supper. You can tell your mother all about it. That'll be just about the last straw if you're going to be accused of stealing, *nom de Dieu*.'

Cisco had seen his friend Riquet home, and had even heard the slap.

'That's pretty rotten,' he muttered. 'And a decent man like him!'

Nonchalantly he retraced his steps. There was no need for him to hurry home, no risk of his being scolded.

Instead of continuing along the Rue du Pot de Fer, which led directly to the poor quarter in which they lived, father, mother, and a swarm of brothers and sisters, he went back to the Trois Tourelles thinking over the events of the day.

He walked on, careless of the time.

'Quite thrilling, this beehive affair,' he mused. 'Certainly Pierrot was splendid. But who could it have been, breaking into the place without making Ranavalo bark? To risk being stung all over just for a few pounds of honey. Doesn't make sense.'

The little poacher was wrong there. He was judging by himself; nothing would have induced him to affront a hive of bees. But there it was! Someone had.

Cisco couldn't help having a sneaking admiration for the chap. Certainly it wasn't anybody in their gang. Not that he had been impressed by that oath. But he knew his pals too well. He would have guessed.

What was going to happen if they one and all kept faith? Of course it was all nonsense, that business of mixing their blood. Though it had been his own idea. As always. Only an idea, all very well in its way, but no need to take it seriously. But of course that was just the difference between him and Pierrot. When Pierrot got an idea into his head, he hung on to it. He even carried it out.

It was the same with the idea of being smugglers. In three or four days Pierrot had got the whole thing planned, set up his headquarters, made arrangements for the booty, and given each member of the gang a particular part to play.

What good had it been? None whatever. Naturally. All the same they'd had a lot of fun for the last month. And there was something in being a gang. It was matey. Like being a band of brothers. No, more than that. For brothers were always bickering, while Pierrot wouldn't allow any quarrelling.

And now they were bound together more closely than ever. Against Piquet and his beastly mean punishment. Ah, that Piquet! He'd find out! He hadn't ever imagined that his pupils had it in them to be cavaliers.

'Blood and Freedom!' muttered the boy, and in spite of himself his hand went up to the wound on his arm.

He went the length of the Rue de la Tour Ardente, then the Rue Bleue, and came to the nasty, lumpy cobbles of the Rue des Halle-

66

bardes, the dirtiest in the whole of Casteilcorbon, down the centre of which ran a gutter littered with household refuse that was washed away only when it rained. The boy, however, was much too used to the smell of poverty to notice it. His father, a mason by trade, rarely had more than one or two days' work in the course of a week. So they had to manage as best they could, which wasn't any too well.

The hovel in which the Guartorellas lived belonged to nobody. Driven out of Spain by Franco's victory, they had simply taken possession of this abandoned building, stopping up the holes with whatever came to hand, without inquiring whether anyone owned it. You couldn't fail to recognize it, even from a distance, for there were never less than two or three *muchachos* crawling about in the dust, showing their bare bottoms to the world. They had running noses, frizzy hair, and magnificent eyes and teeth, and they would no doubt grow up to be as good-looking as Cisco. For all their beauty, they were an object of general pity, which, however, didn't go to the length of offering help. They were pitied, despised, and just a little feared, for they carried their poverty flamboyantly, tattered clothing flying at every window – coloured shirts, underpants with no knees, and frayed petticoats, to say nothing of the nappies of the last arrival and the wet mattresses of the two before.

But if you've been given a name like Francisco Guartorella, and endowed moreover with a lively imagination, surroundings such as these are easily dispelled by day-dreams, dreams of grandeur, luxury, adventure, and even, it should be added, of chivalry and romance. The chief thing was not to notice. Also to keep as far as possible out of sight of his mother, who invariably had some errand to send him on.

As for the father, he was a marvellous companion when he wasn't drunk, and even when he was, he was still good company. Together the father and son had spent many unforgettable hours of vagabondage and pillage. As regards the housekeeping, the great thing was to provide that bare minimum, the five or six litres of wine a day which was needed to preserve domestic harmony. So long as they had that …

No chance of Cisco's getting his ears boxed because he had come home late. That was something! Indeed, it made up for a lot of shortcomings in other directions.

He kicked open the door and at the first glance saw that, without waiting for him, they'd been having a feast. Some greasy paper on the table showed signs of ham and salami, while a row of empty bottles told him his parents had drunk their fill. The head of the house was stretched out full length on the floor in front of the stove. Mme Guartorella was asleep too, sprawling over the table, her head on her arms, her hair dishevelled, happy.

The children had filled themselves with fat slices of *mortadelle* and had gobbled up the sausage, skin and all. Then they had gone to bed.

They were used to this sort of thing. Many an evening finished up like that. Only Raphael, the youngest, two months old, was not yet aware of it. He slept blissfully in his cradle, actually a soap-box.

'All the same,' muttered Cisco, 'they might have left me a snack.'

But he said it without any real resentment. After all, it was his own fault. Apparently his father had had a windfall. It had been promptly consumed by the family, chiefly in drink. Never mind about Cisco.

Ferreting around, he found a hunk of bread, two potatoes that had been boiled in their skins, a raw onion, and the remains of some *pissaladière* – a pickle made of tomatoes, pimentos, and olive oil. There was even a little white wine left in one of the bottles. Not so bad, after all. At least, not to a chap like Cisco.

Munching stolidly, he told himself stories. The ones he invented were the best of all. Sometimes he would go off on wonderful travels. A new Columbus, he would set sail in a caravel to discover desert islands. More often, however, his imagination would conjure up the most extravagant combats, more likely than not in that ancient keep which was always there to haunt his day-dreams. Or the tale might run to love, when the beautiful Éléonore, whisked away from the Count of Roussillon by the three barons and shut up in Casteilcorbon, would play the principal part. A very platonic part, it might be added.

Suddenly the baby stirred in his makeshift cradle and wrinkled his little forehead like an old man with a load of worries.

'Hell!' thought Cisco. 'In a minute he'll be bawling his head off and waking everybody up.'

Shaking himself out of his reverie, he bent over the baby, mildly disgusted by the smell that came up. But at the first cry a curtain was drawn – the curtain which served to cut off the girls' quarters in the one habitable room – and Cisco's eldest sister appeared.

68

She was remarkably grown up for her eleven years. But that was hardly surprising, since the whole weight of the household fell on her shoulders whenever her mother was in her cups, which wasn't seldom. With her hair like a mop, she staggered out of her sleep, picked up Raphael, and tried to calm him down. No use. There was only one thing that would satisfy his demands, and that was a meal.

'What's been going on this evening?' asked Cisco. 'Has there been a wedding?'

Nièves shrugged her shoulders. In spite of her name, *Marie des Neiges*, she was as dark as a fig. She said:

'It was that lout of a Victorin who stumped up four hundred and sixty francs. You can guess what happened.'

'Victorin? Why on earth?'

'Father won them at cards.'

And, jerking her chin at her parents, she added:

'You can see for yourself ...'

She shook her mother vigorously to wake her up, but without success. Raphael expressed his wishes more and more peremptorily.

'Here. Hold him a minute.'

Calmly she unbuttoned her mother's dress and installed the baby in position.

Mme Guartorella opened one eye and so far recovered her maternal instinct as to press him to her.

'*Un vino blanco maravilloso*,' she sighed.

Happy now, Raphael took his fill of milk which, that evening, must have been considerably fortified by alcohol. Nièves yawned, showing dirty teeth. She had to stay there, as the mother, dozing off again already, was quite capable of dropping the child on to the floor when he had done.

'Here, Cisco, what's this story about some honey? Victorin was talking about it just now. You'll let me in on it, won't you?'

But the big brother answered grandly:

'First of all, this is our business, and it's not for girls. Secondly, do you take me for a thief?'

It was now time for the washing-up at the Auberge Daranluz, a dreary chore which returned with the regularity of all unpleasant things. Every evening Marie heaved a deep sigh at the piles of plates before her. Indeed, this last hour's work of the day, spent with her hands in smelly, greasy water, was the hardest of all.

From the café came the confused murmur of voices. Each time the door opened and shut a gust of tobacco smoke was wafted into the scullery, carrying with it the indefinable smell that was made up of sweat, corduroy, and *anisette*. For the men there, this was the best time of all. The day's work was done, their bellies were full, and they could relax, chat, play cards, or listen to Domingo playing the guitar.

The thought of them taking their ease was no encouragement to Maria. But there it was. There was no getting out of the job. Mme Fine never allowed it to stand over till the morning.

So Maria put on her apron, which was made of sackcloth, and plunged the first pile of plates into her basin of scalding water. It was too hot and stung her fingers, which went red. After a while, however, they got used to it and stopped hurting, and then, as the water gradually cooled, pools of grease formed on the surface. Meals were all very well: this was their ugly side. Sixteen people every day: that meant, for the two meals, one hundred and twelve plates, thirty-two forks, ditto knives, ditto spoons, to say nothing of all the dishes and cooking utensils.

'*Oh! là, là.*'

The orphan girl sighed once again. Fortunately there was Fébo to dry for her and put the things away. And there was one consolation, at any rate. So long as she was on that job, the mistress left her alone. Except when something was broken: then she appeared promptly enough. Sometimes there was another. If Pierrot hadn't got too much homework, he came and lent a hand. When that happened, the chore was instantly transformed into a pleasure, the two young people chattering away happily out of earshot of the grown-ups – for Fébo didn't count as a grown-up. And when the latter started telling one of his marvellous tales the time passed more quickly still.

Today Pierrot talked of the honey affair and M. Grillon's threat, and the atmosphere was one of indignation.

'To be kept in for four whole days! Can you imagine what that's like, my girl? Four days copying out algebra!'

Maria had never heard of algebra, but she understood it to be one of the last refinements of torture. She looked miserable.

'Just our luck!' she groaned. 'Just when you'd promised to take me out mushrooming in the Bois de Perdigane.'

'That's true. I'd forgotten about that. Still, it's not the punishment that counts. It's the unfairness of it.'

Gravely, Fébo declared:

'No justice in this world.'

Then he blew his nose skilfully, aiming at the gully that ran from under the sink and scoring a hit.

'What do you mean by that, Fébo? That you'd let yourself be punished unjustly?'

'I'm seventy-two,' the old man answered proudly.

By which he meant, no doubt, that he'd lived too long to have any illusions left, least of all on the subject of fair dealing.

'But what's made him do a thing like that?' asked Maria, with her mouth full. 'M. Grillon, I mean. He doesn't look a bad chap.'

Pierrot shrugged his shoulders.

'I know he isn't. But there you are – grown-ups get queer ideas into their heads. What are you eating?'

'A dried fig. It must have been off Sébastien's plate. He doesn't like them.'

'Give me a bit for Mascha.'

Obediently she stuck two greasy fingers into her mouth and pulled out a bit, which the boy took without the least repugnance. No sooner had he opened his cartridge case than the white mouse peeped out, sniffing to right and left, as though to take in the situation. Then, seizing the bit of fig, it disappeared again to eat it undisturbed in its shelter.

'No, he's not bad really,' went on Pierrot; 'only, he feels he's got to make a stand. If someone owned up, he'd let him off. But he can't just let it slide. You see, he's nuts about bees. Thinks them a sight better than humans.'

Maria stared.

'What? Do you mean he'd do nothing? In that case you've only to say it's you.'

Proud of her cleverness, she stopped washing up and stood with her red hands suspended above the steaming basin.

'I thought of that. But it's no good. It's a point of honour, you see.'

'Honour,' repeated Maria, 'honour ...'

Thoughtfully she picked up some bowls. One of them slipped through her greasy fingers, fell against the edge of the sink, then crashed to the floor.

71

'Maria!' called out Mme Fine. 'What have you broken this time?'

'It was my fault,' said Pierrot instantly. 'But I didn't do it on purpose.'

'What an idea!' came the answer in a softened voice.

Maria gave Pierrot a grateful look.

'A good sport,' she thought. 'Always comes up to scratch.'

She had never really considered the feelings she had for her employers' son. Love? Certainly not. Such an idea had never entered her head. Though she knew very well that that word had more meanings than one. The servant at an inn who spent her days surrounded by cork-cutters and workmen from the quarry and the distillery could could hardly remain for long ignorant of the realities of life, least of all a precocious girl like Maria. She knew what men were made of and how to cope with them. With Pierrot it was quite different. He was only thirteen and not yet in long trousers. Just a boy and quite unconscious of that side of her which appealed to the others. But so nice, so helpful. And each time he called her 'my girl', she wanted to give him a hug.

Of course she'd never dare do such a thing. What on earth would Mme Fine have said? Besides, the boy himself would have been quite taken aback.

'Thanks,' she said at last. 'But I hate to think of your being kept in like that. It's a shame. Quite apart from the mushrooms ...'

Fébo picked up the bits of broken china.

'A pretty one that,' he remarked, examining the pieces. 'Shouldn't be so clumsy.'

'It's not yours,' she snapped back. 'So there's no call for you to start blubbering over it. You'd do better to go and fetch me some more hot water.'

Fébo scowled. He'd have liked the mistress to know who'd dropped the bowl, but after what Pierrot had said he couldn't very well tell on her. Between him and Maria there was no love lost.

All the same, he did as she asked. For it was his job. Only he went extra slowly. Just to show her!

The moment he was gone Maria leant over towards Pierrot.

'He couldn't do anything to me, he couldn't. Tomorrow morning I'll go and tell him I took the stuff myself. He can't eat me. As for a scolding, I get that all day long as it is. A little more won't make no difference.'

She made the offer with a toss of her head that won Pierrot's admiration.

Maria! Who would ever have thought her capable of such magnanimity.

He would have liked to squeeze her hand in gratitude, but both were in the turbid washing-up water. Instead, on the impulse of the moment, he kissed her.

'You're a brick,' he said. 'I'll never forget this. But I won't have you taking the blame.'

Maria swelled with pride at the kiss. She snuffled two or three times.

'All the same,' she argued, 'it's the best way out. And then, with the place shut up on All Souls' Day, we'd go mushrooming after all. If someone's got to take the blame it might just as well be me. As for honour …'

'No. I won't have it. Besides, Piquet wouldn't believe you.'

'Why shouldn't he?'

'Because robbing a hive isn't a stunt for girls. And then – we're going to find out who did do it, and when we do he'll catch it all right.'

'It'll be too late. It won't stop your being kept in.'

'It won't work out like that.'

'What do you mean?'

'Because we're not going to be kept in, whatever Piquet says. There! … But for heaven's sake keep it to yourself. Just watch. You'll see some fun, my girl.'

For a second he was on the point of rolling up his sleeve to show her the mark of the blood oath. But a sudden shyness held him back. Besides, as he had said just now, this was no affair for girls. Another thing – would she understand? He couldn't be sure. More vehemently than ever he repeated:

'You're not to take it on yourself, Maria. I mean it. Seriously.'

'All right. If you want it like that,' the servant answered listlessly.

'You swear?'

'All right.'

'Spit, then.'

And Maria spat.

FOUR

As soon as the washing-up was done, Maria lit her lamp and went off to bed, forgetting to say good night.

'No breeding,' explained Mme Daranluz. 'That's what comes of having no mother or father. But there's one thing to be said for her: she's not nervous. Sleeping all alone in that ruin of a tower – the mere thought of it sends shivers all down my back. Even Fébo prefers the loft. But then he believes in ghosts. But it just shows you ... At first I put up a camp bed in the kitchen. Nice and warm there. But no. Said she couldn't sleep because of Domingo playing the guitar. So she fixed herself up in that room upstairs in the tower. A filthy place it is too, the way she keeps it. Never swept out, and her bed's never made. A little savage – that's what I say. There's no knowing how to handle her. The way she'll answer you back ...'

Mme Fine sighed.

'First I tried kindness. You see, I couldn't help feeling sorry for her. But you might just as well try appealing to the better feelings of a mule. Nor's the other way much better. You can scold till you're black in the face. Sometimes I think she's just laughing at me. If I wasn't so soft-hearted she'd have been chucked out long since. But there you are! You can't change your nature, can you?'

Every night it was Pierrot who put Viette to bed.

The café stayed open till eleven, and later still on Saturdays and Sundays. M. Daranluz had perforce to play cards. He didn't like it, but couldn't very well refuse when he was asked to make up a four. Moreover it flattered his customers to play with the innkeeper.

And whenever he played, his wife had to sit up to serve the drinks. If that didn't keep her busy, she filled in the time peeling vegetables for the morrow, chatting meanwhile with one or another.

Viette didn't make too much fuss over going to bed.

'Sandman, where are you?' cried Pierrot.

And she clambered up on his back.

Perched on his shoulders she was taken the round of the tables to say good night. Upstairs, she had first to say her prayers, kneeling before an Infant Jesus in terra-cotta. After that, Mascha was taken out of the cartridge case and given her to fondle while she was being undressed.

74

Mascha complicated the performance somewhat, as she had to change hands for the second sleeve, and he always tried to escape back to his master, unresponsive to the affection the little girl bestowed on him.

Pierrot tucked her up tenderly in her cot, kissed her on each cheek, and then on her neck to tickle her. Mascha was produced again, as it was always he who had the last kiss.

Sometimes he escaped and dived under the bed-clothes. That was really wonderful. Viette would go off into such shrieks of laughter that her mother would hear her and shout upstairs:

'What's going on up there? Must I come up to see?'

With that done, Pierrot went to his room. He took off his belt, put Mascha on the bedside table, and shook the cartridge case out of the window to get rid of the numerous little bits of liquorice which had accumulated there during the course of the day. The mouse, meanwhile, had a good clean up, sitting up like a miniature squirrel, rubbing its paws behind its ears and stropping its nose as though to make it sharper than ever.

Pierrot poured out its ration of milk into a paint-box pan which contained the exact measure. Mascha lapped it up like a dog, but with a tongue so tiny that it was visible only as a vague pink blur. The boy watched it with admiration as he undressed. Often he talked to it, sometimes even unburdening himself of his troubles. And each time he spoke the mouse lifted up its snout and screwed it round and round like a rabbit, apparently expressing its complete agreement. Then, after carefully wiping its whiskers, it would start lapping again.

Pierrot opened the drawer of the bedside table, and both of them went to bed. For the drawer contained Mascha's bed, the softest and most luxurious bed in the house. It was Tatave who had supplied the material from his mother's shop, a whole roll of cotton wool. A sumptuous present for Mascha, who with immense labour had fluffed it out until the drawer was completely full of a white downy mass in which it had organized – according to its fancy or to some mysterious instinct – a whole system of secret tunnels to make an ideal home.

As soon as the drawer was opened, the tiny white creature disappeared into its white quarters, and it was only by a little quiver of the fluff here or there that one could have an idea which corner of the labyrinth it had chosen for its bedroom.

In bed, Pierrot lay face downwards so as to be sure of not going to sleep. He waited.

Not very long, as a matter of fact. Fébo played two or three tunes on his accordion, sometimes accompanied by Domingo's guitar. Presently the boy's attentive ears heard a door creak and then the old man's cautious steps as he groped his way up the dark staircase. Never did his friend turn in without stopping for a good half-hour, sometimes longer, in Pierrot's room. His mother knew nothing of this, and sometimes the boy had qualms about it; but it was one of the best parts of the day, and he couldn't bring himself to jeopardize it by telling her.

Like all people who can't read, Fébo had a wonderful memory for stories and a great gift for telling them. Sometimes there was more invention than recollection in them, though in his wandering life in France and Spain he had seen enough of men and beasts to fill many books.

In seventy-two years …

Yes, he had been a rolling stone all right, this old Fébo, and had put his hand to many trades. He had travelled with his accordion and a tame marmot, sold almanacs and hot sausages, and fished for mussels and shrimps. He had been a docker at Barcelona, a guide, a warehouseman, a knife-grinder, and had known as many degrees of poverty. He had been more than once in prison. Everyone scrapes through as best he can, and no man had a right to judge him. Only God could do that. And the good God, sitting up there in His Paradise, wouldn't fail to take into account the seventy-two years of hardship and, all too often, of misery.

Now he had come to anchor at the Auberge Daranluz. There he was lodged and fed, that was all. But the days were rare when he didn't pick up a drink or two, from Sébastien, Domingo, or one of the others, when they were in a good humour or had just pocketed their week's pay. As luck would have it, they weren't all paid on the same day, or the days of abstinence would have been more frequent. For the rest, he would earn his tobacco or a little pocket money by rendering miscellaneous services. He was at everyone's beck and call. He rang the church bell for M. le Curé, stacked the wood that belonged to the town, cleaned out the sewer, helped the butcher to kill a pig, raked the paths of the convent gardens, and played the accordion at weddings.

Above all, he was the official, though self-appointed, guide to the Castle of Casteilcorbon. A notice, half washed out by the rain, had been put up by the drawbridge. On it, Pierrot had written in a careful round hand at Fébo's dictation:

For the key ... 2 francs.
(Warning: Beware of loose stairs. Danger.)
Conducted visits: Dungeon, Torture Chamber, &c ... 20 francs.
With explanations and replies to questions ... 25 francs.
Complete tour with history of the castle, prisoner's song, echoes (Recommended) ... 30 francs.
Special terms for parties, children, and members of the armed forces.
Apply to the Auberge Daranluz. Ask for Fébo, authorized guide.
(For the cloister, apply to the *garde champêtre* or the Mother Superior.)

So sight-seers knew just what to expect. Though it should be added that they generally came away thinking that the old man had given them a very good money's worth.

It did stalwart service, that notice. And in summer, when holiday-makers were often tempted off the main road by the sight of the keep on the horizon, the guide would rake in as much as 500 or 600 francs a month, to say nothing of tips and cigarettes.

Tonight Pierrot listened with only half an ear to the old friend who sat in his usual place beside the bed, hardly visible in the darkness, though that didn't prevent him gesticulating all the time, and particularly in the tragic parts of his narrative.

Finally the boy interrupted the story, laying his hand on the old man's knotty one.

'Fébo?'

'Yes.'

'Have you ever seen any thieves?'

Fébo didn't answer at once. Of course he had seen thieves. Hadn't he been in prison both in France and in Spain?

'I mean real ones. Not smugglers or anything of that sort. They're different. Real thieves who go about stealing ... I suppose you can see it in their eyes. Like murderers.'

The old man assured him it wasn't visible at all.

'But you, Fébo, if anyone accused you of stealing, what would you do?'

What indeed! Probably take to his heels. Ever since the day he had been rounded up in a raid on the Barrio Chino, he had decided that it was always best to keep out of the reach of the police, even if you've done nothing wrong. But he answered proudly:

'I'd take and kill him.'

'Splendid! Just what I thought. But it's different with us. We can't very well kill M. Grillon, can we? He says we're thieves, and we're not. He's made up his mind to punish us, and we're not going to be punished. So you see ...'

He sighed. Fébo sighed too.

'We thought of simply going on strike. In some ways that'd be much the best. Only Tatave objected. "It's all very well," he said. "I'd like nothing better. But what can I do when my mother takes me by the ear and drags me round to school? Nothing. No more could you if your fathers grabbed hold of you. Can you see Riquet standing up to M. Martelot or Victorin to M. Muche? And it's worse for me than for anyone, for you can't hit a woman." Tatave's quite right. A strike's a good idea, but we'd never see it through. You understand?'

'Of course.'

'So it'd be much better to clear right out where they couldn't get hold of us at all. That'd be grand.'

'Where?'

'Up in the mountains. Wherever you chose to lead us. For you know every path. I'm the chief of the gang, but you'd be our guide. We've thrashed it all out and everyone's agreed. We've sworn an oath to stand together and they'll all do as I say. If Piquet doesn't change his mind, we'll make off on Saturday afternoon as soon as we come out of school. So get ready.'

The boy gripped the old man's wrist as though to infect him with his earnestness.

'Go on! What are you thinking about? What are you going to eat? Where'd you sleep?'

'The provisions are all ready. We've got sackfuls. And there are farms in the mountains where we could get more. Cisco has worked it out that if we walked all night we'd cross the frontier on Sunday morning. In the afternoon at the latest. But it might be better to keep under cover during daylight. If we had you for our guide we couldn't lose our way.'

Fébo said nothing. Was it possible the boy was serious?

At first he had thought the boy was taking a leaf out of his own book and freely mixing fantasy with reality. But Pierrot went on in such a determined, matter-of-fact way that his words couldn't be taken otherwise than in earnest.

'There are two plans. Mine is to make straight for the frontier and get out of the country as soon as possible. Cisco wants us to go for Andorra. There's an old woman there who's a cousin of his, and she could hide us if need be. Besides, Cisco says there aren't any gendarmes there. That's an advantage certainly. Only it's awfully far.'

Fébo listened, hardly able to believe his ears.

'In the end we decided to leave the choice to you. You see, we all believe in you absolutely. Besides, there's another thing. People might think it a bit queer to see a party of boys together, but so long as there's a grown-up with us it'll seem quite natural. They'll sell us bread and cheese and milk, and perhaps even let us sleep in their barns. Victorin's promised to bring some money.'

'Good.'

The old man couldn't help being touched by this mark of confidence. What a boy, this Pierrot! Quite undaunted. Fébo could see he was quite capable of leading his companions into this preposterous adventure. Lucky he'd talked about it. It gave the old man a chance of stopping it.

'Mind you're ready, Fébo. The day after tomorrow evening. Pack up what you need. We're taking all the food we can carry. At least, all we can carry easily and without slowing down the pace. We've got to do the first stretch as fast as we can. For the moment the important thing is not to let the cat out of the bag. It's a deadly secret. Six o'clock Saturday night. That is, unless M. Grillon changes his mind.'

'And how'll you go? Will you all march off together?'

Pierrot shrugged his shoulders in the darkness. Was his friend joking?

'Of course not. What do you take us for? We've got it all worked out. It's dark by five nowadays. Each one will go off separately as though we had errands to run. Only Victorin and Tatave will together. You see, we're not too sure of Victorin. But two together won't attract any attention. Then we'll all meet at the top of the Perdigane Hill, just above the pine-wood. You know ...'

'Yet.'

'We'll gather in old Féroulet's hut. You'll go up there in advance

79

and start getting a meal ready. You'll find everything you need. We'll have a good tuck in, so that we'll be able to walk all night. Cisco's idea is that we might spend the night there and start off fresh in the morning. It's possible. Anyhow, the hut's there if we want it. No one's used it since old Féroulet died. What do you think?'

'Me …?'

The old man didn't know what to say. He was completely taken aback by this cut-and-dried plan.

'Still, I can make up my mind about that tomorrow,' went on Pierrot. 'I think it might be risky to stay. A search-party might find us there. Besides, however early we started, we'd meet the people from the mountains coming down to Mass, and they'd say which way we were going. That'd make it easy to catch up with us.'

'Do you really want to leave your *padre* and your *madre*? And little Viette?'

Pierrot sighed. Fébo had raised the one objection he didn't want to think about.

'No. I don't want to leave them. It's for the sake of the others. They don't mind leaving home. In fact, that's really the chief attraction … But I'm the leader. I can't very well stand out.'

'Why do they want to?'

'It's difficult to explain, Fébo. Here at the inn we're all so happy. With them it's different. Take Riquet, for instance. He gets knocked about all the time, and it's more than he can stand. Victorin hates school, but his father makes him stay on, and gets on to him every day for being a dunderhead. Of course he is. But it gets under his skin in the end. At Cisco's all the money goes in drink, and if Riquet and I didn't give him the snacks we take to school he'd be eating bricks.'

'Bricks?' asked Fébo in astonishment, his mind jumping to the fact that Cisco's father was a mason.

'Well, anything you like. What I mean is that he's often nothing to eat and just has to tighten his belt. As for Tatave and Georget, that's something more complicated. In fact, I don't think I really understand myself. I shouldn't think Piquet's much of a father. Still, he doesn't knock Georget about. What I can't make out is Tatave. His mother makes no end of a fuss of him. Sometimes she even comes to fetch him back from school, as she's frightened of his catching cold. Yet in spite of everything I think he ... Well, there it is – I think he hates the sight of her. It's a funny thing to hate your mother, isn't it?'

No. Fébo didn't think it funny. As a matter of fact his own ideas on the subject could hardly have been drawn from personal experience. He was a foundling. He had been discovered on the steps of the Séo d'Urgel seventy-two years ago, though the figure could hardly be vouched for.

'Anyhow, they all want to go. And as I'm the leader I've got to go too. Besides, it's the only way to get out of being kept in. It's a matter of honour, you see. There's really no choice.'

Fébo softened. It was difficult not to be won over by all this boyish enthusiasm. What touched him more than anything was the way this Pierrot counted on his help without a second's misgiving. But what an extravagant idea, all the same! It wasn't going to be easy to stop it without letting them down and earning his young friend's resentment.

Still, there was nothing like a good night's rest. Wiser counsels would no doubt prevail in the morning.

'We'll see,' he said to himself.

'You quite understand, don't you?' asked Pierrot. 'Six o'clock on Saturday ...'

The customers generally left the inn about eleven. Mme Fine always found that last hour the longest of all. She glanced at the clock, whose hands moved with such deliberate slowness. She was so tired that she felt as though with each minute something of her life went from her. She yawned, though she never failed to put her hand in front of her mouth and turn her head away from the company towards the dying fire. For she was the one to get up early. Always down first in the morning.

Often her husband made her a sign suggesting she should go off to bed. He was only too willing to close the place up himself. But it was no use. She always shook her head, and that made her yawn again.

It was all very well – her Benoît had the best intentions in the world. Most considerate. But men were like that. They meant well. But you could never count on them. Not for the little things. No, Mme Fine had to see for herself that everything was ship-shape before finally going upstairs. She banked up the fire and attended to the lamps. Ah,

81

that electricity! So long promised, yet just as far off as ever. Again and again the mayor assured them he was doing his best to get it supplied to the town. But he had a private plant of his own for the distillery (and for his house, of course, into the bargain), so that he wasn't really interested.

While her husband counted up the takings – you could never do that in front of the customers – she pinned the notes in bundles and slipped them into a black bag which she would presently take upstairs with her for greater safety. Finally she would go round for the last time to see that all the doors were properly locked and bolted. Her husband used to tease her about it. Said she was fussy. But there you are! That's just why you can't leave things to men.

With their muzzles in the air, Boulou and Barbette followed her about. They were waiting for their dish of fresh water. Before pouring it out, Mme Fine filled a large glass for herself, to which she added sugar. As soon as they heard the sound of her spoon as she stirred it, the two dogs started wagging their tails and pawing at her knees. She smiled at them, took another lump of sugar, and gave them each half, with a last pat for the night.

That was all – at least downstairs. By this time Benoît would already be undressed and in bed. She went upstairs on tiptoe. The last little duty was a sweet one – to have a peep at her two sleeping children.

Cautiously she approached the cot in which Viette was sleeping, her arms outspread, like the Child in the crib.

'How pretty she is!' thought Mme Fine, with a pride which at that time of the day attained its maximum. She was tempted to call Benoît so that they could rejoice together in this marvel they had created. But no. He would make too much noise. Even barefoot and taking all the care in the world, he always managed to wake Viette up. Then, with typical inconsistency, she couldn't resist the temptation to hold her lamp right over the cot to contemplate the slightly open mouth showing two rows of milk-white teeth. Immediately the child's eyelids flickered and her nose was screwed up.

She mumbled a few words, but when her mother kissed her she promptly fell asleep again.

There was no need to tiptoe into Pierrot's room. Once he went off, the boy was plunged into a sleep like death – a comfortable little death – and it was quite a job to shake him out of it in the morning.

Mme Fine looked reprovingly at the open drawer, the clothes scattered carelessly anywhere, the empty cartridge case on the washstand, the shutters he had forgotten to close.

'What hopeless creatures boys are!'

She picked up a sock that had lost its partner, folded up his crumpled overall, unknotted his tie and hung it over the back of a chair.

Inquisitively, Mascha poked his nose out of the cotton wool to find out the meaning of the light that was wandering about the room. Then, satisfied that the intruder was harmless, he retired again.

'And just look at those trousers,' muttered Mme Fine to herself. 'All rolled up in a ball. And the pockets full to bursting.'

She turned them out, examining their contents.

No handkerchief, of course. That was the last thing he'd think of having. But then the other things were far more useful! His knife, for instance, which was kept on a chain.

'Pity I can't chain his handkerchief to him,' thought his mother. 'There'd be some sense in that.'

Then there was a bit of cheese-rind in which Mascha's teeth-marks were clearly visible, two lengths of catapult elastic, and a bit of leather, a wooden whistle made by Fébo, another of metal, a ball of string, an envelope full of foreign stamps, a nail, four marbles, and a bit of blotting-paper on which was scribbled $v = \pi r^2 h$.

That was all in one pocket. In the other was a box of matches, the fork of the catapult – which by the way had made a hole in the lining – a nearly toothless comb, the butt end of a blue pencil, a top polished by long use, a bit of much-chewed liquorice root, an india-rubber, and a magnet.

Pierrot's mother laid these treasures on the mantelpiece. Then she shook the trousers, scattering a few bits of mouse-dung, for on cold days Mascha preferred a warm pocket to the cartridge case.

Something else fell on the floor. Holding out the lamp, Mme Fine stooped and picked it up. The sound of its fall disturbed Pierrot in his sleep, but he merely turned over without waking.

It was a bit of candle with the end whittled away, apparently to make it fit into a bottle.

She was puzzled. A candle and matches! What on earth could he want them for? Some diabolic fancy, no doubt!

As with Viette, she bent over him and studied his face. A line which betokened strong will rose from between his eyebrows, but it meant nothing to his mother. He was her little boy who slept dreaming of the angels. She knew nothing about the other Pierrot, Pierrot the *preux chevalier.*

FIVE

On that Friday the 28th of October M. Grillon was in a thoroughly bad temper. He had the painful impression that everyone was conspiring to make a fool of him. He felt strongly about human dignity, and not least about his own, and this was something he couldn't pass off with a shrug of his shoulders.

Then he had had a bad night. Lying awake, he had turned over in his mind Georget's *démarche* of the previous day again and again, sometimes with indulgence, sometimes with the utmost severity. The poison of the bee-stings had given him a slight temperature, and all sorts of resolutions formed themselves in his mind, only to fade away and give place to others.

It was morning when he finally went off to sleep. Then he slept so soundly that the alarm clock had for once stolen a march on him, going off before he could silence it.

That was the first defeat of the day.

Matters were not improved when he looked in the glass. The swelling had gone, but the skin was still tender and discoloured in places.

It wasn't long before his troubles began.

Maria came five minutes early – no doubt, he thought, to make up for her defection the previous day. When Déodat entered the classroom to have his first look round she was sprinkling water all about her, making dusty drops run across the floor. She stopped at once, planted herself in front of him, and, leaning on her broom, said:

'So you've had thieves here?'

There was a certain effrontery in her manner and a slightly derisive curl on her lips.

'*Bonjour*, Maria,' he answered coldly, intending to put her in her place.

'What a fuss! All for a bit of honey, and with your cupboards full of it! Yet you've never even thought of giving me so much as a spoonful, have you?'

M. Grillon winced. It was true. No, he'd never even thought of such a thing. Yet she was often there when he and Georget breakfasted, and she might well have cast an envious glance at their slices of bread fairly plastered with the stuff, when she came into the kitchen to fetch a duster or a broom. Moreover, he was disconcerted by her manner, against which he could find no defence.

'And is it true you're going to punish the whole class because of it? Rotten thing to do. Thank the Lord I'm not one of them.'

The schoolmaster shrugged his shoulders and tried to move away. The cheek of the girl! The best thing was to leave her severely alone. But she ran after him.

'Look here, Monsieur; there's something I wanted to say to you. The thing is – if it suits your book to say it's me that took your honey, I've no objection. There's plenty worse been said about me. A little more won't make no difference, and the world'll go on turning round just the same, you know.'

Déodat Grillon was nonplussed. Maria had never said so much in all the time he'd known her. In spite of her offensive way of talking, he couldn't help thinking that some quite laudable intention might lie behind it.

'My poor child,' he answered, 'what on earth makes you think it might suit my book, as you say, to accuse you falsely? Your reasoning doesn't make sense. And please don't imagine that it's merely the cost of a few pounds of honey that worries me. Just think of it for a moment. One of my hives was robbed. The whole swarm would have died if I hadn't come promptly to the rescue. Think of those poor bees who had been working all through the summer to provide me with honey, those innocent creatures who would have died of hunger. That's what makes the theft so odious, Maria, and that's what I feel obliged to drum into the heads of these thoughtless boys ...'

M. Grillon was well away now, waxing eloquent on his favourite subject, which offered so many lessons in moral philosophy. Maria listened, scratching her nose and thinking:

'It must be wonderful to be able to talk like that.'

Yet it was with admirable good sense that she answered with a smirk:

'But, M. Grillon, whoever took it, it wasn't for that, believe me. He ust wanted to stuff some of your honey into his mouth – that's all.'

A little later Victorin slunk into the building as though he didn't want to be seen. M. Grillon found him sitting at his desk fidgeting with impatience. The boy lost no time in coming to the point. Waving a five-hundred-franc note with about as much discretion as those people who make signals with a handkerchief, he blurted out:

'M'sieur, M'sieur … Here. This is for the honey.'

'So it was you, was it?' said M. Grillon sadly but very gently.

But Victorin answered with the utmost candour:

'Me, M'sieur? Oh dear, no! A fat lot I care for your honey. Why, our house is full of it.'

The schoolmaster frowned. That was hardly the language to mollify him.

'I don't understand you, Muche. If you weren't guilty, what do you mean by bringing me that money?'

'Because you were going to keep us in. It was my mother who gave it me. She knows I'm not a thief. And she said: "Take him five hundred francs and let us hear no more about it." '

Déodat was incensed. Nothing could have been more humiliating. It showed a total lack of understanding on the part of the boy's parents. Here was the mayor's wife treating him like a servant, to whom one gives a tip to repair wounded feelings. But of course that was just like rich people. They think they can settle everything with money. They despised him, did they? Well, he despised them for doing so. Hated them too.

'Young man! Go back home immediately. Take that note back to your mother and tell her I am not a beggar. What's more, you can tell her that I would give five hundred francs myself – yes, and a lot more – to find out who it was who broke into my garden and robbed the hive.'

He spoke with such vehemence that this hefty lout of a Victorin stared at him open-mouthed, not knowing whether to do as he was told or sit down again. Hovering between the two, he looked stupider than ever.

'As for you, my boy,' went on the schoolmaster, a little ashamed of his outburst, 'if your object was to cover one of your school-fellows, it shows at least that your heart's in the right place. But it also shows how woefully you have misunderstood my attitude. Do you really think it was the value of the honey I was worried about?'

'No, M'sieur.'

'Then what did you think?'

'Well, I thought five hundred francs was always worth having. But if you want to keep us in just for the fun of it, there's nothing more I can say. Except this: a lot of good it'll do you!'

That was going altogether too far. Not only was this lumping great fool incapable of understanding anything, but, like Georget the evening before, he seemed vaguely to be threatening something. One thing was quite clear: these boys were as thick as thieves. As thieves! The idiom seemed peculiarly apt.

'Very good,' he snapped. 'You can sit down.'

Victorin obeyed passively. His mind was a blank. He didn't even wonder why Piquet always said 'very good' just when things were as bad as they could be.

All through the morning the schoolmaster thought about this unexpected conversation. He had plenty of time while his pupils laboured over the arithmetic problem he had set them. Since the one about the hive would have been tactless, he had raked up another about two trains which left the same station at different times and different speeds. At what time would the fast one overtake the slow one?

'There's something to keep you busy,' thought M. Grillon.

But instead of the silent concentration which the problem demanded there was an atmosphere of restlessness in the class. At the end of a quarter of an hour, he distinctly saw that a bit of paper was being circulated.

'There they go,' he thought, 'cribbing.'

Keeping watch out of the corner of his eye, he suddenly pounced on Henri Martelot, who tried heroically to swallow the note. He only succeeded in coughing, however, and the master seized it, or at any rate a sizeable piece of it, wet and crumpled, with the violet ink running. But what was his astonishment when he recognized the writing as that of Pierre Daranluz, his best pupil. The note ran as follows:

Kit necessary – spare pair of boots, nailed if possible, and woollen stockings, a knife, a ...

The rest of the note was wending its way down Riquet's alimentary tract.

'Young men,' said the master, 'this is neither the time nor place to play Boy Scouts.'

In the middle of the day, when M. Grillon was washing his hands at the pump in the courtyard of the Auberge Daranluz – a thing which he did every day before sitting down to lunch – Fébo suddenly appeared from nowhere. With his finger on his lips and making mysterious signs, he drew the schoolmaster into the dark corner by the ruined tower.

'Serious, Monsieur. Very serious.'

'What's serious, my friend?'

'The punishment. Boys very angry.'

'If that's all you've got to tell me ...'

'Something else too. Monsieur shouldn't punish without knowing. Won't bring you *fortouna*. I tell you ...'

'What are you talking about with your "*fortouna*"? I can't understand a word of it.'

Fébo had been speaking French for many years. A queer half-Spanish French, admittedly, but nothing annoyed him more than not being understood. After all, Mme Fine never made him repeat anything, nor Pierrot, nor even little Viette. Yet this schoolmaster, who ought to know better ...

'Honey,' he explained angrily. 'Honey. I'm telling you the boys didn't take it. I know, I tell you.'

'In that case you must know who did take it. If it was you, out with it, and we'll say no more about it.'

'Steal the honey! *Robar la miel! Ah! qué non!* What an *accusatione!* Honey – never touch the stuff. Makes me sick. I'm seventy-two years old, *y nunca yé mangé la miel. Pouh!*'

Fébo put both hands to his stomach to express his disgust.

What a coarse fellow! thought M. Grillon. Not to like the nectar of nature. But what was the fellow driving at, anyway?

'Understand. Monsieur must understand, or great *disgracia* comes. Those boys. Terrible boys. Musn't punish them. Your honey – yes, I stole it, *yé lé robada,* so you mustn't punish the boys. *Claro?*'

Good heavens! Here was yet another turning up to accuse himself. Who would it be next? The Mother Superior, perhaps! It was quite obvious: everybody was making fun of him, pulling his leg. This old servant – what right had he to come butting in on something that was no business of his?

At that moment Maria appeared with a dirty cloth over her arm.

'M'sieur, M'sieur,' she called, 'wherever have you got to? Your chop's been on your plate these ten minutes, and it'll be stone cold if you don't come quick.'

It was when Maria was serving the coffee that M. Muche came into the inn. Without removing his hat, he walked straight across the room, coming to a halt in front of the schoolmaster's table. Boulou and Barbette, usually quiet, suddenly started barking furiously.

Four of the distillery workmen, who always took their meals there, stood up respectfully, but M. Grillon, seeing that the mayor kept his hat on, was determined to be no politer himself, and he remained in his seat, calmly stirring his coffee.

'Quiet,' shouted M. Daranluz.

The dogs lay down again, grumbling. All conversation ceased, and when the mayor spoke, in his rough, aggressive voice, it was for all to hear.

'What the hell's all this fuss about?'

Apparently not noticing the schoolmaster's frigid attitude, he seized a chair and sat down beside him.

'Liqueurs for everybody,' he ordered.

An appreciative murmur greeted this lavishness, which was typical of M. Muche. When he had occasion to enter the Auberge Daranluz he didn't miss the opportunity to boost his popularity.

'Georget,' said M. Grillon, 'run along and play with Pierrot.'

There was a dead silence. Then Maria came in with a bunch of liqueur glasses in each hand. She brought one for herself too. Hadn't the mayor said: 'Liqueurs for everybody'?

The two knights exchanged anxious glances as they made for the door, followed by Viette, who was playing trains, hanging on to Pierrot's belt.

'Puff … puff … puff …' she cried.

'Viette. Stay here,' called Mme Fine, 'or you'll be catching cold.'

'M. Grillon,' began the mayor again, 'would you mind explaining …'

He pushed his hat to the back of his head.

'Not for me,' said the schoolmaster, waving the bottle away. 'I never take liqueurs. Deadly stuff.'

Pierrot and Georget looked at each other again. Things were starting well. Or badly. It depended on how you looked at it. It was a pity they were going to miss the fun.

The remark was taken as a direct affront to the products of the Distillerie Muche.

'My damn-fool nincompoop of a son,' he snapped, 'tells me you accuse him of stealing. I won't allow ...'

'You've been misinformed.'

'Misinformed? Then perhaps you'll tell me ...'

'Certainly. Those boys know who robbed the hive. That's all. And I mean to make them ...'

The café had already resumed its normal animation. Though she pricked her ears, Maria could only hear above the buzz of conversation a few isolated phrases – 'five hundred francs', 'the cabbage patch', 'Ranavalo' ...

M. Grillon spoke in a low voice, holding up his right hand in a didactic gesture to reinforce his words.

M. Muche warmed his liqueur in the hollow of his hand. He said nothing, but his face grew redder every minute.

Suddenly he burst out:

'Stuff and nonsense! The whole thing's a storm in a teacup. And let me tell you this: if a theft has been committed I'm the person to come to. Am I the mayor of this town or aren't I? Or you could have gone to the *garde champêtre*, who is one of my officers. Allow me to say that you have behaved like a nitwit, M. l'Instituteur.'

This time M. Grillon stood up. In contrast to Guillaume Muche, he had gone very pale, which showed up still more the marks left by the bee-stings. In Maria's eyes he looked more pitiful than ever. She was thoroughly enjoying herself. Nothing pleased her more than to witness disputes between men, though she couldn't have told herself why.

'If you have any observations to make to me, M. le Maire, you could choose a more suitable place than this public resort. And I might point out that in school I am my own master, free to act as I think fit, subject only to the control of my academic superiors.'

'Academic yourself!' cried Muche, who, though he had only the vaguest idea of the meaning of such words, had the art of flinging them back in the adversary's face.

'If you think you're going to find the thief by punishing the whole class or by appealing to lofty sentiments, you're barking up the wrong tree. It won't get you anywhere, *mon pauvre Monsieur*. But whether it does or not, I repeat: my son's a damn-fool nincompoop, as big a one as you like, and we won't argue about that. Still, that doesn't make him a thief, M. Grillon, and what's more, he's not one. Is that understood?'

To ram his words home, he tossed off the rest of his liqueur and put down his glass in a way that seemed to brook no contradiction.

Déodat's moustache quivered.

Forgetting for the first time in his life to fold up his table-napkin and return it to its box-wood ring, he stumped over to the hat-stand, put on his hat, and came back to the mayor.

'And now I've got something to tell you, Monsieur,' he said. 'If at half past five tomorrow afternoon I have still not been informed of the name of the culprit, my six boys of the first form will be kept in over the All Saints' holiday, Master Victorin Muche like the others, be he the son of a mayor or no. Though of course you are perfectly free if it pleases you to send me a medical certificate attesting his unfitness to attend ... Good afternoon, gentlemen.'

He took his hat off with a wide sweep and stalked out of the place with great dignity. Maria rushed after him.

'M'sieur, M'sieur, you've forgotten your coat and your scarf. You'll catch your death of cold.'

He had to retrace his steps – with considerable annoyance, for he had been inwardly delighted with his exit.

Abandoning the game of marbles he and Pierrot had started, Georget trotted beside his father, trying to keep up with him, for under the stress of strong emotion the schoolmaster walked very fast. Pierrot was left alone beside the pump surveying the triangle they had scratched in the earth, in which lay the three marbles Georget had left behind him in his haste. The promptitude with which the boy had dashed off in obedience to a sign from his father had made a queer impression on Pierrot.

'How powerful they are – grown-ups!' he mused.

The day before, in the Tour de la Reine, he had experienced a moment's intoxication. The solidarity of his classmates, their eagerness to prove themselves equal to the occasion, and their complete confidence in him had been wonderful. When Cisco had first suggested running away, every eye had shone. There was exaltation in the air. They felt strong, strong with the righteous indignation which flares up against unjust suspicion.

That moment had passed. Gazing at the abandoned game, Pierrot came down to earth, and with the sense of reality came fear.

'Won't they all cry off at the last minute?' he asked himself. 'If one of them flinches, it'll be all up with us – I know that.'

Six boys – knights, of course, but schoolboys none the less – six boys making for the frontier to start life afresh elsewhere! It raised a lot of problems, didn't it?

'Still, we'll have Fébo,' thought Pierrot, banishing his misgivings. 'He'll be a great help.'

Not that the old man could take the lead. No question of that. But his knowledge would be useful, and the mere fact of his being a grown-up was an asset in itself.

Maria came out of the house, her shoulder pulled down by a bucketful of leavings for the hens. She was still limping.

'*Tiens!*' said Pierrot to himself. 'I ought to have asked her why.'

From every corner of the yard the hens came scurrying, anxious to get the biggest possible share of the feast. Only a white cock stood aloof, fluffing up his dirty feathers in order to look more important, crowing reprovingly, for his harem had not waited for him to give the order before rushing at their food.

Two of the hens, more pushing than the others, had already got their necks into the pail before Maria had time to empty it. She scattered the contents all over them, raising a chorus of protests.

Suddenly she noticed Pierrot and came over to the pump. Putting the bucket upside down on the ground, she sat down unceremoniously. Their necks craned and their heads on one side, some guinea-fowl looked on with a fierce eye, apparently shocked by her behaviour.

'Pity you weren't there,' said Maria. 'It was a fine dust-up.'

The hens came up to her clamouring for more, but she sent them flying with a kick.

'He got quite an earful, that Piquet of yours.'

'Tell me … what did he say?'

'Oh, it was about that silly honey business.'

'Well, I knew that much. But what did the mayor want? Did he ask him to lay off, so that Victorin could get his holiday?'

He was torn between the hope of some such intervention and a vague resentment at grown-ups barging into their affairs.

'Couldn't say for certain. Something of that sort, I suppose, for he started off by standing liqueurs all round. In the end they fairly went for each other. It was grand. But it won't calm Piquet down much. He'd already had a couple of rounds with Fébo before he ...'

'Who? M. Muche?'

'Go on. Can you see that old fool standing up to the mayor?'

Maria burst out laughing at the very idea. Pierrot, however, with a strangely tense look on his face, began to ply her with questions.

'Are you quite sure Fébo and Piquet had a talk together?'

'I wouldn't have said so if I wasn't. I saw them. Piquet was just starting to wash his hands. He dropped the soap. There it is, on the ground.'

'What on earth's taken hold of him?' she wondered, seeing the boy's face grow hard. He was frowning and his jaw was thrust forward, making him look like a young bull-dog in a bad temper. She knew it took a good deal to upset him.

The hens were approaching again, clucking gravely, grumbling at a repast they considered inadequate. Even the white cock came over towards the pump, strutting solemnly, looking right and left, as though counting his concubines. Finally, unable to think of anything better to do, he flapped his wings to attract attention.

After all, he was the chief, wasn't he?

The afternoon lessons that Friday passed off uneventfully. M. Grillon tried to explain what square roots were. For Victorin, the only roots of any interest to the human race were those of the gentian, which were distilled by his father to make a tonic appetizer.

The other boys were hardly more attentive. The one thing which relieved the monotony was a ribald bit of doggerel, which was passed surreptitiously round the class.

Pierrot had torn it up, however, considering it in bad taste on the occasion. Cisco was dreaming as usual, while Tatave practised squirls to embellish his signature. Georget was the only one to pay any real attention, for fear his father might question him afterwards.

In the four o'clock break Pierrot gave his hunk of bread and bit of

94

chocolate to Cisco, who didn't seem to have had much to eat that day. Then, breaking away from the others, he went off on his own, walking thoughtfully across the playground, kicking a stone in front of him.

'With every second it gets nearer,' he thought. 'At this time tomorrow there'll only be that last grammar lesson, and then …'

A shiver went down his back. To comfort himself, he took Mascha out of the cartridge case, but the wind was too cold for the mouse, and it ran up his sleeve.

'Whatever's the matter with me?' Pierrot wondered.

He couldn't put a name to it. But one thing was certain: he must shake it off at once.

'Cisco,' he called.

Cisco ran up, eager to know what was worrying the chief and flattered at being the one chosen to hear it. Yet he asked no questions. He had finished the bread and chocolate and was gnawing a piece of bark.

What could be wrong? Hadn't everything been thought of? They could even make a fire in Féroulet's hut if it was cold. He had been up that day and collected a good heap of fir-cones. As a matter of fact that's why he had had so little to eat. By the time he'd got home the others had polished off the dish of *garbanzos* without waiting for him.

But Pierrot said nothing. He was absorbed in his stone. The thing was to kick it in a dead-straight line so that he didn't have to deviate from his course. And it was with the natural superstition no children are free from that he said to himself:

'If I miss, it'll mean the whole thing will fall through.'

The four others, standing in a group in front of the lavatories, watched them walking side by side.

'It must be something serious,' said Tatave, snuffling.

He looked absurdly small in his voluminous clothes. His face was very grave and not really childish at all. In fact he looked rather like a middle-aged man in miniature. His complexion, always a bit yellowish, was more than ever so at this moment. For he was suffering pangs of jealousy, and he hated Cisco with all his heart.

'Time to g … go in,' stammered Riquet. 'I'm going to p … pee.'

'Wait for me,' said Victorin. 'I'm coming too.'

As soon as they were out of earshot, Georget made haste to ask Tatave:

'What's the news? What did they do yesterday?'

'Nothing. At least, there was only a letter. She'd stuffed it in her apron pocket.'

'Let's see it.'

'Don't be an ass. D'you think I took it? I only just had time to read it when her back was turned.'

'What did he say?'

'Oh, silly things. Better you didn't know.'

For a moment phrases swam before Georget's eyes ... *Mon Dédé chéri* ... *Ma toute petite* ... Could these two be saying things like that to each other now?

He ground his teeth.

'But things can't go on like this,' Tatave went on. 'We're off. That'll teach 'em.'

'Yes,' growled Georget savagely, 'that'll teach 'em.'

Teach 'em what! They could neither of them have answered that. What connexion could M. Grillon and Mme Grosbelhomme see between their children's flight and their own clandestine manoeuvres? But that didn't matter. As the boys saw it, the important thing was to act. No matter how. Tatave had put it in a nutshell. Things couldn't go on like that.

One thing was quite certain – Tatave's mother was going to be at her wit's end with anxiety, and he revelled in the thought.

Pierrot took another kick, and this time missed the stone altogether. He was tempted to have another shot. But no. That wouldn't be playing the game. Master Daranluz had strict ideas about cheating, even when he was playing against so treacherous an adversary as fate.

For a second or two he thought of unburdening himself of his anxieties over Fébo's talk with M. Grillon. It would do him good. But, as with the stone, he restrained the impulse. What was the use of sowing panic among his followers? If he had made a mistake in taking the old man into his confidence, it was up to him, and to him alone, to put things right.

Suddenly he asked:

'What about that little fox? Has your father still got it?'

'He killed it. I told you. But he was too drunk yesterday to skin it. It's always the same. When it stinks too much, my mother'll throw it on to the rubbish heap. Then it'll be lost. We never seem to manage to bring anything off.'

'What a shame! A little fox must be great fun. I wish I'd had it. I'd have tamed it and kept it as a pet.'

Mascha had gradually worked his way up, and was now poking his head out from under the collar of Pierrot's jacket, tickling the boy's cheek with his whiskers.

'Why are you always talking to me about that wretched fox?' asked Cisco, disappointed. 'What's the idea?'

And the little chief answered:

'Oh, nothing.'

'Who'll put Viette to bed tomorrow?'

That was the question which gnawed at Pierrot's vitals as he went up to his room that night. He felt utterly discouraged. Humiliated too, humiliated and angry at the consciousness of his own weakness.

What would his brothers-in-arms say if they knew of the misgivings which assailed him? What would Cisco think? And Tatave and the others? They believed in him wholeheartedly. They had never questioned his orders.

At that moment Pierrot envied Mascha. He had just put him in his drawer of cotton wool, where the little creature ferreted about without a thought for the morrow.

'I must get Tatave to bring some cotton wool along with him,' he thought. 'I'll line the cartridge case so that Mascha won't be cold during the journey.'

He got into bed, making up his mind not to go to sleep till he'd seen Fébo. It had happened once or twice. Then Fébo had tiptoed out of the room again. Tonight he kept the lamp burning. He wanted to look into the old man's eyes.

He waited.

Downstairs, Domingo was plucking at his guitar. A thin trickle of notes, which seemed to be always the same, floated up into the bedroom. Sometimes he ended abruptly on a chord, Spanish fashion. Then he began again.

No sound from Fébo's accordion. Surely he couldn't be long now. The boy decided to be severe, or at any rate firm. He had to know what had passed between the old man and the schoolmaster. Yes, that was essential. But he mustn't badger the man too much. He was necessary. They couldn't do without him. Particularly when they got across the frontier. Cisco could speak the language all right, but he'd never been to Spain. They must have somebody who knew the ropes.

With the frontier guards, for instance, the presence of a grown-up among them would make all the difference. Not that Fébo was altogether a grown-up. There was a subtle difference. But nobody was to know that.

A door opened and shut below. The old servant's rope-soled feet came slowly up, for with his seventy-two years he wasn't very good at stairs. There! That was the sixth, which always creaked. Ten to go before he reached the landing.

No. He mustn't be rough with the old man. He'd speak to him *as man to man*. That was an expression he'd picked up from his father, who was always using it. Pierrot wasn't very clear about its exact meaning, but he employed it for any conversation of particular importance. It was one of those phrases, like M. Grillon's *human dignity*, that seemed equally apt on all occasions.

Three steps more. Then two, then one.

A hesitation. There was no mistaking it. Pierrot was quite sure.

Was it possible? No! It couldn't be!

Yet it was. The footsteps went on, up the next flight of stairs. For the first time, Fébo had refrained from coming. And on this night, of all nights! Just when the boy was going to speak to him as man to man.

It gave the show away. Completely. There was no room for doubt. Fébo had let him down. He had proved himself unworthy of the trust. He had gone over to the other side.

A bitter disillusionment, felt with the cruel keenness of all childhood's sufferings, when there is no experience to soften the blows of adversity: all the more bitter because it was he, the chief, who was responsible. It was he who had confided their secret to an outsider.

Through his fault, their project was now compromised. Perhaps everybody already knew. Perhaps all the grown-ups were laughing at them.

Even if the secret wasn't out yet, tomorrow when they took to the road there'd be one old man left in Casteilcorbon who knew their plans, and it wouldn't be long before he gave them away.

Fébo loved to make people think he knew everything that was going on.

The whole point had been to take everybody by surprise. By the time their parents had finished running round in circles and wondering what had happened, they were to have been well on their way to the frontier.

Yes, it was all up. And his fault too. Tomorrow he'd have to tell the others it was no good, just because he'd opened his mouth too wide. He had proved himself unfit to be their leader.

But what made him more ashamed than anything was that, in spite of everything, he couldn't help feeling relieved that the scheme had fallen through. Was he then just a coward, after all?

He ought to have run after Fébo and dragged him into the room. It was too late now. The old man was nervous and always locked his door and bolted it as well, being scared of the ghosts which were supposed to haunt the castle and which might well attach themselves to the official guide and follow him back to the inn.

SIX

On that last Saturday of October the sky was painted in fresh colours and the streaks of blue looked as wet as in an unfinished water-colour.

The Abbé Escoutou came out of the church, rubbing his hands. He had only to cross the square to reach the presbytery, where he would be greeted by the smell of the toast and hot coffee which his house-keeper, Valérie, would have ready for him. He stopped, however, at the top of the church steps to take a deep breath of the delicious autumn air. It really was a wonderful day, and for a second he thought of rendering thanks to his Creator for it. But after a quarter of an hour's prayer, which, if not inspired, was at least conscientious, his contact with the Almighty was temporarily suspended. There was a time for everything, and for the moment he felt entitled to enjoy the physical satisfaction of being alive on this radiant morning and hungry for the breakfast that awaited him.

'Splendid!' he murmured out loud.

It was a favourite word of his, which he used in season and out, even in the confessional when his parishioners boggled at admitting some sin.

'Splendid!' he would say, encouraging them to take the plunge.

Seizing on a pretext for enjoying the morning air a little longer, the priest remembered that he had to see Fébo as soon as possible, as his help was needed for the thorough clean-up of the church which was always undertaken in preparation for the All Saints' celebrations. It meant a little extra expense, of course, but the old man was not exact-ing in his demands. At the same time he would arrange with him for the ringing of the bells.

The Allée des Trois Tourelles was bathed in sunshine as the portly Abbé Escoutou turned down it, his rubicund face, round as a Dutch cheese, beaming good-naturedly. On the steps of the disused *gen-darmerie* François Tistounet, the *garde champêtre*, was sitting at a bowl of soup. He gave a military salute which he had conserved from the days when he was a corporal in the Spahis.

'Well, Tistounet? How are you getting on?'

'As you see, M. le Curé. With a good appetite ...'

'Splendid!'

A little farther on he was greeted by Grisouille, the convent donkey. Between his duties, which were far from numerous, the latter was allowed to wander freely about. He never strayed very far, as there were too many friends near at hand, too many doors at which it was worth while to wait patiently for an eventual pat and a lump of sugar. Coming up, he rubbed his warm, velvety, though somewhat moth-eaten nose against the priest's ear, then he leant on the latter's shoulder as though saying:

'Just feel how heavy my head is.'

M. le Curé stopped and scratched the proffered nose, while the donkey closed his eyes in sensuous delight, waiting for the titbit which he well knew the priest would presently produce from his pocket.

Hoping for a second helping, he followed the priest – who was in no way embarrassed by his company – in the direction of the Auberge Daranluz, where every entrance was decorated by a pine branch. Mme Fine was sweeping the steps.

Boulou and Barbette, quick to recognize a friend, gambolled round the priest. The donkey stopped and held himself aloof, thinking their demonstrativeness out of place.

'Splendid!' murmured the priest, trying to keep the dogs from spoiling his cassock.

But it was already covered with dusty footmarks.

'And what can we do for you, M. le Curé?' asked Mme Fine, leaning on her broom and smiling all over her face.

She didn't like to ask him in, as a café was no place for a priest. But she was highly flattered by his visit and pleased to be seen talking to so important a personage.

'Is Fébo there?'

'I'm afraid he isn't. The baker's borrowed him to get in some wood. He hadn't a stick left in the bakehouse. You know, we always help each other out when we can ... So that's why you find me sweeping down the steps.'

She laughed gaily. She was still young and comely.

'Splendid!' said the Abbé Escoutou.

'Can I give him a message?'

'If you wouldn't mind telling him I'd like him to lend a hand with the cleaning first thing tomorrow morning. And then for the bells – at least a dozen peals between six and seven o'clock on Monday. And on All Saints' Day ...'

'Wait a moment. My boy's just finishing his breakfast. If he's quick, he can nip round to the Bastide before going to school. He'll find Fébo there, making up faggots, and he can bring him here. Then you can tell him just what you want him to do with the bells. That'll be much better than my explaining it ... Pierrot! ... Pierrot! ... Come here a minute ...'

The boy came running out with his mouth full.

Maria left the kitchen to see what was going on. Unobserved by the others, she stood at one of the windows of the café. She saw the fat priest pat Pierrot's cheek, while her mistress, leaning on her broom, purred with pleasure. A few yards away, Grisouille also looked on, but kept a wary eye on the dogs.

Having seen Pierrot make off in the direction of the castle, Maria glanced enviously at his unfinished coffee. She had to be content to breakfast off soup, the stuff that was left over from the previous evening. 'Second-haul' soup, she called it resentfully.

Mme Fine went on holding forth, her features composed into that Sunday expression which she automatically adopted every time she put on her best clothes to go to Mass.

'Splendid!' muttered Maria mockingly.

She took up the coffee and drank it calmly without taking her eyes from the window. Then, putting the bowl down on the floor, she whistled for Boulou to come and lap up the dregs, as Pierrot did every morning.

Barbette came instead. Carefully she polished off the last grains of sugar that remained at the bottom, then went all over the bowl again to make sure none had been forgotten.

So everybody was happy, even Mme Daranluz when she saw that Pierrot had had time to finish his breakfast.

'You're lucky to have a boy like that,' said the Abbé Escoutou. 'He's one of the best. I've rarely seen a boy so quick-witted and at the same time straight as a die. And so obliging. You can thank God for having given you such a son. For my part, it gives me the utmost pleasure to see him in the catechism class. His mind never wanders. If he goes on like that, you can be sure he'll make his way in the world.'

Mme Daranluz didn't doubt that. Still, she knew a mother oughtn't to boast of her offspring, and answered with becoming modesty:

'Oh, he's got a will of his own, M. le Curé. Indeed, he can be quite headstrong at times. You don't see him every day. As a matter of fact, now that we're talking about him, he seems to have changed these last few days. You'd hardly know him. Shut up in himself, he is. Generally he tells us everything. As open as the day. But now he hardly says a word. He's got something on his mind. It's that honey that was stolen from M. Grillon, if you ask me. Ridiculous I call it.'

'I know, I know. Valérie told me. I'm worried about it myself. It seems I shan't have any servers for the celebrations if M. Grillon carries out his threat. But I can't believe he will. He's an excellent man, M. Grillon, and he's got much too much sense to do a thing like that.'

'I'm glad to hear you say so, M. le Curé. You see, we can't very well say anything ourselves. M. Grillon's a customer of ours, and when you're in trade ... But we hate to see our Pierrot going about like that.'

'Splendid! Of course you do. But don't worry. I'll find an opportunity of having a word with him before the day's out. Of course we all know he's an unbeliever – prides himself on it – but that doesn't alter the fact that he's one of the best men in the world. I've a great opinion of M. Grillon. The way he devotes himself to his pupils! And considering what the schools are nowadays, I'm grateful to Providence for giving us a man like that, for he's much too scrupulous to use his position to undermine the faith of his pupils.'

'I'm sure you're right, M. le Curé. Yet to punish a whole class for the fault of one – you must admit that it's not fair ...'

'Never mind about that, Madame. Those brats have got to learn sooner or later that there's injustice in the world and they've got to put up with it. They'll meet with plenty of it later on in this valley of tears. When they do their military service, for instance, they'll often find themselves in a scrape that's not of their own making.'

'Yes ... But they're so young, M. le Curé ...'

'Suffering is no respecter of age,' answered the priest, and he went off into another speech which Mme Daranluz found very eloquent.

She nodded her head approvingly from time to time, particularly at those passages which she couldn't follow very well.

At the same time she kept glancing towards the drawbridge, expecting at any minute to see Pierrot reappear with Fébo in tow.

'So don't worry about it any more, Mme Daranluz,' concluded the Abbé Escoutou. 'I'll have it out with M. Grillon. Just leave it to me. If I don't run into him in the course of the day, I'll go and beard him in his school. It'll be all right, I assure you, and you'll have your Pierrot going about as carefree as ever.'

'Ah! There he is,' she exclaimed.

Pierrot was running, waving something above his head. He passed Grisouille, who came trotting behind him.

The boy was out of breath. He seemed excited.

'Fébo's not there,' he burst out. 'I couldn't see him anywhere. Here's the key. I found it in the door. As for faggots, he's hardly done any.'

'Splendid!' said the curé. 'It doesn't matter. I'll see him later. Thanks all the same.'

Still very red, Pierrot muttered something in reply.

'It's for him to thank you,' put in Mme Fine. 'Just think of it, Pierrot: M. le Curé's going to put in a word for you with M. Grillon and everything's going to be all right. Come on! Say thank you.'

Pierrot frowned.

'Why? Do you mean you're doing that for me?'

'You see, I need you. I need you and Henri Martelot to act as servers,' the priest answered with a roguish smile.

But he saw the boy's features harden with annoyance.

'No, M. le Curé, please don't do that. If we're being kept in, I'm standing in with the others. I'm sorry about the service, but it can't be helped. You'll …'

The rest was lost as Grisouille suddenly started braying.

'Pierrot! What are you thinking about?' burst out Mme Daranluz angrily.

The priest was quite taken aback by the boy's vehemence.

'I'm sorry, M. le Curé,' repeated Pierrot politely but determinedly, 'but whatever you do'll make no difference. Thank you all the same … I must be getting to school now, or I'll be late.'

He darted off in the direction of the school gate, which could just be seen in the distance. Grisouille followed him at a trot.

'Dear me!' said the Abbé Escoutou thoughtfully. 'There's something wrong with the boy. We'll have to keep an eye on him … We'll have to keep an eye on him.'

At lunch-time there was still no sign of Fébo.

'Funny,' said Mme Fine, cutting thin slices of *saucisson de Bayonne* – three slices to each plate with a sliver of gherkin. 'I can't make it out at all. He's never failed me like this before.'

'Did you notice anything queer about him this morning?' asked Benoît.

'No. He seemed just as usual. A bit sulky, perhaps, and he had words with Maria over something. But then it's like that every day. It's funny how those two can't stand the sight of each other … Are you listening, Benoît? What's the matter with you this morning, yawning your head off? … Then Guste came round and said he'd no wood left in the bakehouse, and could Fébo fetch some in for him. The old man looked pretty sour at him, but after Guste had stood him a drink he seemed to think better of it. He fetched his billhook and slouched off just as he was, in his sabots. That must have been about seven o'clock.'

'It wasn't as late as that,' put in Maria. 'It couldn't have been more than a quarter to, as Pierrot hadn't come down yet.'

Mme Fine pursed her lips. Why did the girl always have to put her oar in? Still, she happened to be right this time, so her mistress couldn't very well say anything.

Benoît yawned again. He'd got up late that morning, as the distillery didn't work on Saturdays. It was always like that: the more he slept the sleepier he was.

'Then, just as I was sweeping down in front, who should turn up but M. le Curé? By the way, I must tell you what he said to me about Pierrot. But what he really came for was to see Fébo about the church-cleaning and the bells. I sent Pierrot to the Bastide to fetch him. He found the door unlocked and the key in the door, but no sign of Fébo anywhere. We couldn't understand it at all. Then Guste came round and asked why the old man hadn't come ... By the way, I ordered six *fouaces* for tomorrow evening. I thought we ought to have something a bit special.'

'Quite right.'

Boulou and Barbette began to show signs of excitement, and indeed the next moment Pierrot appeared, returning from school. With Viette, they rushed to meet him. He was unresponsive to their blandishments, however, and plunged into the study of a map printed on the back of a calendar that hung on the wall.

'I was just telling your father about Fébo. Couldn't find him anywhere, could you?'

He confirmed the statement with a vague grunt.

'Oh! And while I think of it – I've ordered six *fouaces* from the baker's. They'll be ready at six o'clock, so you can fetch them on your way back from school ... I'm speaking to you, Pierrot. Can't you answer?'

'Yes.'

'Should say "Yes, Mum" – it's polite,' Viette corrected him sententiously.

'To come back to what I was saying – Guste went along to the castle and he couldn't find Fébo either. There was just one faggot ready – that was all. He came back to tell me. And of course he had another drink while he was about it.'

'A good customer, Guste. Yes, I'm glad you ordered those *fouaces* ...'

His wife beamed on him. Pierrot went on studying his map with a scowl on his face.

Fébo's defection was noticeable in a variety of unperformed chores. It was a nuisance. And what with Pierrot in a bad temper ...

'Never mind,' said the innkeeper. 'He'll turn up all right. There's nothing to worry about. The smell of his dinner'll bring him home, if nothing else will.'

'Perhaps he's drunk,' suggested Maria maliciously. 'You'll probably find him laid out in a ditch.'

Pierrot scowled at her, but said nothing. His mother, however, didn't let the opportunity pass.

'Trust you to barge in where you're not wanted! There's no call to say things of that sort, anyhow. If you'd get on with your work instead of letting your tongue run away with you ... Just look at the way you've laid the table! It's like a ...'

She broke off, unable to find a comparison, and, as she hadn't yet let off all her wrath, she rounded on Viette, who was stuffing herself with sausage.

'If I catch you putting your fingers in the plates I'll give you a slap you won't forget in a hurry.'

They seemed endless, those last lessons on Saturday afternoon. The hands of the clock seemed determined not to move. A veteran like M. Grillon couldn't fail to be aware of the shuffling feet and general restlessness of his pupils. There was something queer about those feet. It was funny that the boys should one and all, as though by common accord, have put on their heavy hob-nailed boots. Though he noticed it, however, the schoolmaster's mind probed no further.

As a matter of fact, he himself found it difficult to concentrate, and the Latin lesson dragged on lifelessly.

Barely two hours to go. He had a momentous decision to make. And he must make it quite calmly. He must remain absolutely self-possessed.

It wasn't so easy. Four times he had been aware that a message was being passed round the class, and he could have sworn they all came from Pierre Daranluz. Fortunately, in the other class the little ones were being admirably quiet and industrious as they copied the drawing of a bee which the teacher had chalked on the blackboard.

He was starting to explain what a colloquialism was. The sound of that somewhat cumbersome word seemed to wake the class up.

'Can anybody give me an example of a colloquialism? What about you, Muche?'

The moment he was addressed, Victorin stood up, but by the expression on his face you might have thought the word colloquialism was some sort of personal insult. Tatave smirked.

'You can't think of one? Very well. Sit down.'

Victorin slumped down on to his seat.

'I'd like to ask my father what a colloquialism was,' he said to himself.

And suddenly the thought that within a few hours he'd be far from school, far from home, far from all the people who couldn't leave him alone, filled his heart with a marvellous lightness.

'What are you shrugging your shoulders for, Muche? I can assure you this is nothing to sneer at.'

He dictated a passage, then set the boys to write it out afresh, transposing all the idiomatic phrases into formal French. Then he turned his attention to the younger boys, whom he finally sent off a quarter of an hour early.

Half past five. Slowly the big hand of the clock started to climb up again. Sitting at his desk, M. Grillon wrote out a note for each boy to take home to give his parents official intimation that the class would go on as usual during the All Saints' holiday.

Between each letter he looked up, and each time his eyes met his son's, which were anxious and full of supplication.

Ten to six. Five to six. And finally the clock gave that little double click which announced that it was going to strike.

The master got up from his chair and stepped down from his platform. He began to hand round the notes he had prepared.

And when he came to Georget it took him a couple of seconds to realize why he had no letter for him.

'At last!' thought Pierrot as he held out his hand for his.

When she arrived at the Auberge Daranluz, Mme Grosbelhomme went straight through the café, taking no notice of the innkeeper, who stood behind the bar rinsing out a bottle. With that sprightly step so common with plump women, she sailed into the kitchen and accosted Mme Fine.

'You haven't seen my Tatave, have you?'

Viette was playing with a potato, rolling it along the floor, while Boulou and Barbette watched for an opportunity of pouncing on it. She babbled as she played.

'Be quiet, Viette. What is it, Mme Grosbelhomme?'

'Tatave. You haven't seen him, have you?'

At that moment Viette threw the potato farther than before and there was quite a rumpus as the dogs made a rush to it.

'Dear, dear! We never get any peace with this little wretch about. Viette, come here and keep quiet. I'm talking to Mme Grosbelhomme … Sit down, Mme Grosbelhomme. It's not often we have the pleasure of seeing you here …'

'It's about that boy of mine. He hasn't come home, and I thought he might be with your Pierrot …'

'Good gracious! It's nearly seven o'clock. I'd no idea it was so late. With all these men to cook for I don't seem to find time to look at the clock.'

'It smells pretty good, I must say, whatever it is you're cooking.'

The kitchen was indeed filled with the odour of the mushrooms and spices Mme Fine had just put in her stew.

'I dare say Tatave is with Pierrot. We haven't seen him yet.'

'Do you mean Pierrot's not back either?'

'Not yet, but he won't be long now. He's never later than seven. On Saturdays, you know, they're in no hurry to get home, as they can always put off their homework till the next day. So they loiter about and amuse themselves as boys will ... Do sit down, Mme Grosbelhomme.'

'You think they're all right?'

'Of course they are. Pierrot was late yesterday, but he turned up all right in the end, and before this pot comes to the boil you'll see the dogs jump up to meet him. They know he's coming when he's still a hundred yards away. Just look. They're waiting for him.'

'But Tatave knows very well I'm nervous and easily get upset. He was late yesterday too. And when I saw it was after half past six I began to get really worried.'

M. Daranluz appeared in the doorway with a bottle of Basque liqueur in his left hand. His right hand seemed at first sight as though it was heavily ringed, but what he was carrying between his fingers were three cut-glass, gold-rimmed liqueur glasses. Putting them down on the table, he filled them expertly, jerking the neck of the bottle up just as the yellowish-green liquid rose above the gold rim, without allowing a drop to spill.

'You'll have a glass with us, Mme Grosbelhomme, won't you? This is good stuff this – the real thing.'

'I came round about my Tatave. He hasn't come home.'

'I expect you'll find him there when you get back.'

'No. I left a note for him to follow me round here.'

Benoît smiled. They were all the same, these women. Like hens that have hatched out ducklings.

He was reassuring, and in the serene and comfortable atmosphere of that kitchen Mme Fabienne began to feel ashamed of her alarm. Perhaps she was making a fool of herself, and she hastened to explain:

'You see, when you're all alone you easily get worried over nothing. As long as I'm busy in the shop I'm all right, but as soon as I put up the shutters at six o'clock I start listening for his footsteps. And this evening as the minutes went by ... Of course, I know I shouldn't worry. But you can't help the way you're made, can you?'

Benoît wiped his hands on his apron and picked up his glass.

'Here's your health, Mme Grosbelhomme; and don't think any more about it. There are enough troubles in the world without inventing more.'

'All the same, it's not often Pierrot's as late as this,' remarked Mme Fine.

It was her turn to start worrying. And suddenly struck by the coincidence she added:

'We've already been wondering what on earth's become of Fébo.'

'Fébo?'

'Yes. Would you believe it, since seven o'clock this morning ...'

The story of Fébo's disappearance lasted a good five minutes. Mme Fine's hands were as busy as her tongue, and with fat sizzling in the frying-pan she had to speak at the top of her voice. One of the customers in the café had to clap his hands to attract the innkeeper's attention. Nearly all the regulars had arrived by now, but no one seemed in a hurry for supper, and round after round of *anisettes* were called for. In that respect it was much like any other Saturday.

Dragging her feet, Maria dawdled over laying the tables. When the men tried to joke with her, she snapped back at them irritably.

For the tenth time Mme Grosbelhomme looked at the clock and sighed. Progressively the two mothers worked on each other's nerves, each feeding the other's anxiety.

Fear is an infectious disease.

Suddenly Mme Fabienne could stand it no longer.

'I'll run round to the Martelots,' she announced. 'Their boy'll be able to tell us.'

'If you'll wait half a minute, I'll come with you.'

They might have gone to the mayor's house, which was only just over the way, but nobody cared very much to knock at that door.

Victorin's mother was always polite, even amiable, yet you couldn't help feeling you were disturbing her.

'Maria, Maria, come and take my place for a moment. And be careful, or the soup'll boil over.'

Before they could even see the glow of the forge, the smell of a burning hoof told the two women Martelot was still at work. Standing in the arched doorway, his figure silhouetted against the fire beyond, he was shoeing the last horse of the day, swearing steadily because Riquet wasn't there to hold the horse's foot, and the owner, who had offered to take his place, was doing it very clumsily.

'*Nom de Dieu!* If you can't hold the damned thing properly I'd do better all alone.'

Standing in the shadow, Fabienne and Fine nudged each other, each urging the other forward.

Then a window opened above and the blacksmith's wife poked her timid face out and looked up and down the street. She was on the point of withdrawing again when Mme Grosbelhomme called out as loudly as she dared:

'Mme Martelot! Mme Martelot! Have you seen anything of Tatave?'

'No,' answered Riquet's mother, shaking her head and putting her finger to her lips.

She glanced apprehensively in the direction of the smithy, from whence came a series of hammer-blows which seemed to symbolize the blacksmith's wrath, and she signalled to her visitors to come round to the back door.

What cleanliness indoors! Everything polished as only the women of the north know how. White-and-red check curtains. Copper saucepans burnished like mirrors.

Mme Martelot's colourless hair was done *en bandeaux*. Her cheeks were like red apples, and you might have thought she polished them too. She always seemed to be looking at something beyond the person she was talking to, which gave her eyes a vagueness that was not without its charm.

She promptly put some bowls on the stove – for the table was already laid – and began filling them with café au lait.

'Riquet's not back either.'

She had been worrying too, thinking of the scene her husband would make when the boy finally returned and the rain of blows that would fall upon him. She suffered from those blows, though she never lifted a finger to ward them off. She was a good wife, but devoid of imagination and altogether unskilled in the many little deceits to which indulgent mothers have recourse.

Even in the house they could still hear the oaths of the blacksmith. He would be busy for a while yet, and Mme Martelot suggested they should go round to the Guartorellas. From the bottom of the garden they could get into the Rue des Hallebardes without attracting attention.

'That's a good idea,' approved Mme Grosbelhomme. 'Perhaps Cisco's back ... Oh, these boys!'

'Just a minute. I'll fetch the lantern.'

And the three women threaded their way past the cabbages in single file.

It was Nièves who opened the door, and she stared wide-eyed at her unexpected visitors. Mme Fabienne led the way, and they entered the sole room of the hovel, which smelt of rancid oil.

'Have you seen my Tatave?' she asked once again.

With the exception of Cisco, the whole Guartorella family was there, sitting round their roughly improvised trestle table, on which was spread as roughly improvised a meal. The latter was forgotten, however, as all eyes were trained on the new-comers. Only the baby was unconscious of the strangeness of the visit, but as his mother, in her surprise, had abruptly pushed him from her breast, he was the first to react, protesting vociferously at the interruption.

The mason was still a fine-looking man. Drink had aged him, but had not obliterated his regular, Catalan features. His grey, curly hair was parted in the middle. As was usual with his countrymen, he wore a small beret, dusty with mortar, on the side of his head. Quickly he snatched it off, however, as he rose to his feet.

'*Buenas noches, señoras.*'

Without stopping to button up her dress, his wife made haste to perform her duties as hostess. Two children were swept off the packing-cases they sat on, so that they could be offered to the ladies.

In the middle of this confusion, Fine and Fabienne began talking at the same time. With the baby still howling, Mme Guartorella found their explanations difficult to follow. In any case, how could she understand the anxiety of these three mothers? If Cisco didn't turn up for a meal, it was assumed he was cadging one elsewhere. So much the better if he was. If, on the other hand, he turned up later hungry, there wasn't very much she could do about it.

M. Guartorella, having invited the ladies to sit down with a lordly sweep of his arm, relapsed into silence with his eyes fixed on Fabienne Grosbelhomme. He admired women of that sort, plump and rather bold in their way of looking at you. Mme Martelot was, in his opinion, not worth looking at at all. He'd as soon have admired a guinea-pig. As for Mme Fine – she was much the best looking of the three, yet he kept his eyes averted.

It's embarrassing, when you owe money, isn't it? It was a long time since he'd set foot in the Auberge Daranluz, unless invited by his pal Domingo.

There was some red wine left in the bottle on the table, and in obedience to the laws of hospitality, Mme Guartorella pressed it on her visitors, and Nièves hastily washed three glasses in a basin of rather doubtful-looking water.

If it hadn't been for the girl, heaven knows when they'd have come to the point.

'Cisco came back just after six,' she informed them. 'Just dropped in to fetch his stick and his rucksack. He snatched up something to eat and was off again. Victorin was waiting for him. I saw him standing at the corner of the Rue Bleue.'

'And Tatave?' asked the herbalist.

'I didn't see him.'

'There you are!' cried Mme Fine. 'When they go about in pairs like that it means they're up to something.'

She was anxious now to get back to the inn, where the men would be wanting their supper. She couldn't trust Maria to rise to the occasion.

Mme Martelot didn't say a word, aghast as she was at the sight of the dirt and disorder in the Guartorellas' dwelling.

'There's nothing for it but to go to the Muches,' said Fabienne.

Bravely she finished her glass, wondering what would be happening to her inside as a result of the café au lait on top of the Basque liqueur and now the coarse red wine on top of that.

She carried the day. The three women stood up.

'To the mayor's?' asked Mme Guartorella, suddenly alarmed. 'Then it must be something serious.'

And falling into the spirit of the affair, she quickly rolled Raphael up in a bit of torn blanket and followed the others out into the Rue des Hallebardes.

Picking her nose, Nièves said to herself:

'For once I'd have done better to keep my mouth shut.'

They had to pass the inn, and Mme Fine said to the others:

'I must see Benoît and tell him we're going to the mayor's. Come in a moment.'

But the mayor was already there, holding forth in the middle of the café. Open-mouthed and with arms akimbo, Maria gazed at him and listened, while a smell of burning floated in from the kitchen. Nobody had sat down to supper.

Mme Daranluz rushed to the kitchen stove, crying:

'*Mon Dieu! Mon Dieu!*'

The dogs barked at the lantern which Mme Martelot was still carrying, waking up Raphael, who, after a second's reflection, wrinkled up his forehead and started howling again. Hoping to calm him, his mother sat down and unbuttoned her dress, Viette standing squarely in front of her, greatly interested in the operation.

'That nitwit of a schoolmaster! What do you think he did when he saw me? You'd never guess if you stayed up all night.'

M. Muche paused dramatically.

'As soon as I opened the kitchen door, the nitwit jumped to his feet and came and grasped me by the hand.

' "It's good of you to have made the first move, M. le Maire," he said.'

'But the children? Where are they?' interrupted Mme Grosbelhomme.

'I haven't the faintest idea, my good lady. And that's why I went to see him. Not to shake hands with him, you may be sure. Making the first move, indeed! My wife, for some inexplicable reason, was longing for the return of her dear boy, that jackass of a Victorin …'

'We've all been worrying. When my Tatave didn't come home …'

An exasperated voice came from the kitchen.

'Maria! Maria! The soup tureen ...'

'Well, if you ask me, they must be somewhere, the young monkeys,' put in Benoît placidly. 'What does M. Grillon think about it?'

'You should have seen his face when I challenged him to find his son. "Georget!" he called through the doorway. "Georget, my boy." But of course there was no more Georget than there are feathers on my backside. The bird had flown ...'

'Will you sit down to supper, gentlemen?' screamed Mme Fine. 'Why, it's nearly nine o'clock.'

In vain. She bustled from table to table, ladling out the steaming soup, but distractions were rare in Casteilcorbon and nobody took any notice of her.

Thereupon the blacksmith appeared. Nervously his wife edged up to the herbalist, convinced there was going to be a scene. But, like many a man who roars the house down at home, he was easily intimidated in public, and he stood passively by the door, listening and trying to make out what all the fuss was about.

'It's absurd,' Mme Grosbelhomme was saying indignantly. 'Didn't he tell you where my Tatave was?'

'I don't know where your Tatave is, my good lady. Neither does M. Grillon. We don't know where any of them are.'

'Please sit down,' implored Mme Fine. 'Or the soup'll be stone cold.'

'Something's got to be done ...'

To add to the uproar, Domingo started bawling something in Spanish to Mme Guartorella.

Fabienne was almost out of her wits.

'Really, something's got to be done. You can't go on standing there idle. With these chilly nights my Tatave'll catch his death of cold. Those children must be somewhere.'

'You don't mean to say so!' observed the mayor sarcastically.

He didn't like women to do the talking.

'Yes, I do mean it,' she snapped back. 'And what's more, when it comes to a bit of trouble you men are no use whatever.'

'Now, now!' intervened the innkeeper. 'We shan't get anywhere by quarrelling. Come on! Sit down and have your supper, friends. There's nothing like sitting down to a meal for making people turn up.'

The soup smelt delicious and there was at last a general move to the tables.

'Maria, lay places for these ladies and for M. le Maire ... Oh yes, you must. A plate of hot soup'll put new heart in you ...'

At last they had all settled down, some at the small marble-topped tables, the others at the big wooden table in the middle. There'd never been so many.

'Just my luck!' thought Maria. 'With Fébo away, and Pierrot not back yet. Let's hope he turns up in time for the washing-up.'

To make his contribution, the blacksmith ordered drinks. M. Muche followed suit.

'We'll have some white wine for these ladies,' he said with clumsy gallantry.

So the improvised meal began to look rather like a wake in honour of their departed boys.

And with each glass of wine some fresh explanation was suggested.

'If you ask me,' said the innkeeper, 'they've done something silly and don't dare face us now.'

'Quite right,' answered the blacksmith. 'My Riquet loses nothing by staying away, and well he knows it. I'll give him such a kick up the arse as he'll remember on his wedding day.'

With that he tossed down another glass, as though to make a pledge of it.

It was then that Mme Muche joined them. She came in timidly, abashed by the many eyes fixed upon her. Never before had she crossed the threshold of the inn, but the circumstances were exceptional. Mme Fine couldn't help a feeling of pride when the first lady of Casteilcorbon was persuaded to sit down next to her husband.

'What can I offer her?' she wondered.

If only she had had those *fouaces* she had ordered from the baker. They would have been just the thing. She had forgotten all about them. It was Pierrot who was to have fetched them on his way back from school.

'Maria. Maria, run round to the baker's. Tell him ...'

The girl listened, snuffling, then did as she was bid. As things were, that much extra made no difference.

Surrounded by a respectful silence, the mayor was explaining:

'The whole thing's just a practical joke – idiots that they are, those boys. Yes, I tell you it's just a practical joke, and the best thing we can do is to take no notice when they do turn up. We'll each simply take our own brat home. Once there, we'll deal with them as they deserve. I'll certainly teach mine to think twice about playing any more jokes on me.'

'Me too,' agreed the blacksmith. 'I'll give my Riquet something to remember.'

As anxiety increased, threats of vengeance grew in the same proportion. Mme Martelot cried a little every now and then, and that irritated her husband. People ought to control themselves in public. From time to time he dug his elbow into her ribs, but she went on dabbing her colourless eyes with her rolled-up handkerchief.

'What's the good of that?' he snarled at her finally. 'It isn't crying that'll bring him back.'

Maria returned empty-handed. But she had brought with her some news – and Guste the baker, who was anxious to deliver it in person. He had merely slipped on a jacket over his bare skin, and by way of a waistcoat there was nothing but the hair on his chest, white with flour.

Soon after six Pierrot had come round as arranged to collect the *fouaces*.

'I weighed them out myself,' Guste told the assembly. 'And they came to just over seven pounds. My wife lent him a basket, and we put paper in between because of the jam.'

On the whole, these details were reassuring.

'He could hardly have got very far, with a pile of cakes like that to carry,' suggested Mme Fine.

'Just what I told you,' said the mayor. 'They've been and made pigs of themselves with those *fouaces*, and now they don't dare come home.'

'Pierrot might have taken me along,' thought Maria wistfully, picturing the feast.

'And what about Fébo?' asked the baker. 'Has he turned up?'

They'd all forgotten the old man. Not Guste, however, who was worried about his faggots. What with all the baking he had to do for the holiday …

The old man's name fanned the general anxiety, as everybody jumped to the conclusion his disappearance had something to do with the missing boys. The old man was an unknown quantity, which fitted him for the role of sorcerer. Belief in witchcraft dies hard in the country. Tongues were loosened. Tales were told. An accordion was just as good as any other musical instrument, and Mme Martelot could see the old man, like the Pied Piper, leading her boy into the side of a mountain.

Fortunately, however, the instrument in question was there on the window-sill, wrapped in its green cover.

'Look here,' said M. Muche. 'We'll wait till eleven. If they're not back by then we'll make up search-parties. Just the men, of course. I'll take one lot out on the Perdigane road. Sébastien and Domingo – you'll make for La Chênaie. M. Daranluz – you'll search one side of the cemetery and M. Martelot the other, meeting at the quarry. That leaves the road to the sea. We'll send a party under François Tistounet that way. Will someone go and fetch him?'

'I'll go,' volunteered Maria, who was not displeased to be running about the place at night.

'We'll have a gun with each party. And whoever finds the wretches will fire two shots in the air to let the other parties know. Then we'll all gather here again and you'll drink my health in punch.'

He spoke light-heartedly enough, but to his wife, who knew him, his words rang hollow. He was really far more worried than he cared to admit over the disappearance of his hefty lout of a son.

No one else saw through the blustering manner, however, and he was listened to with the utmost respect. Even by his workmen, who in their hearts detested him.

'You have to take your hat off to him,' muttered one of them grudgingly. 'He certainly does know how to manage things.'

Yes. He could take the initiative all right, and he carried everyone with him. All the men offered to join the search-parties. It might be added that the prospect of a midnight hunt was also rather exciting. Lanterns were fetched, guns and ammunition.

'You're not going to leave us women all alone, are you?' whined Mme Martelot.

'I'm going with one of the search-parties,' declared the herbalist firmly.

The other women looked at her disapprovingly.

'Just like her!' snorted Mme Fine as she carried an armful of plates into the kitchen.

She looked round at the piles of dirty crockery stacked everywhere. All that washing-up to be done. Only Maria to help, and heaven alone knew when she'd get back, now that she'd found a pretext for gadding about the town.

A wave of discouragement broke over her.

'*Mon Dieu!*' she sighed. '*Mon Dieu!*'

It was only a few minutes to eleven. The groups were forming up. Men were draining their glasses. Suddenly Boulou and Barbette began barking and everyone stopped talking.

'There they are,' said Mme Fine.

Tatave's mother rushed towards the door, but when it opened it revealed only the tall figure of M. Grillon, and there was a groan of disappointment from the women.

At the sight of the mayor, he almost turned round. That would have been undignified, however, and he stood his ground, merely asking:

'What's going on?'

He had made up his mind not to show how worried he was.

No one answered.

'I've been thinking things over,' he went on, 'and I've come to the conclusion that we are in the presence of nothing less than a deliberate revolt of the most reprehensible character. The whole of the class – all the elder boys, that is – have run away in protest against a punishment which I had quite rightly imposed on them. That being the case, I think it behoves us to consider what attitude to adopt in order to uphold the authority of the family no less than of the school.'

This speech was greeted by a hostile silence which was almost harder for him to bear than the blow he had received when he realized his own son had fled. He looked for a ray of sympathy in Mme Grosbelhomme's eyes, but all he could see there was a mother's anxiety – and a mother's reproach.

Finding the silence unbearable, he added:

'Sooner or later, the stray bee returns to the hive.'

At that, the mayor took three steps towards him and bluntly expressed what everyone was thinking:

'You can go to hell with your damned bees, you silly chump.'

M. Grillon swayed. The cup of bitterness overflowed. Pathetically he glanced at the herbalist, whose presence made the insult all the more painful. But she, with the cruelty of the barn-door fowl who rounds on the cock that has been beaten in battle, responded with a vicious peck:

'After all it's his fault ...'

The other fowls hastened to join in.

'What a way to treat children!'

'If he'd only kept an eye on them when they left school.'

'It's a shame!'

Déodat was overwhelmed by the tide.

'Anyhow, are you going to volunteer?' asked M. Muche.

'Volunteer for what?'

M. Grillon had only been there for barely a minute, but no one made any allowance for that. The mayor's insult had completely disconcerted him, and the quaver in his voice did nothing to add to his stature.

'For what?' snarled the mayor. 'He asks for what! Why, to go fishing for frogs, with a butterfly net, my good man!'

A servile titter went round the room.

Poor M. Grillon! He was a pathetic sight. Mme Muche was the only one to take pity on him. She couldn't very well stand up for him against her husband, but she tried to turn the conversation by saying:

'But what can they be thinking about, those children? It's simply terrible not knowing where they are or what they're doing.'

'I can tell you where they are, Madame!'

The voice came from the doorway, in which stood François Tistounet, the *garde champêtre*, one time corporal and trumpeter in the Spahis, who stood to attention and gave a military salute.

'Yes, M. le Maire,' François was saying, 'I can give you my word for it. There they are, shut up in the Bastide. We were coming along the Allée des Trois Tourelles, Maria and me, when suddenly we heard no end of a shindy. That's right, isn't it, Maria? A rattling of chains and I don't know what. So I said to Maria, I said: "We'd better go and have a look. Maybe there's some tramp wandering about who's up to no good. After all, you never know, do you, what may be ..."

'Still, never mind about that ... So we turned, we did, up the slope leading to the Bastide. Pitch dark it was. We couldn't see a thing till we were almost there. Then suddenly we saw something moving right in front of us. Bless my soul! You could have knocked me down with a feather. For there it was … You may not believe it, M. le Maire, but it's as true as I'm standing here … The drawbridge … It went up as we stood there. Right before our very eyes it did …'

PART TWO

ONE

THE look-out – or, to give him his proper title, the Knight of the Guard – sneezed three times and had to wipe his spectacles.

In his subconscious mind his mother's voice kept nagging at him.

'Keep out of the draught, Tatave ... Turn your collar up, or you'll catch your death of cold.'

He shrugged his shoulders. A look-out doesn't catch cold, still less when he's a knight.

All the same, he pulled the bottom of his Balaclava helmet down over his shoulders, thinking with satisfaction that in the distance it must look exactly like the hood of chain-mail worn by the knights of old. Huddling under the battlements, he tried to get a little shelter from the wind, which at that height was rather keener than he'd bargained for.

At one corner of the square keep was a small overhanging look-out turret, which would have provided shelter enough. Indeed, they had intended to use it until it was discovered that the bottom had fallen out. The mere thought of that gaping hole with a drop of a hundred feet was enough to make Tatave feel slightly sick.

The dawn on that last Sunday of October promised well. Two tinted clouds, like rosy cheeks, peeped over the lavender-grey line which blurred the horizon of the sea. In the west, the sky, still black and heavy, weighed down on the Perdigane hills, making the Canigou hardly visible. It was from there that the rain came, but today the sunshine was obviously going to prevail.

At the foot of the Bastide, the little town slept. From this height the houses looked like those little roofed cubes that children play with on the floor and forget to put away when they go to bed.

Nevertheless a few chimneys were already smoking – those of the presbytery and the Auberge Daranluz, for instance, and one belonging to the convent. And there was another. No mistaking which it was, since the house stood up alone between the Impasse des Suisses and the obelisk of the war memorial. It was Mme Grosbelhomme's.

Stoically, Tatave banished the thought of the creamy hot chocolate he always had for breakfast on Sunday mornings, in which his mother beat the yoke of an egg 'to build him up', as she would never fail to say.

There were other things too. But no. He wouldn't think of them.

'I'd much sooner have a bit of *fouace* any day,' he muttered.

And gazing defiantly at his home, he had the pleasurable feeling that he was getting his own back.

'I'd like to see her face now,' he mused. 'She and her cod-liver oil!'

That was another thing. She wouldn't be able to push that stuff down his throat. No, not for many a long day …

Rubbing his hands together, he went over all his grievances one by one, gloating over his new-found emancipation.

'She'll be in a state, I bet. And what'll she say to M. Grillon when she finds out it's all his fault?'

The day grew lighter.

As soon as he could see to write, Tatave, who wasn't given to wasting time, selected a fountain-pen from the formidable array hooked on to his inside breast pocket, and wrote:

No signs of enemy activity. Quiet night. Morale excellent. Nothing special to report, but keep out of the watch-tower or you may get a surprise.

P.S. The beastly rooks have been shrieking like pole-cats.

On second thoughts, he crossed out this last note, as the comparison didn't seem quite apt.

It was broad daylight now. Taking out his own private note-book, the boy settled down to write the second chapter of *Les Chevaliers de Casteilcorbon*.

He took a long time trying to think of a suitable heading. Finally, in green ink this time, he wrote:

FIRST NIGHT

and beneath it:

LIBERTY, SWEET LIBERTY

It hadn't been as sweet as all that. Victorin, for one, had hardly stopped grumbling about the weight of Riquet, who was kneeling on his shoulders.

The chains which lifted the drawbridge passed over two sheaves and then were attached to the opposite ends of a huge copper tank which, when filled with water, formed the counter-weight.

Not having been used within living memory, and no doubt much longer than that, it was hardly surprising that the tank leaked.

In Tatave's narrative several paragraphs were devoted to the prowess of the Chevalier Henri du Martel, who might more soberly be described as the blacksmith's mate – if that. Whatever his status, however, there could be no doubt of one thing: it was Riquet's little store of technical knowledge which gained the day. So perhaps prowess wasn't such a bad word, after all.

Kneeling on Victorin's shoulders, he scraped away the verdigris and soldered up the holes. There seemed no end to them, but patiently the boy worked on. There wasn't much the others could do but watch and hand him up the tools he asked for.

It was a trying time for Pierrot. He was the leader. He was responsible. And now for the first time he was forced to realize that the success or failure of their enterprise depended, not on his will and judgement alone, but on the skill of another's hands. It worried him, it disconcerted him, but he concentrated on keeping up the morale of his troops.

'Shut up, Victorin. Stop grousing. Every time you open your mouth you move. How can Riquet do the job if you don't keep still?'

'Here's another,' cried Cisco, who was inside the tank helping to locate the holes.

His voice had a strange metallic resonance.

With the road-mender's lantern, they had only two packets of candles, which had been procured at the last moment. Cisco had been sent on that mission. He had been to the grocer's and asked for some liquorice root, knowing well that old Mme Broc kept her stock of it behind the shop. When her back was turned he had quickly pounced on the candles and stuffed them inside his trousers under his belt.

'Go on. Stick it,' urged Pierrot as Victorin groaned again, for Riquet's knees seemed to be digging right into his shoulder muscles. 'We shan't be much longer now.'

Indeed, a few minutes later Riquet clambered down.

'I think that'll hold.'

He clapped his hands and rubbed them together exactly as his father did when he was pleased with the job he'd done.

'But why are we here at all?' asked Victorin. 'That's what I'd like to know. I thought we were going to …'

Pierrot cut him short.

'I'll explain that tomorrow. The only thing that matters now is to get the bridge up … Of course if you'd rather not stay … If you've got cold feet … We don't want to keep anyone against his will …'

Victorin swallowed the rebuke.

'There's one thing left to do,' said Riquet. 'We've got to oil the sheaves.'

This was done. The great moment approached.

'Noble knights …' began their leader.

All sorts of ideas ran through his head. He would have liked to tell them …

But his voice was unsteady, and it was as much as he could do to utter the words:

'Open the sluice.'

The water from the moat gushed through the sluice and thundered into the tank.

'Steady,' called out Riquet. 'Not too fast, or it'll bust.'

And a few seconds later:

'It's holding! … It's holding!'

The chains tautened. The sheaves creaked. Then slowly the bascule moved upwards. It was an awe-inspiring moment.

But the most terrifying was to come. Just as the drawbridge reached the vertical it automatically released the catches which retained the portcullis, which with a tremendous roar came crashing down, narrowly missing the gallant Victorin, who, a foot or two farther forward, would have been impaled by one of its ferocious spikes.

All this was recorded in the *Veracious Chronicles of the Sieur Gustave de Grosbel*.

Veracious? That word certainly did give rise to occasional misgivings in the noble chronicler's breast. But he had no great difficulty in brushing them aside.

'Paladins,' they heard in their chief's stentorian voice, 'we have now cut ourselves off for ever from the wickedness of the world. Sleep. Sleep in peace my brothers-in-arms. I myself will keep watch over this fortress till cockcrow.'

At those words, the knights took off their armour and stretching their weary limbs upon the floor sank into a refreshing slumber.

They had some straw to lie on, but it was damp and there was not nearly enough of it. The cold stone of the huge paved guardroom was very hard indeed. Preferable, however, a hundred times preferable to the *soft couch of slavery*.

Pleased with that phrase, Tatave sucked the butt end of his fountain-pen, waiting for further inspiration. Deceived by the boy's immobility, a rook flew down and alighted on the battlements.

'Shoo!' cried Tatave, and the bird decamped precipitately.

It went and complained to its fellows that their battlements had been invaded by strangers, and the birds one and all croaked with indignation.

'Abracadabra!'

Georget's head emerged from the spiral staircase that led up to the platform. Rather out of breath, he came towards Tatave, his mouth smeared with jam. Behind him trailed a long train of coloured stuff.

'Abracadabra!'

The watchman put down his fountain-pen and crossed his fingers.

'Blood and Freedom!'

'Just look at this, Tatave. Isn't it wonderful?'

'Where did you find it?'

'In one of the storerooms downstairs. Riquet was able to open the door with a bit of bent wire.'

'Yes, it's a splendid flag. Are we going to hoist it somewhere?'

'I should jolly well think so.'

It had been the emblem of a Friendly Society, the *Mutuelle Vieillesse des deux sexes réunis*, which had been liquidated some years back, since when the flag had been forgotten. It was not unsuitable for its present purpose. On a red-and-green ground were two clasped hands with the words *One for all, all for one*, the whole thing being bordered with a tarnished gold fringe.

After attaching it to the lightning conductor, the boys stood back to admire it.

'Fine!' said Tatave. 'It might have been made specially for us.'

Freshly inspired, Gustave de Grosbel opened his note-book again and wrote:

When daylight came a banner could be seen floating in the morning air over the keep, bearing in letters of gold the watchword of revolt ...

'What are you scribbling in that exercise book?'

Tatave closed it at once, answering evasively:

'Oh, something ...'

Georget didn't inquire further, captivated as he was by the magnificent view of the town and its surrounding hills and woods.

'There! Get along with you now. I'm on guard. We've kept you a bit of *fouace*. And Pierrot's got a job for you. He wants a list of all our provisions.'

He looked at his friend and was suddenly sorry for him.

'Go on. Go and get warm. Your nose is purple and your cheeks green. You'll see – Riquet's made a lovely fire. There's any amount of wood down there.'

Tatave hesitated.

'The thing is: I wanted to ...'

Georget understood at once. Thrusting his hand into his pocket, he pulled out the treasure of treasures, the telescope.

'Don't you worry. You leave it to me. With this gadget I'll keep an eye on them all right.'

It was indeed quite a handsome object, with its leather fittings. Georget removed the cap over the object-glass and the little slide over the eyepiece and pulled the telescope out to its full length.

Conscious of looking like one of those sea-captains of the illustrated story-books, he put it up to his eye, and, as with Tatave, his first concern was to inspect his own home.

All he could see was a blur, and he was fiddling with it for quite a time before an image suddenly came sharply into focus. Then he had a marvellous view. Ranavalo's kennel, the beehives, the lavatories on the far side of the playground – everything was there in the minutest detail. The place looked deserted.

'Perhaps he's still asleep,' thought Georget, assailed by a slight pang.

He trained his telescope on the neighbouring streets. It was a funny feeling being able to look down so intimately into other people's back yards. Then he picked up a moving figure.

Ah! That was the Abbé Escoutou crossing the Rue de l'Église. The figure danced up and down in Georget's field of vision, for it was difficult to keep a steady hand when you were following a moving object.

The priest stopped. And there was another person now in the picture – none other than Tatave's mother, who had no doubt been waiting for him by the church door. They were joined by a third. Without seeing his face, Georget at once recognized the uniform of François Tistounet, the *garde champêtre*.

There was some gesticulating. They seemed to be looking at him and pointing, yet Georget felt sure he was invisible, crouching as he was behind the battlements.

Others joined in. There was Guste the baker, François' daughter, whose red head made a splash of colour, the cobbler in a brilliantly white shirt. Yes, and there was the Reverend Mother herself. It would have to be something quite extraordinary to bring her out into the street to jostle with the crowd.

And all heads were tilted. Everyone seemed intensely interested in the top of the Bastide.

The crowd grew, and Georget found it most entertaining to watch the expressions on their faces. Of course he couldn't hear a word, but they seemed to have plenty to say to each other. The curé rubbed his hands and was no doubt saying:

'Splendid! splendid!'

Mme Grosbelhomme was angry – that was as plain as a pike-staff. But what on earth could they be looking at?

Suddenly he understood.

'What an ass I am! Of course, it's the flag. They're admiring our flag!'

The priest detached himself from the group and went up the church steps. In the entrance he stopped. Georget could still see the lower part of him. But what was he doing? One of his feet – he wore buckled shoes – seemed to be groping for something. Then the foot went up and down.

The next moment the church bell was ringing. That was it. The priest was ringing the bell for eight o'clock Mass. But why should he be doing it himself? Where was Fébo?

Fébo! Yes, indeed, what had become of him? Fébo, who was to have led them into Catalonia?

Georget didn't pursue the question. There were too many interesting things to look at. He shifted his ground, and from each side of the Bastide he discovered a new and fascinating aspect of Casteilcorbon. It was all so familiar, and yet so fresh.

He discovered another staring group outside the Auberge Daran-luz, and yet another in the Place de la République, in front of the mayor's house. In the poor quarter, the Rue Bleue, it was just the same. All over the town, people – they looked from Georget's altitude like black ants – had come out into the streets to gaze at the banner of liberty and exchange comments on the situation.

Finally Georget's attention wandered back to the school. The windows of his father's room were wide open now.

'He's up,' thought the boy.

And once again there was that brief pang.

'He must be out of his mind with worry.'

Unable to see any more, he resolutely rubbed the lenses of the telescope, refusing to admit it was his own eyes that needed wiping.

His vision re-established, he inspected the garden. There was Ranavalo basking in the slanting rays of the sun. A little farther on a spade stood, planted in the earth, on the edge of the cabbage patch. He had been using it himself yesterday and had forgotten to put it away.

Yesterday! What a long time ago that was!

Lifting the edge of the telescope, Georget followed the line of gooseberry bushes at the bottom of the garden, and a shock went through him when he recognized his father's straw hat hovering about among the hives.

Was it possible?

Yes, it was. When all the town was agog with what had happened, when people hurried to and fro, angry or bewildered, discussing the situation, here was his father, unmoved by the crisis and apparently indifferent to the fate of his child, looking after his bees.

'It beats me,' grumbled Victorin. 'Instead of leaving, here we are. Shut up, too. Might just as well be in prison. What I'd like to know is ...'

He had slept badly. After the excitement of the night before, the early morning painted a much less romantic picture of their situation. It was all very well for the others. They were only kids. But for him! Pretending to be a knight, at his age! He should never have let them drag him into it. They had gone too far this time. The whole thing was obviously going to be a flop. His father would see to that. Trust him!

To make matters worse, the hefty lout had a stiff neck – a thing which doesn't make life any the rosier. With draughts everywhere ...

'What is it you'd like to know?' asked Pierrot menacingly.

He pulled Mascha out of the cartridge pouch, feeling the need to touch something warm and friendly. Really it was too bad. A malcontent already. But he might have known it would be like that with Victorin. Anyhow, he must act promptly. Half-heartedness must be nipped in the bud.

'What is it you'd like to know?'

'How long it's going to last, this joke.'

'So you think it's a joke, do you? Well, let me tell you this, Victorin Muche: it's nothing of the sort. And if any proof's wanted that it's not a joke, we've got a prisoner already ...'

Everyone sat up with a jerk. A prisoner? Had Pierrot really said 'a prisoner'?

'Yes, a prisoner. Or, if you like, a hostage. In fact, that's why I've summoned you all to a council of war. But first of all let's have no more grumbling. The situation's much too serious for that. Victorin Muche, go up and relieve the look-out. We'll have you back in the council when you're in a better mood.'

Crushed by the rebuke, the hefty lout left them and started up the spiral staircase. Half-way up they heard him stumble and swear to himself.

'He puts up a pretty poor show for a knight, I must say,' groaned Cisco.

'But he's not a knight,' corrected Tatave. 'He's only a squire. At least, that's what he is in my scheme, as I've just been telling you. You couldn't make the mayor's son a knight ...'

'That'll do,' said Pierrot. 'You let me speak.'

He stood up to affirm his authority, the others remaining squatting round the fire with their chins on their knees.

'From now on you will all take titles worthy of your new life,' he said gently. 'They have been chosen by our friend, Tatave ...'

'*Gustave de Grosbel*,' corrected the chronicler.

'Yes, of course. I'm sorry. But you know we really ought to earn our titles by deeds of valour. And as a matter of fact the only one who's done anything extraordinary so far is Riquet ...'

'*Chevalier Henri du Martel* ...' Pierrot was again put right.

Cisco, always a bit of a flatterer, chipped in to say:

'But what about you, Pierrot? After all, you've been in charge of everything. We wouldn't be here if it hadn't been for you.'

'That's different. I'm in charge, and what has to be has to be.'

A little vaguely put, perhaps, but they all understood his reasoning perfectly. And it was unanswerable.

There was the sound of steps scampering down the stairs and then Riquet appeared.

'Whatever have you been d ... doing to the hefty lout?'

'You mustn't say hefty lout any more,' said Tatave, who was a stickler for form. 'He's now a squire.'

'Oh! Well, what you been d ... doing to him?'

He pulled out a bit of liquorice, covered with grey fluff from his pocket, and began sucking at it with relish.

'Don't bother about Victorin,' said Gustave. 'The thing is that while you've been upstairs, you've been knighted.'

'Ah!'

'Yes, you're the *Chevalier Henri du Martel* now. What do you think of that?'

'All right with me. Whatever you say. What I want is to get my head down.'

His tone showed him to be completely insensible of the honour that had been done him.

'Did you say something about a prisoner?' asked Cisco.

'Yes, but I'll come to that later. First of all we've got to get organized. And the two most important things are to keep a good look-out and to see to the food.'

'Bravo!'

That was from Tatave.

'Shut up! There's nothing to go bravoing about ... Now listen – there are six of us, and we'll work in six watches all round the clock, two hours at a stretch as look-out man up top and another two hours attending to the fire down here.'

'What's it matter if it goes out?'

'The point is, we've got plenty of wood, but not too many matches. Only two boxes, and they're soon gone if you're not careful ... Now, *Gustave de Grosbel*, you get it all written down, the names and the watches, so there'll be no arguing about whose turn it is ... And then there are the other things to be done – we'll take them all in turn – getting the food ready, clearing up, cutting wood ...'

'And don't forget the "break", Tatave,' chimed in Georget, who was quite irrepressible that morning.

Gustave de Grosbel was delighted with the idea of compiling the roster. He would do it in five colours, giving the knights their full titles, leaving space for their coats-of-arms, those having not yet been decided on.

But there was a practical matter to clear up first:

'How shall we know the time?'

'Victorin's got a watch,' said Cisco. 'A silver one. His father gave it him for his first Communion. It's a beauty.'

He spoke without envy. He knew there was little chance of his ever possessing such a treasure and accepted his fate philosophically.

'That's true,' said Pierrot. 'Then we must requisition it. We'll hang it up there over the fireplace. Only, he'll be the only one allowed to touch it and wind it up. We'll hang Tatave's list up beside it.'

'And the chap on guard – how'll he know the time?'

'By the church clock, silly.'

Their chief had an answer for everything. He put Mascha back into his cartridge pouch, feeling no longer in need of comfort.

'I said there were two things – keeping watch, and the food ...'

'We'll have to drink too,' put in Cisco.

'There's no lack of water,' said another.

'You mean the stuff in the moat? It's full of weeds and frog-spawn.'

'That'll do for salad.'

Pierrot frowned.

'You can keep your jokes till afterwards, Georget. This is a council of war, and we've got to be serious.'

'But I am being serious. Only I couldn't help thinking ...'

'Thinking what?'

'Can't tell you, or you'll say I'm joking.'

He burst out laughing, and his mirth was so infectious that they all followed suit, without knowing really what they were laughing at. It did them good. For the last twenty-four hours they had been strung up, with fear gnawing at their guts. This was the reaction – rather like the laughter at a funeral reception.

Mascha was so astonished by the noise that he poked his nose out and studied the situation.

Tatave was the first to come back to the business in hand.

'We could sterilize the water. Of course we've got no chloride … nor permanganate of potash …'

'Come off it, Tatave. We're not in school now.'

'I only want to save you from getting typhoid. The point is that, as we've no chemicals, we'll have to boil the water. At a temperature of …'

'What'll you boil it in?'

Tatave's learned dissertation was brought to a halt. Certainly there were some things that hadn't been thought of. Apart from the barrel of herrings – and they could hardly boil water in that – they had really no receptacle at all. Everyone started talking at once, but Pierrot silenced them.

'Write down: *The Council requests the Chevalier Henri du Martel to look into the question of something to boil the water in. If it leaks he can mend it.*'

Riquet had no idea he was being referred to until everyone turned to look at him.

'To come now to the provisions …'

'Lucky we were smugglers before being knights,' remarked Georget.

And once again Pierrot frowned. Being smugglers had been merely a game, and he didn't like the present adventure being put on the same level. He was already vaguely conscious of the difficulty of commanding people who always flew off at a tangent, or made things sound funny, which was worse. Georget particularly. Such a nice boy. So gay and companionable, so obliging. Yet that didn't prevent him constantly interrupting their deliberations with frivolous remarks.

The list of provisions was soon drawn up.

Potatoes	52	
Gammon	1	
Salted herrings	84	about, judging by the number in the top row
Jujubes	1	box not quite full
Liquorice root	1	packet
Chocolate	2	slabs

'Is that really all?' asked the chief, struck by the paucity of their reserves. 'What about the provisions for the road?'

'They were all taken up to Féroulet's hut,' answered Cisco. 'Those were your orders, seeing as how ...'

'Yes, of course,' interrupted Pierrot, biting his lip.

'I've got something in my pocket left over from yesterday afternoon,' said Riquet.

And he produced the butt end of a loaf stuffed with two pieces of sugar.

'Good,' went on Pierrot. 'Then we've still got a whole *fouace*, besides the half that was left over from this morning.'

'We'll have to have rationing,' declared Gustave de Grosbel with sombre asceticism. 'I'll work out a scheme. So much per head per day.'

'There's nothing to worry about,' said Cisco superbly, accustomed as he was to taking no thought for the morrow. 'We might find some food here. We haven't had a good look round yet. There are several more rooms locked up. Besides, didn't you hear the rats last night? If they can find something to eat, so can we. What's more, we could eat them. I'd catch them all right.'

'Eat rats? How awful!'

'I'd sooner eat the prisoner,' said Georget. 'Since Pierrot says we've got one ...'

At that they all laughed again.

'All the same,' said Cisco, 'there's one thing I would like to know, and that is: why are we here, shut up like animals in a cage? We'd have just about reached the frontier by this time. After all, that was the plan, and I can't make out ...'

'There's no need for you to make out anything,' snapped Tatave. 'Do I bother my head about such things? I just carry out orders and keep my mouth shut.'

Well said, Chevalier de Grosbel! Pierrot was pleased. Nevertheless he came to Cisco's rescue by saying:

'It doesn't matter – you've a right to know. When we're in council we're all equal. Just brothers-in-arms. It's the majority that decides everything. Unless of course it decides something silly. In that case ...'

He completed the sentence with a gesture. But Tatave resumed the offensive:

'If anybody doesn't like being here, he needn't stay.'

'The door's wide open.'

And Georget pointed to the portcullis which had so nearly cut their hefty lout in two the night before.

Another laugh, and the little storm blew over.

'The thing is,' explained Georget, 'we're a republic of knights who vote for whatever their leader wants. That's simple, isn't it? And now, Pierrot, what about showing us this prisoner of yours?'

Pierrot hesitated.

'Not yet,' he said finally. 'We must wait for Victorin.'

'Why?'

'He's strong. He's almost a man. We mightn't be able to hold the chap without him.'

TWO

'My poor Fine, you won't change anything by taking on.'

'I'm not taking on.'

'You haven't stopped once. All night long you were tossing and turning in the bed, with your *Ah! Mon Dieu* and your *Jésus Maria.*'

'How do you know, since you were fast asleep?'

'I was nothing of the sort.'

'There you are! You see!'

'See what?'

'That you're just as worried as I am. As if I didn't know you.'

'Worried? I dare say I am. But I don't let go.'

'Much better if you did. You're so busy not letting go that you don't do anything else.'

'What do you want me to do? Wander about with my mouth open like everyone else, gaping at that blessed Bastide?'

'Oh, you men! You're all alike. Spend your time keeping your dignity, instead of ...'

'Instead of what? ... Besides, what's the hurry? We know where they are now – that's the chief thing. And where they are they can't fly away, can they?'

'Still, there are lots of things you could do. You could go and see M. le Maire and the other parents. Instead of just doing nothing.'

'Give me a chance to shave first.'

'Very well, I'll go myself. I can't bear to stay here any longer.'

Behind her Viette came down the stairs, one step at a time. Maria had already opened the shutters, and in spite of the early hour several customers were already sitting in the café. From time immemorial, the last Sunday of October at Casteilcorbon was market day for hazel-nuts. From far and wide the farmers came streaming in, their pockets bulging with samples of their crops. The buyers, pastry-cooks, nougat-makers, and middlemen of all sorts, gathered in the Avenue Neuve and the part of the Allée des Trois Tourelles which was close to the Auberge Daranluz.

With little note-books in their hands and pencils over their ears, they fingered the nuts, cracked them, munched them with their eyes shut. Sometimes they spat them out quickly, not to be rude, but just to show they were experts who couldn't be taken in.

There were also people selling sweet and bitter almonds. Honey, too, since in the Roussillon most of the farmers kept bees. Thus all day long there was an air of thoughtful animation in the little town, buying and selling being a serious and even quite a cunning business.

The deals naturally were concluded round a bottle in the inn.

'What a day to have the place full of people,' sighed Mme Daranluz.

More were coming in already.

'*Bonjour*, Mme Fine. It'll be three coffees for us with a drop of *aguardiente*.'

'It doesn't look as though I'll get much chance of getting away,' she thought.

But she managed to smile at her customers as she bustled to and fro serving them. These three were the biggest growers in the district, she knew. It was they who set the pace, and they were trying to agree on a minimum price. A stiff one, of course. Though each in his heart knew he wouldn't keep to it. At any rate, not to the extent of losing a good bit of business.

Their little bags of nuts were laid on the marble-topped table.

'Mme Fine! Can you lend us some scales?'

'In a minute ... Maria! Maria! ... Where on earth has that girl got to now?'

A man came in, accompanied by two ladies. They wanted to see over the Bastide.

'I'm afraid you've fallen on a bad day, Monsieur. The guide's gone – disappeared. Not that that would have mattered very much if it hadn't been for ... You'd like to have lunch here? Yes, Monsieur. Certainly ... Meanwhile can I get you something?'

Mme Fine led them to the table nearest the window.

'Chocolate? Café au lait?'

There was laughter and conversation all round, and Mme Fine was being hailed on every hand. If only Maria had been there ...

'Viette, let go of me. How can I serve the customers with you clinging to my skirt? Here! Go and find Maria.'

'That's a pretty little girl you've got,' said one admiringly.

'Oh, she's that all right. A handful, all the same. Still, I can't complain. It's when they get older that they ...'

Near the door, a peasant rapped on the table.

'Coming …'

'And what about those scales, Mme Fine?'

The three farmers were getting impatient. They were still in earnest discussion, examining each other's samples.

Outside, people passed, then passed again. Generally they came in in the end. And Mme Daranluz, normally completely mistress of the situation, hardly knew which way to turn. Still, she struggled bravely to cope with it, hurrying to one table with the coffee-pot, to another with an armful of bottles. But she couldn't for long keep off the subject that was on her mind.

'Would you believe it? They've gone and shut themselves up in the Bastide. Been there the whole night, they have …'

People listened gravely and nodded. Yet she could see they were really more amused about it than anything else.

'The little devils!' said Pépé Combasil.

But there was a note of admiration in his voice.

'Oh, I'm sure they didn't mean to,' said Mme Fine, ready to find excuses. 'They must have shut themselves in – just for a lark, I suppose – and then found they couldn't get out.'

'Children! They're always up to something,' said a farmer's wife, a thin, goat-faced woman who talked with her lips pursed. 'Why, at our place the other day my grand-daughter took her little brother out of his cot and climbed up a ladder with him. Right up on the roof of the barn. Then she got frightened and couldn't get down again. So she started hollering for all she was worth. We were all out in the fields. Luckily the neighbours heard. Just think of it! A little girl of eight!'

'Yes,' said Mme Fine. 'But our boys aren't hollering. That's what gets under my skin.'

When he was thirsty, Grisouille used to push open the church door with his velvety nose and calmly walk in to drink the holy water in the stoup. Nobody was really shocked. Had not the Abbé Escoutou been the first to laugh? Perhaps it would have been otherwise had any other donkey done it. By belonging to the nuns, Grisouille had acquired some sort of religious status himself, and it seemed almost an act of loyalty that he should prefer holy water to any other kind.

Besides, he was quite extraordinarily discreet about it. Some sixth sense appeared to tell him that it wasn't the thing to do on Sundays. Then he would betake himself to the fountain in the Impasse des Suisses. Though it was farther, he was rewarded by the fact that some very succulent grass grew round it. And then there was Mme Grosbelhomme in the vicinity, she being readier than most with a lump of sugar. Tatave, moreover, was not one of those boys who couldn't see a beast of burden without wanting to clamber on to its back.

This morning, however, he loitered in vain. Hoping to attract the herbalist's attention, he nibbled at the yellowing nasturtium leaves in the window-boxes.

On the other side, in front of the shop, whose two shuttered windows faced on to the Place de la République, a little group of peasants had collected. They were less patient. They knocked, and knocked again.

The *garde champêtre* came by.

'Hallo, Tistounet! Isn't the shop open?'

'You can see it isn't.'

'I wanted some yeast.'

'We've been waiting quite a time,' grumbled Pépé Combasil.

'No right to shut on a Sunday,' said another. 'It's the only chance we get to do a bit of shopping.'

François Tistounet was always ready for a chat. He posted himself in the middle of the group, half sitting on his stick. For a moment he twisted his moustache, looking important. Finally he said:

'If it's Mme Fabienne you want, you're not likely to find her. Not today, you won't. She's just about out of her mind with worry.'

'It's some lotion I was wanting to grease my cow's teats.'

'A little soap'll do just as well, and won't cost you half as much.'

'What if it gets in the milk and gives it a bad taste?'

François was obliging. Moreover, it was part of his job to give information.

'There's the nuns. They do sometimes open the dispensary after the ten o'clock Mass. And when anything special's wanted, the Reverend Mother will make it up for you. You've only got to ring.'

Pépé Combasil spat to show his contempt.

'That Reverend Mother! It's not her that'll see the colour of my money.'

'Why not, Pépé? What's wrong with her?'

'I'll tell you why. She sold my wife a candle. She's dead now – my wife, I mean, rest her soul – and it brought us nothing but trouble it did, that candle ...'

'What did it do to you?' asked François, who always liked to make people talk.

'Well, you see, she was frightened of thunderstorms – my wife, I mean. And the Reverend Mother said: "With this you won't have no more to bother about. It's a special candle. It's been blessed by the priest." So my old woman took her word for it, and every time there was a storm she shut herself up in a cupboard with the candle ...'

'What harm was there in that?'

'That's what I'm coming to. D'you remember that storm we had twelve years ago come April? It was all round us from the Canigou to the Alberres. And all at once there was a crack right overhead such as you never heard. Knocked the missus right off her feet it did, and she flopped down where she was. In the cupboard ...'

'Did it kill her?' asked Tistounet, who knew the answer very well.

'No. Of course not. But with that candle burning she set fire to the house.'

'It might have been worse if you'd been struck by the lightning,' said an old woman. 'So there's no knowing but what the candle did you a good turn, all the same.'

'Look here,' said the good-natured François; 'if you won't go to the convent, follow me. I can take you to Mme Fabienne. I saw her just now with the other mothers outside the mayor's house. You can explain what you want to her. There's no use waiting here, I tell you, not if you were to wait all day. You see, this isn't an ordinary Sunday. The whole town's upside down because of them boys.'

'Seems they stole the schoolmaster's honey.'

'And the baker's *fouaces*, every single one of them.'

'What did I tell you? The children nowadays!'

'At their age, there must be a deal of wickedness in them to hoist the flag of the Revolution like that.'

'What can you expect in these days, when they've driven the priests out of the schools?'

'For All Saints' Day too. What'll all the people think who come to the town?'

'Come on,' said François; 'we mustn't make too much of it. I know them. They're not thieves. They're not bad boys at all. Take

143

that Pierrot, for instance, or Georget, or the blacksmith's boy – you couldn't wish for better. Don't know that I could say as much for that Tatave. A bit sly, I dare say. As for Victorin, he hasn't brains enough for much mischief. If you ask me, it's Cisco that's at the bottom of it all. I doubt he'll come to much good, that one. Spanish. And with a father that drinks – to say nothing of his poaching – and a mother who whelps every time the clock strikes. No, there's nothing in that family to give one confidence. There's no getting away from it. And if anybody was to tell me it was Cisco who had swiped M. Grillon's honey … Well, enough said …'

'And how are you going to get them out of the Bastide now that they've shut themselves in?'

The *garde champêtre* took a pinch of snuff. That was the very question he'd been asking himself all the morning, and he hadn't yet found a satisfactory answer.

'The best thing is to do nothing at all,' he said at last. 'It can't be much fun for them in there, poor devils. To my mind the less we say to them the sooner they'll see reason. It can't go on for ever. Play a waiting game, I say. Keep calm, and they'll soon get tired of it.'

It wasn't till the bell had been rung for the fourth time that Guillaume Muche buttoned up his waistcoat, strode across the hall to the front door and flung it open, glaring like an angry watch-dog at the women who had had the temerity to drag him away from his breakfast.

His hair was ruffled, his cheeks aflame. Mme Muche followed, holding his jacket out for him.

'Think of your heart, Guillaume.'

At the bottom of the steps stood Mme Grosbelhomme, Mme Martelot, and Mme Guartorella, encircled by a small crowd of onlookers who were determined not to miss anything.

By this time news of the escapade was all over the town, known not only to its inhabitants but to all who had come in from the surrounding country. It was on everybody's lips and effectually eclipsed the various other attractions that were provided. Scant attention, for instance, was paid to the gypsies whose caravans were drawn up round the war memorial and even to the beautiful girl in the red turban who played the tambourine to a dancing bear. Still less was paid to the big buyers who arrived in their fine cars from Perpignan and Carcassonne, from Castres, Toulouse, and even Montélimar. For the hazel-nuts, almonds, and honey of Casteilcorbon were famous.

At the mayor's appearance, everyone stopped talking. There was even a tendency to edge away out of reach. The mason's wife took cover behind another woman, while Mme Martelot buried her face in her handkerchief. Only Fabienne Grosbelhomme stood her ground. Indeed, emboldened by a wounded mother's feelings, she even took two steps forward.

She pointed to the Bastide.

'Look at that,' she said tragically.

Instinctively the mayor turned to look, but being short-sighted he saw nothing.

'What is it?' he asked.

'Up there. On the battlements. It's him. I've seen him. I could tell who it was by the pompom on his Balaclava helmet.'

'Who?'

'Tatave. He's up there with the others. I know he'll catch cold ... M. le Maire, I beg you, give me back my Tatave.'

His shirt-sleeves rolled up, M. Muche crossed his hairy arms.

'My good lady, we know very well that your nitwit of a son is up there with the other nitwits.'

'Ooh! Oh!' wept Mme Martelot. 'It's past believing.'

'If they're there,' went on the distiller, 'it's because that's where they want to be. And it's no reason for pulling my bell off the door and causing a breach of the peace in front of my home in the early hours of a Sunday morning.'

'But, since you're the mayor, it's up to you to open up the Bastide and bring back my Tatave.'

'Well, you can go and fetch him yourself, and leave me alone.'

Stung to the quick, Fabienne drew herself up, following his example in crossing her arms.

'M. Muche, in the name of every mother, I call upon you to get that bridge down and return my son to me.'

The mayor thought it best to smile at this aggressive little woman who stood there with her chest thrown out. With the mixture of gallantry and effrontery so characteristic of him he said:

'By the way you talk, my little lady, anyone might think I'd thrown your Tatave into prison. If you've got any complaints, you might at least keep a civil tongue in your head.'

He loved to say things like that. It was his way of being disarming. For if anyone had a civil tongue in his head it certainly wasn't Guillaume Muche, whose wealth and whose violent character allowed him to be just as rude as he pleased.

But Mme Grosbelhomme was not so easily disarmed.

'Just as you like,' she answered. 'But for my part I'm going to telephone to the Gendarmerie at Perpignan. Then we'll see whether …'

Now M. Muche didn't like gendarmeries. It was an instinctive distaste, formed in the struggling days of his youth, and which he had never lost, not even when he had become one of the 'pillars of society'. François Tistounet, the *garde champêtre*, with his képi and his big moustache, he considered a sufficient embodiment of law and order, and the Perpignan gendarmes could stay where they belonged – in Perpignan.

'You can go to the devil with your gendarmes,' he roared. 'Do you think we don't look silly enough as it is? Just at the time of the *féria*, when the whole place is swarming with strangers! Is that all you care for the dignity of your town? Is that your idea of patriotism?'

Patriotism! The word hit her like a slap in the face, and for a moment she was silenced. Not for long, however.

'Well,' she began again, 'what are you going to do?'

'I'm going to do damn all – that's what I'm going to do. I'm going to mind my own business, and it'd be a lot better if others did the same. Now, be off! The whole lot of you. And don't come plaguing me with your idiotic questions.'

'Ooh! Ooh!' whined Mme Martelot. 'What does he take us for … It's past believing …'

'*Garde champêtre*, disperse the crowd.'

'*A vos ordres, M. le Maire.*'

Tistounet gave a military salute, but, instead of lowering his hand, he kept it at the peak of his cap in an attitude that was at the same time respectful and questioning.

'What is it?' the mayor condescended to ask.

'Meaning no disrespect, M. le Maire, it's about that red flag up there. It doesn't look well – not on a day like this, it doesn't.'

'What red flag?'

Every head was turned towards the Bastide.

There it was, the flag of the defunct *Mutuelle Vieillesse des deux sexes réunis*, half wound round the lightning conductor, in such a way that only the red showed.

'Hell on earth!' bellowed the mayor. 'Why the devil couldn't you tell me before, you damn fool?'

The distiller always claimed to be a progressive, and red was far from being an obnoxious colour in his eyes, particularly when it figured on election posters. And if there was another reason for his not disliking it, it lay in the hope he cherished of one day sporting the ribbon of the *Légion d'Honneur* in his buttonhole.

But a red flag – that was quite another matter. That spelt one thing, and one thing only: Revolution. There were painful memories of an occasion when his workmen had even hoisted it over the distillery.

'Hell on earth!' he bellowed, his face growing purple. 'Tistounet! Get that rag hauled down, and get it done at once. If not we'll be having another *garde champêtre* in Casteilcorbon, and no later than this very evening.'

'My dear Guillaume,' begged Mme Muche, holding out his jacket. 'Your heart ...'

Tistounet's eyes were filled with terror. Standing more rigidly at attention than ever, he stammered:

'Meaning no disrespect, M. le Maire ...'

But he broke off helplessly, cutting a pathetic figure. All at once he remembered that he had been ordered to disperse the crowd. Hoping to prove his zeal and recapture his prestige, he set about it with a will. Brandishing his stick he shouted:

'Move on there, will you? Do you hear me? Get a move on.'

Solemnly M. Muche put on his jacket. He was suddenly quite calm, but there was a frown on his face as he said icily:

'You could at least keep a civil tongue in your head, Tistounet.'

The Abbé Escoutou was in the act of putting on his amice when Mme Grosbelhomme barged into the vestry. Behind her came Mme Fine, dragging Viette by the hand, and Mme Muche, perfumed and blushing, while the two other mothers brought up the rear, Mme Guartorella still carrying her baby.

The neat little room, smelling of stale incense and white wine, was soon full of exclamations, sighs, and protests. With five women talking at once, one of them in Catalonian dialect, it was little wonder if the priest was at a loss to know what they'd come for.

'Splendid! Splendid! Of course I can understand how you feel. It's not very nice for me either. I've got to go without my servers.'

'But something must be done, M. le Curé.'

'Just think what I feel like, with my Tatave up there. And I don't suppose he's had a morsel for his breakfast.'

'Quite so. Quite so, Madame. You have all my sympathy, but what can I do?'

With a sweep of his hand, he indicated the vestments he was putting on and the holy vessels which one of the nuns had set out for him.

'As you see, I was just getting ready. In ten minutes the third bell for High Mass will be rung. At least it would have been if Fébo had been here. As it is, I suppose we'll have to go without. I can't very well ring it myself, dressed like this. Come back later, will you, and we'll talk it over?'

'Keep still, Viette,' said Mme Fine sharply. 'And don't let me see you touching anything.'

'It won't do,' said Mme Fabienne. 'Later, I mean. Something's got to be done at once.'

'At once? But what about the Mass?'

'That's just the point. If you don't help us now, those children won't come to Mass. And it'll be partly your fault.'

'My fault? ... Quite so. Quite so. There's something in what you say. I hadn't thought of it in that light. They'll miss the Mass without a valid excuse, and that's a grave sin certainly. And such good boys too ... Quite so ... But I don't see what I can do. You should go to the mayor.'

'We've been. He's furious.'

'Splendid! And what does he think of the situation?'

The herbalist nudged Mme Muche.

'You tell him.'

The lady mayoress swallowed.

'My husband ...' she began.

'She doesn't like the idea of coming to you on behalf of her husband because he doesn't go to church,' explained Mme Fabienne. 'But, as I said to her, "Your husband may not believe in God, but ..."'

'Then what do you want?' asked the priest, feeling more and more at sea. 'If he doesn't believe, it would be hypocrisy to …'

'That doesn't stop him having good ideas,' said Mme Daranluz placatingly. 'Religion's one thing, intelligence another, isn't it, M. le Curé?'

The priest looked from one to the other of them with kind but puzzled eyes.

'My husband,' went on Mme Muche, 'intends to call a special emergency meeting of the Council.'

'Splendid!'

'But before they meet, he thought … he thought you might be so kind as to … You know Guillaume easily gets carried away. On the other hand, our poor dear Victorin has let himself be led on by the others …'

There were protests on all sides.

'I can't let that pass. You've got it the wrong way round. It's my Tatave who's been led on. Victorin's much the oldest, and …'

'And the stupidest,' they all thought, but this they kept to themselves.

In any case, he was only Mme Muche's stepson, which prompted Mme Fine to observe charitably:

'You can't hold yourself responsible for what you haven't made yourself.'

'You know,' continued Mme Muche, 'that my husband has a very bad heart. Any excitement may prove fatal. On the other hand, we all know you've a great influence over those boys …'

'Yes,' added Mme Fine. 'No one knows how to get round them like you do. I suppose it's your training.'

The blacksmith's wife said nothing, but from time to time her lips moved and sometimes she dried her eyes.

'Quite so. I understand. Or rather I don't. What is it that the mayor wishes me to do?'

'It's quite simple,' explained Mme Grosbelhomme. 'This is what I suggest … We'll all go up on to the church tower and you'll come with us …'

She was interrupted by a cry of alarm from Cisco's mother.

'*Qué va! Cuidao!*'

'Viette! Viette! Come here, you naughty girl …'

Too late. A shower of coins rained on to the floor and rolled away in every direction, some, with particular malice, making for the most inaccessible spots under the furniture.

Attracted by a beautiful shining censer, the little girl, her pink bow standing up proudly on her head, had pulled herself up on to the credence to examine it more closely. She had almost attained her goal when the Spanish woman gave the alarm. Frightened, she clutched hold of the first thing that came to hand, an old biscuit box in which the priest put his offertories.

The money rolled and rattled, the women uttered cries of dismay, and Viette naturally added to the din by howling as though she'd been hit. Not to be outdone, Raphael joined in too.

Down on their knees the women picked up the coins, handing them to M. le Curé, who thanked them profusely. Occasionally he threw an embarrassed glance at Mme Guartorella, who had promptly opened her dress to silence her baby in the only way she knew. For after all a vestry is hardly the place for ...

'Splendid!' he muttered from time to time.

In the Allée des Trois Tourelles people stood with their heads in the air. Little groups were gathered at the junction of the Montée de la Reine and the Avenue Neuve. The strangers didn't mix with the locals, but they were hardly less interested. They, too, sauntered up to the castle to contemplate the bridge which overnight had become a door, a huge iron-studded door which fitted neatly into the Gothic archway that formed the entrance to the Bastide. To see better, they came right up to the edge of the moat, standing on the very ground on which yesterday the drawbridge had rested.

'Steady there! Don't push behind. You'll have us in the water in a minute. And it's deep.'

'You wouldn't recognize the place,' said Mme Broc, who kept her geese there.

'Look! There's smoke. They must have made a fire. Making the place nice and warm, I suppose.'

'I'd warm their backsides for them.'

'Go ahead, Martelot. If you know how. We're not stopping you.'

'Pretty good joke, I call it.'

'We'll have to get a boat and break down the door.'

'Just look at my geese. Poor things! They can't understand what's happened to them.'

Mme Broc called to them coaxingly, but they held aloof, gathered round the lower postern, looking suspiciously at the crowd of sight-seers.

The tourists who had that morning asked to see over the castle were there too. The father of the family was holding forth while his wife and daughter listened attentively. With his white cap and gold-rimmed glasses, he peered into the Baedeker, looking just like the Englishman of comic operas.

'What we see here,' he explained, 'is the remains of one of the most formidable strongholds of the Middle Ages. The earliest part dates from the thirteenth century, at a time when Jaime I, King of Majorca, ruled over the Roussillon. This was his summer residence.'

The family took it all very seriously.

'Just think! The thirteenth century!'

His nose in his book, the man went on:

'His successor erected the outer defences, and the keep was made practically impregnable. Indeed, in the whole course of its history, the fortress of Castillocuervo, as it was formerly called, never suffered the shame of capitulation.'

What a pity Tatave was unaware of these details, which were re-lated as eagerly and proudly as if the man had played a heroic part in the story himself.

'It resisted Louis XI during his wars against the King of Aragon. It resisted François I in 1542. It resisted Richelieu ...'

Gaping with admiration, the women stared up at the battlements. They weren't the only ones, for the inhabitants of Casteilcorbon were seeing their Bastide in a new light that morning. It had only needed some boys to make the drawbridge work and the whole town had been thrown back a few centuries. Until that Sunday morning no-body, not even Tistounet, so proud of his native town, had ever realized just how effective a fortress could be as a place in which to resist a siege.

Everybody seemed to be out, Nièves among the others. She had just brought off a coup, 'lifting' a couple of small bags of hazel-nuts from a lorry parked outside the Auberge Daranluz. Generously she had divided them between her brothers and sisters, keeping only a large handful for herself, which she had poured into the pocket – a sort of booty bag – hanging underneath her skirt.

Sitting down on the bank of the moat, her legs dangling over the water, she was enjoying herself. Every other minute her hand dived under her skirt and another nut went into her mouth, to be cracked between her teeth, then chewed as slowly as possible so as to prolong the pleasure. She thought of nothing as she gazed placidly at her nut-shells which floated on the still water.

Yes, she was happy like that, enjoying the general animation, though taking no part in it.

Suddenly she started as a hand was laid on her shoulder.

'*Dios mio!* Maria, how you frightened me.'

'What are you eating?'

'Nuts. Want one? Sit down.'

'Where did you get them?'

'Given to me.'

'You're lucky. I've been serving drinks to people all the morning that had them by the handful, yet they never once thought of offering me one. Those peasants! They're that mean …'

These girls seemed to be of the same race, dark, thin, with tousled hair, burning eyes, and dirty knees, two mountain goats, with a wild cunning in their slanting eyes, encircled by shadows.

'Does your mistress let you out in the mornings?'

'What an idea! No, she's gone to church, and I just slipped out. Had about enough of it. Since Fébo made off, everything comes back on me. It's Maria this and Maria that till I don't know whether I'm coming or going.'

'And the boss?'

'Oh, he doesn't say anything. He's all right. But the old woman … Down on me all the time. Never misses a chance. Today more than ever because of Pierrot … Is your brother there too?'

'Looks like it. He didn't come home last night.'

'Like Pierrot. And to think he never breathed a word of it to me! Did Cisco tell you?'

Nièves snorted.

'Cisco tell me! Not him! He never talks to girls if he can help it.'

'What do you think they're doing in there? … Give me another.'

Politely Nièves cracked a nut between her teeth and offered it all shiny with saliva.

'I don't know. Shouldn't be surprised if they found it pretty dull.'

The two girls chewed in silence, each following her own train of thought. Then Nièves asked:

'Would you like to be in there with them?'

'I should think I would.'

Her eyes shone more brightly.

'What would you do; shut up in there with a lot of boys?'

'I shouldn't do anything special. I'd just like being there. I'd look through one of those loopholes or whatever they call them. I'd laugh at all these staring louts. It'd be fun.'

'Why would it be fun?'

Maria looked superior as she answered:

'It's no use trying to explain. You're too young to understand.'

Nièves was hurt. As the eldest girl at home she was something of a little mother, and she felt very grown up indeed.

'Go on. Tell me. We're pals, aren't we? Besides, I've given you some of my nuts.'

That was a good argument, Maria had to admit. She racked her brains, but it was difficult to put her thoughts into words.

'It's like this,' she said at last. 'Those boys in there are getting their own back on the grown-ups. That's what I'd like too – to wipe my boots on them.'

'What'd you get out of it?' asked Nièves, who had a keen sense of profit and loss.

'Nothing. Perhaps a clout or two when it was all over.'

'There you are! You see ...'

'I told you you were too young to understand.'

THREE

SINCE the council of war, the garrison had gone from discovery to discovery, each lock yielding to the dexterity of the blacksmith's apprentice, the Chevalier Henri du Martel. And with each new find their courage soared.

'They didn't half make solid walls in those days!' exclaimed Tatave.

'With enough food, we could hold out for years.'

Though classed as a *monument historique*, the Bastide had remained the property of the municipality, and it was put to practical use as a warehouse by many of the town's worthies. As members or honorary members of the Council, they could do this without paying any rent. It wasn't quite in order, perhaps, but the mayor winked at the practice.

As a matter of fact Guillaume Muche had been one of the first to avail himself of this privilege to conceal surplus stocks from the eyes of the Excise.

In the first room, opened with no great difficulty, were rows of sacks of wheat which Guste had received from local farmers in exchange for a daily supply of bread. But the baker was careful not to take all this fine corn to the mill, preferring to sell some of it for seed, buying inferior produce in its place. That was nobody's business but his. And a profitable business it was.

The boys filled their mouths with wheat. The mastication of it was certainly laborious, even for young teeth, but in the end a paste was produced that was quite pleasant in taste.

'Like chewing gum,' remarked Georget, 'except that you couldn't pull it out in strings.'

'I tell you what,' said the ever-ingenious Tatave. 'We could chew some up, then add a bit of sugar and a few drops of crème de menthe. Then we'd roll it and dry it and cut it up into squares. It'd be scrumptious.'

He made a note of it then and there.

In the rooms set aside for the town archives which had already yielded a flag they found piles and piles of back numbers of the *Journal officiel*, reaching right up to the ceiling. They were done up in six-monthly bundles tied with red string.

'They might come in useful for lighting fires,' said Pierrot.

'We mustn't waste the string,' added Cisco.

'What ... what do you w ... want the string for?'

'Just an idea.'

There were also stacks of public notices that hadn't been used. One relating to a country-wide campaign against rats had been unceremoniously nibbled at the edges by the very creatures it referred to. Sacks of sulphur and copper sulphate and two cloud-guns awaited the spraying season and that of the hailstorms. A hand-pump. Hundreds of feet of hose-pipe. A variety of traps and snares. Fascinated, the boys pounced on each object in turn. But it was Tatave who, opening a cupboard, came upon the firemen's helmets, the swagger ones that were used on state occasions such as Bastille Day and Armistice Day, or at the funerals of local notabilities.

These noble headpieces of gleaming brass stood in a row on an upper shelf, each with the owner's name beneath it.

Cisco was the first to cram one on. His frizzy hair acted as a pad, as did Tatave's Balaclava helmet. Pierrot stuffed his with straw, while Riquet used a copy of the *Journal Officiel*. Georget, who had an enormous head, was the only one who needed no padding.

Magnanimously they decided that Victorin must have one too.

'He'll look splendid in it,' said Tatave, whose own face looked more wizened than ever under his.

That wasn't noticed, however, and they all admired each other unstintingly.

'Look at that axe.'

An enormous axe that would have been a credit to any executioner.

Riquet appropriated it at once. Pierrot armed himself with a small coil of rope, and the exploration went on. Tatave brought up the rear, looking carefully round to make sure nothing had been overlooked and entering every item in his note-book.

Whoever had designed the interior of the Bastide had apparently been animated by a hatred of straight lines. Apart from the huge guardroom and one other, which were rectangular, the interior was a maze of narrow corridors with steps up and down at unexpected places, of winding staircases and blind alleys. Sudden buttresses projected awkwardly. Indeed, the place might, by the look of it, have been intended for a glorious game of hide and seek.

The boys had been in the building before and played there.

Somewhat apprehensively, it should be added. In fact, frightening each other had been the principal source of amusement.

'Look out! The bogie-man's coming.'

And there would be a panic-stricken flight, all the more thrilling because the boys were *almost sure* there was no bogie-man at all.

But now the cavaliers had taken possession of the castle and were at home there. Talk of bogie-men would have been in bad taste. Though Georget did say at one moment:

'The place smells of ghosts.'

Meant in jest, of course. But the jester was not quite so light-hearted as he wished to appear.

'Go on! That's the stink of b ... bats' dung.'

In a corner, dimly lit by a narrow loophole, clusters of bats hung motionless, head downward, from the vaulted ceiling.

'I wonder if I could tame one,' muttered Pierrot.

He liked the idea. A tame bat would be rather like Mascha with wings.

The end of the room they were in was blocked by a partition of roughly nailed planks. Riquet struck one of them with the back of his axe. The blow echoed from corridor to corridor, and in a moment the air was full of soft, noiseless fluttering.

He struck again, and one of the planks gave. Pierrot held up his lamp, and through the gap they could see a lot of mouldy straw and on it a row of demijohns containing neat spirit – 500 litres of it, 500 litres on which M. Guillaume Muche was intending to pay no duty.

One was uncorked and sniffed at. A finger was put in, then licked.

'Whew!' exclaimed Cisco. 'That's a find.'

'We're not going to touch that stuff,' said the chief firmly.

'Oh, come!'

'No. It's deadly poison.'

Involuntarily, Pierrot had slipped into the phraseology of M. Grillon.

The plank was replaced. The knights moved on.

They went along a passage that gradually got narrower, then down two flights of steps into the basement. It was difficult to see where they were going, and they advanced cautiously, step by step, feeling their way along the walls. Only Pierrot seemed quite sure of himself.

'Shut up,' he ordered as they turned a corner. 'We're almost there ... Be quiet. We don't want to frighten him.'

Indeed, every sound echoed queerly.

They came to a hole in the floor, as if one of the flagstones had been taken up. Pierrot knelt down.

The others were impressed. They knelt down too, leaning over the hole till their helmets touched. Pierrot held up his lamp.

Coiled up in a corner of the dungeon, the prisoner was fast asleep.

A whole day and night in an oubliette is nothing to laugh at. Not even at the age of seventy-two, when one has become accustomed to vegetate for hours without a thought passing through one's head. But that was generally in the sun or in front of a fire. Anyhow, not in the damp and darkness of a dungeon.

How often had not Fébo himself evoked the terrors of the place, depicting in his own peculiar jargon the lot of the unfortunates who had been buried alive there at the whim of some feudal lord, to the visitors he took round, the thirty-franc ones who were treated to all the gruesome details.

'*Qué gran miséria, Messieurs! ... Qué terriblé destino! ...*'

His gestures were expressive. He trembled with terror as he acted the part, playing to the gallery. But never for one moment had he imagined that he was himself destined to experience the *gran miséria* in its stark reality.

He had started by squatting down patiently and waiting.

It was Pierrot who had snatched away the ladder, after having enticed him there to sing him the prisoner's song. The boy had asked so nicely, and it was difficult to refuse him anything. Fébo had sung:

> *Ay de mi alma!*
> *Ay de mi cuerpo!*
> *Ay de mi novia!*
> *Ay de mi pueblo!*

And when he'd turned back to the ladder it was gone. Of course it was only a practical joke of Pierrot's – the little scamp. Though there had been a note of gravity in the boy's voice when he said before leaving:

'I'm sorry, Fébo. I can't help myself, d'you see? ... The thing is ... But it'd take too long to explain. Don't worry. I'll be back.'

All right. He'd be patient. And he was for a bit. Then he began to get anxious, and little by little the anxiety turned to panic and despair in that black, mouldy hole. In the company of skeletons and rats – that's what he used to say so dramatically to the sight-seers. As a matter of fact there were no skeletons and no rats. But woodlice, any amount of them. He couldn't put his hand anywhere without feeling them. Sometimes he flicked on his lighter, and they'd beat a momentary retreat. If only he'd had a cigarette to light with it! That would have been some comfort. But no such luck.

It was useless to shout. He knew all about that. After all, he was an authority on the subject. It was a strange acoustic effect which he used to demonstrate to his listeners. The dungeon swallowed up the voice, which only reached the floor above as a faint distant cry.

The darkness made the time pass slowly, terribly slowly. And the more Fébo thought it over the more desperate did his plight appear. Vaguely he guessed the reason for his imprisonment – so that the boys could make for the Spanish frontier without fear of his giving their plans away.

Of course they'd be overtaken and brought back. But how long might that take? Meanwhile ...

With luck their escapade might last a week, possibly longer. If that was the case, his successor as official guide – *ay de mi!* – would be able to affirm without exaggeration that human bones lay in the oubliettes of the Bastide.

All the same, he tried calling for help. Not that he had any real hope, but the sound of his own voice kept him company.

At the end of two hours spent in the gloomiest of forebodings, his stomach, accustomed to being nourished with scraps and tit-bits at every hour of the day, was so famished that he was firmly convinced he had been imprisoned for as many days.

With that he wept into his beard, and then fell asleep.

'Poor old chap!' thought Pierrot.

He reproached himself for not having come at once to deliver him. But he'd had so much to do, so much to think about. Besides, he'd felt bad enough himself about Fébo, and he didn't know quite how the others would take it. To imprison a grown-up took a bit of doing, still more an old man of seventy-two. For the moment, he had thought it more prudent to bear the responsibility alone.

'W ... what are we g ... going to do with him?'

'Prisoners are tried,' answered Tatave coldly. 'And if they're found guilty …'

He didn't quite like to finish the sentence, but he squinted at the blade of the axe.

'But first of all we've got to get him up,' said Georget.

He had already got hold of the ladder, which lay on its side against the wall, when Pierrot stopped him.

'Wait till I tell you to. As I said, we need Victorin first. Fébo's still pretty strong, in spite of his age. Last week, when we killed a pig, I saw him pick it up all by himself and carry it off on his shoulders. He could easily deal with any of us.'

'We might tie him up while he's still asleep. Pierrot's got a rope …'

That was Tatave again. He was always for extreme measures. The Chevalier de Guartorella gave him a contemptuous look.

'Tie him up? You? With those little arms of yours?'

That roused Tatave's anger and the sparks would soon have been flying if Pierrot hadn't intervened.

'That'll do. There's no point in quarrelling. Besides, you might wake him up. I said we'll wait for Victorin. Stand back now. We'll come again later.'

He had spoken too loudly. Though he could not see them, the captive realized someone was about.

'*Socorro! por Dios!*' he wailed.

The knights had never heard the lost voice of the oubliette. It seemed to come right out of the earth and to reach them from across the centuries. They fled helter-skelter. All except Pierrot, who stood his ground. After all, he had already heard the old man sing his *Ay de mi alma.*

Kneeling down again, he held the lamp up to his face, so that Fébo could see who it was.

'It's me, Fébo. There's no need to howl like that. We haven't forgotten you. Here! Catch this. You'll find a bit of *fouace* there and two bars of chocolate … I'm sorry about this, but I had no choice. After all, it's your own fault …'

Fébo was standing up now and holding up his arms beseechingly.

'*Por Dios!*' he pleaded again.

He was half comic, half pitiable. Pierrot didn't know whether to laugh or cry.

'Don't worry. We shan't let anything happen to you ... And another thing – you know all that stuff you've told me about ghosts and doors that opened and shut by themselves. You don't need to be frightened, because it's all rot. If there are any ghosts about, it's us.'

'*Favor*,' begged the old man.

Only just woken up, he was slow to understand. He gazed up, but there was nothing but darkness through the hole now. Pierrot had gone.

Fébo tried to strike a light, but there was no fuel left in his lighter. He groped about for the packet the boy had thrown him. Ah! There it was! His fingers trembled as they opened it. Then he quickly filled his mouth with the stale cake and started munching.

There! That was better! Even in the dark life was still worth living. And it wasn't bad at all, that *fouace*. It wasn't bad at all.

'Where are you?' cried Victorin. 'Hallo there! ... Hallo!'

For ten minutes he had been dashing to and fro along the corridors of the Bastide in search of his companions.

'Hallo! ... Hallo! ...'

No answer.

'A dirty trick they're playing on me if they've made off,' he grumbled to himself. 'Leaving me all alone to face the music. And I was the one who never wanted to get into this racket at all. Just my luck!'

He turned down another passage.

'Hallo! ... Hallo! ...'

Suddenly he came upon the brass helmets as the gang emerged from one of the cellars.

'Quick,' he shouted, waving his arms excitedly. 'Hurry. You're wanted.'

'What is it?'

'It's M. le Curé trying to talk to us through a megaphone.'

They all scrambled up the spiral staircase as fast as they could, jostling each other. They always tended to get out of hand when Pierrot wasn't there to remind them of their dignity.

The upper platform was bathed in blinding light, for once again in that exceptional autumn the sun had come out in all its splendour. The firemen's helmets shone; the boys blinked.

'There!' said Victorin, pointing. 'Look ...'

The church tower was no more than sixty yards away, and the priest was clearly visible in the bull's-eye window over the clock. One hand was held up to shield his eyes. In the other he held an aluminium megaphone, which also glittered in the sun.

It magnified his voice, but also transformed it into a blurred bellow, like a loudspeaker that's not properly adjusted.

'What's going on?' asked Pierrot, joining them.

'Hush. The curé's saying something. Preaching, perhaps.'

Pierrot leant over the battlements.

'Give me the telescope.'

He had a little trouble getting it into focus. Then, as though by magic, every detail stood out clearly.

'I can see your father, Victorin. He's hiding behind the Abbé Escoutou. He doesn't look any too pleased.'

A shiver went down Victorin's spine.

'Yes. And there's Tatave's mother. And others too.'

'I'd like to see her face,' muttered the chronicler.

Pierrot recognized the megaphone at once. It belonged to the inn, and was used to make announcements at fêtes and dances.

Again the voice floated over, comically distorted.

'Sounds like a cow that's lost her calf.'

'Shut up, Georget. You're always trying to be funny. Can't you be serious for a moment?'

And again that frown appeared on his forehead which made him look as though he had been born to wield authority.

'Don't answer, anybody ... I'm the only one who can parley with the enemy.'

'If they want an armistice, they ought to hoist the white flag,' said Tatave.

Cisco was the first to distinguish a few words.

'It's about the Mass. He's talking to us about the Mass ... He must have a swelled head, to think we're interested in that.'

Cisco never went to church.

'It's t ... true ... I'd for ... gotten it was Sunday.'

'Oh, one Mass the less won't kill you.'

It was Georget who said that – in all simplicity. He had been brought up on strictly secular lines, and professed a complete indifference to all religious matters, though it should be added that M.

Grillon had imbued him with a deep respect for all Christian principles.

It was different with the others. The priest's appeal weighed heavily on the consciences of Pierrot, Tatave, and Riquet. Nor was Victorin indifferent. In the church was a prie-Dieu marked with his name, standing beside his mother's in the very front row.

And the megaphoned exhortation came floating through the air, most of it unintelligible, but none the less persuasive.

'And there are the other days too,' thought Pierrot. 'All Saints' Day, in particular. He'll blame us for that too. Rotten luck! We ought to have thought of it. But there you are! One can't think of everything.'

'Can you still see my father?' asked Victorin.

He blew his nose with feeling.

'Put that handkerchief away,' snapped Tatave. 'If they see that, they'll think we're surrendering.'

'What are we g ... going to d ... do? ... I don't want to miss g ... going to church.'

Pierrot thought hard. Neither did he want to miss it. He had to find some way out. There was no time to be lost. His position as leader depended on his decision and resourcefulness.

Suddenly he had an idea.

'Look here ... We'll send them a message.'

'A message?'

'Yes. You'll write it out, Tatave. Take down what I say.'

The note-book was already open.

'Shall I write it in red or blue?'

'Whichever you like.'

Tatave chose green.

'All right. Fire away ...'

'At the top put: Casteilcorbon. Sunday 30 October. Message No. 1 ...

'Then start:

'Dear M. le Curé,

You have always been very kind to us and we should hate to let you down. We would like to come to church, but we can't this morning, as we are standing up for Rights and Justice. Please tell the others that we are not thieves, so the punishment was unjust.'

'Steady on,' said Tatave. 'You're going too fast.'

He had his tongue between his teeth in his effort to keep up.

162

'How are you g … going to p … post it?'

Pierrot had already thought of that.

'Go down and bring up one of those newspapers. We'll make a dart.'

'… unjust …' repeated Tatave, inviting Pierrot to continue.

'I think we can arrange it, all the same, M. le Curé. In the catechism class you told us that for going to Mass it was sufficient …'

'How many f's in sufficient?'

'Three,' said Georget, once more incurring his chief's displeasure.

'Don't be silly. Two …

'It was sufficient to see somebody who could himself see what was going on. That gives us a solution.'

The fountain-pen hesitated again. How many l's in solution? Tatave didn't like to ask this time again, so he boldly decided on two.

'If you have the doors open, the men who always stay outside will see what is going on. And as we shall see them we shall be all right. The same on All Saints' Day.'

The others gaped, silently admiring their chief's theological subtlety.

'Is that all right?' he asked.

'I should think it is! Wonderful!'

'You'll have to finish up with something, or it won't be polite,' said Tatave.

There was some argument over the respective merits of various formal endings, from *sincères salutations* to *respectueux hommages*.

While it went on, Victorin tried in vain to adjust the telescope to his own sight. Though dreading it, he was longing to have a look at his father.

'For him to have climbed all the way up there, it looks as though …'

Sometimes he imagined him in a paroxysm of fury. At other times – though more doubtfully – he nursed the idea that he had been overtaken by a sudden access of tenderness. It never occurred to him that his father was, after all, the mayor of the town, and in that capacity was approaching a state of frenzy.

'Come on,' said Pierrot at last. 'We'll never get anywhere at this rate. Put simply, "affectionately".'

'Who's going to sign it?'

'We'll all sign, of course.'

'Not me,' objected Cisco. 'I've got no use for the old boy. Nothing affectionate about me. Not where he's concerned.'

'Same here,' put in Georget. 'Not that I've anything against him. It's just that I've nothing to do with this church business.'

Pierrot looked at them reproachfully.

'I think it's rotten of you. You ought to sign just for the sake of standing in with the rest of us. Still, I can't force you to. Have it your own way. And since you're not interested in the Mass you can make yourselves useful. Chevalier de Grillon, go down and look after the fire. And you, Chevalier de Guartorella, see if you can make a broom of twigs and sweep out the guardroom.'

They were taken aback by these blunt orders. They obeyed a little sheepishly, feeling that they hadn't put up a very good show in defending liberty of opinion. Rather sadly, Pierre Daranluz watched them go. This was the first time there had been a division in the ranks. Just when solidarity was most needed – in the face of the enemy. Oh, this question of religion – what a nuisance it was! Still, there it was: you couldn't get away from it.

'Very well,' he said at last, 'we shan't sign it, any of us. Just put: "The Knights".'

Tatave was disappointed. He had been looking forward to listing all their styles and titles. It would have been an opportunity to use several different colours, which would certainly have impressed those people down below.

It was a pity he couldn't engross their message on parchment in Gothic characters, with a seal and a red ribbon …

To make up for that, he finished with a flourish:

Abracadabra. Blood and Freedom.

As an afterthought he added:

By Air Mail.

Meanwhile Riquet, the expert in aeronautics, was constructing, on a principle known to them all, a huge paper dart.

He chuckled with glee.

'We've n … never thrown one from so high as this. P … perhaps it'll go right out of the t … town.'

He gave it its final touches, then tucked the letter into the folds.

'Here she goes!'

The dart left the battlements, hesitated a second, trembling as though astonished to find itself so high above the ground, then glided down towards the town.

'Good shot!' exclaimed Victorin.

All eyes were fixed on it. The message it was bearing was now forgotten, everyone intent on guessing where it would come to rest.

It swerved, and circled back towards the Bastide.

'Blast!'

Striking the wall, it began to fall like a dead leaf. Miraculously righting itself, however, it again soared gracefully away.

'That's better.'

There was quite a crowd now in the Rue de l'Église and the Allée des Trois Tourelles. All heads were in the air. Children shouted. At the last minute there was a rush of small boys towards the Impasse des Suisses, as it now looked as though it was there that the missile would alight.

François Tistounet, the *garde champêtre*, lumbered after them. He had just received a megaphoned order from the mayor to secure the incriminating document at all costs.

Entering into the spirit of the occasion, Grisouille trotted in his wake.

FOUR

THE aerial missile lay now in the Town Hall, on the green table-cloth round which the councillors were wont to deliberate. Having delivered up its message, it lay pathetically with its wings crumpled, to receive another angry hammer-blow from the fist of Guillaume Muche every time he wanted to drive home a point.

'Those damn-fool brats of ours have taken leave of their senses. Listen to that: Blood and Freedom! Abracadabra! Unless they're just pulling our legs ... What do you think?'

The councillors nodded, prudently saying nothing. It was always like that in the Council. The chief thing was not to offer yourself as a target for one of the mayor's explosions.

Benoît Daranluz was there; so was Guste the baker and old Jou, one of the richest landowners of the district. Besides them there were M. Belaigue, manager of the grey marble quarry at Estagel, Tarasse, Captain of the Fire Brigade, and a few others, all of whom had been hastily rounded up after Mass by the *garde champêtre*, who had been ordered to summon them to an extraordinary meeting.

Far from pacifying the mayor, this tacit approval merely added fuel to the flames.

'Can't you say anything, instead of just sitting there on your back-sides like a lot of damn-fool nitwits? Have I got to do it all myself? Is there nobody in this damn-fool town who's ready to lend a hand? Serve you right if I resigned.'

His face was as red as a tomato, contrasting with that of the plaster bust of *La République* which stood immediately over his head.

What would she have said, this Marianne, had she been able to speak? Probably, like Mme Muche:

'My dear Guillaume, think of your heart.'

'You can't be judge and prosecutor at the same time. And there are two of us here, Benoît Daranluz and me, who – to our shame, let me add – have children of our own among those ... those damn-fool boys ... I'd like to use a much stronger word, but we'll leave it at that – those damn-fool boys who've given us nothing but trouble since yesterday evening. So for once it's not for me to make a decision. It's up to you: to the Council as a whole.'

Having said that, Muche relapsed into silence. One after the other, he scrutinized the faces around him, though perhaps less in the hope of getting them to speak than of discerning signs of flattering approval. But this time the notabilities of Casteilcorbon were more cautious than ever, betraying neither by word nor look what was going on in their minds ...

He decided to tackle them one by one.

'What about you, Jou? You've been here longer than any of us. What would you do in my place?'

Old Jou had no teeth left, and when he swallowed, his mouth went right in.

No response. A damn-fool of an oyster. Muche turned to Guste.

'Looks to me as though we're up a gum tree, M. le Maire. Of course those kids – they're just silly.'

Another bang of the mayor's fist.

'Silly! They got the better of you all right, didn't they? If you hadn't let them get away with your *fouaces*, like a damn fool, we shouldn't be where we are now.'

Guste hung his head, looking down his long nose at the table-cloth. He had burnt his fingers. But, then, he should have known better. What was the point of getting drawn into discussion with a volcano? Not knowing what to do next, the mayor picked up the knights' message again and read it through, holding it at arm's length, as he'd forgotten his glasses.

' "Standing up for Right and Justice," ' he muttered. 'Damned cheek! And do you know what M. le Curé said when he learnt of this ineffable piece of impertinence?'

They all knew, of course, but it was wiser to affect a polite curiosity.

'Instead of helping me to enforce law and order,' the mayor went on, 'instead of putting the screw on those little guttersnipes who have been demoralized by communist propaganda, instead of trying to make them haul down that filthy red flag which disgraces our town just on the very day when people are flocking here from all over the country – instead of that, what do you think he said? "Splendid! ... Splendid!" And rubbing his hands and beaming on everybody, he had the church door opened before he started saying Mass. He carried out their orders! That's what our wretched country's come to! That's how the Church supports lawful authority!'

Taking his courage in both hands, M. Belaigue came out of his shell.

'All the same, we mustn't exaggerate. The whole thing's only a lark, though a very regrettable one, I must admit. And I can't see that ...'

'Ah! You can't see, M. Belaigue, you can't see! And, do you know, I'm only half surprised at your lack of perspicacity. For the last half-hour I've been sweating my guts out trying to explain to you all that these damn-fool boys are making us look even bigger fools than they are, and you call that *only a lark*. Have you no blood in your veins, M. Belaigue? You're thinking: *M. Muche will soon settle things, as he always does.* You're in a hurry to sneak off to have an aperitif with certain other nitwits who are sitting not very far away, leaving everything on my shoulders. And you'll go off saying: "Splendid! ... Splendid! ..." like that damn-fool priest.'

Unfortunately, Mme Muche wasn't there to enjoin him to be calm. His whole face had gone a nasty lurid purple – something between the colour of raspberries and bilberries.

Meek as he normally was, the manager of the marble-quarry wasn't going to lie down under insulting language of that sort, and a fine row ensued.

'Really, gentlemen ... Really ...' pleaded M. Daranluz, getting up to shut the window so that their squabbles could at least be fought out in private.

When twelve o'clock struck they were no nearer a decision than ever.

'We'll have to break into the place, that's all.'

'Yes, but how?'

'All the same we've got to teach them a lesson.'

'We might try with ladders.'

'If we once got inside,' said Guste, 'we'd soon make the brats put down the drawbridge.'

And so they went on, round and round in circles without advancing an inch.

Hasty and hot-tempered though he was, Guillaume Muche didn't lack common sense, or he would never have succeeded either in business or in local politics.

'You make me laugh!' he said, though he had never been farther from laughing in his life. 'You make me laugh! Do you know anyone in this town capable of scaling a hundred-foot wall? Do you know anyone who's got a hundred-foot ladder?'

'They might use climbing-irons.'

'Climbing-irons yourself!'

'And there's mountain climbers. They can get up anything.'

'But what about the Fire Brigade? Haven't they got ladders?'

Everyone turned to M. Tarasse, the Captain, who had one of those credulous faces that seemed to invite you to play him a practical joke.

'The ladders?' he answered. 'But you know they're all in the Bastide with the pump and all the rest of our gear.'

At that old Jou burst out laughing. For him the Fire Brigade with its pump and its brass helmets was nothing but a standing joke.

He was very old indeed, and even the mayor forbore to reprove him for his ill-timed mirth. He was able to make up for this restraint a moment later when Tarasse suggested calling in the Perpignan Brigade, who were real professionals and had a proper fire-escape.

'Are you out of your mind, Tarasse? Don't you think we look silly enough as it is? Do you want to make us the laughing-stock of the whole department, if not the whole of France? And *who* will everyone be laughing at, do you suppose? Not you. Me. Just because I've been idiot enough to interest myself in the welfare of this town ... So, if you've nothing better to suggest, Tarasse, you may as well keep your mouth shut.'

'But we're all agreed that something's got to be done,' said M. Daranluz cautiously, 'so it's simply a question of seeing what *can* be done.'

'Unless we leave them to it and simply starve them out,' answered M. Belaigue.

Guste was thinking of his stock of corn, but he didn't like to allude to it. As a matter of fact the mayor's mind was on a similar track. What would happen if the little wretches got hold of the demijohns of alcohol?

'The real question is this: is it or is it not possible to break down that door?'

'Nothing easier, if you want to,' said the manager of the quarry. 'My people could do it easily. A couple of sticks of dynamite suitably placed ...'

Benoît Daranluz couldn't let that pass.

'What if one of the boys is behind the door when you blow it up?'

Nor could the mayor.

'You're a nitwit, M. Belaigue. You jump from one extreme to the

169

other. First you want to do nothing and let them starve, then you want to blow the place up.'

That idea tickled old Jou, who started laughing again, but his mirth was cut short this time by an attack of asthma.

It looked as though the meeting would last all day.

Then Benoît Daranluz made a suggestion which everyone thought reasonable. Muche threw open the window and shouted for the *garde champêtre*.

'Tistounet, go and fetch the mason. Bring him here at the double.'

Since it was a holiday there was more reason than ever for M. Guartorella to be drunk. All the same, he wasn't too far gone, and after a lot of persuasion he consented to come. Before knocking at the door, François whisked off the Spaniard's cap and put it into his hands.

'Come in!'

Tistounet pushed Cisco's father into the room, and took the opportunity of slipping in too.

'Guartorella,' began the mayor, 'you've a boy of your own in the Bastide, and it's your duty to help us deal with this situation. Do you understand?'

'*Sí, Mossié lé Maire ...*'

'You don't look as if you did ... Now, listen to me. How long would it take you to put up a scaffolding on the east side of the Bastide?'

'Scaffolding? Right up the top?'

'Yes. Right to the top. So we can get in and knock the little bastards' heads together. And don't give me a roundabout answer, as you generally do when you're asked for an estimate. We want to know how long it'd really take.'

'*Una andamiada!*' exclaimed the bewildered man. '*Qué trabajo!*'

'Naturally we'd supply all the labour you wanted. And the saw-mill will furnish the planks ... It's got to be done quickly.'

'There's no need to go right up to the top,' protested M. Belaigue. 'Up to the first loop-holes is quite far enough. My men could easily cut away a bit of masonry and enlarge the hole sufficiently to ...'

'No good, my dear sir. No good at all. You'd be damaging a building classed as a *monument historique*, and we'd never hear the last of it. Don't you know we're not allowed to do even the most trifling repairs without first asking permission? ... You seem determined to have a crack at that Bastide. First you want to blast your way in, and now ...'

The row flared up again. Guartorella stood looking on, wondering who'd had most to drink, he or the municipal councillors.

Suddenly the mayor came back to the matter under discussion.

'Well? How long would it take?'

'I don't really know. It's difficult to say. What with the holidays and all ... Perhaps six weeks ...'

The mayor gasped, completely taken aback. Then suddenly he roared:

'Six weeks! Is that what you're telling me? Six weeks! Do you think we can wait six weeks while you ... Get out of here! And do it quickly before I ...'

But the mason had already vanished.

François Tistounet thought it best to disappear with him, and it was impossible to say which of the two was more relieved to find himself once again in the street.

And when they sat together at their large glasses of Pernod, the *garde champêtre* delivered himself of a piece of homely philosophy.

'The way people change their minds! They turn quicker than the earth goes round. Such a fuss! And what for? Will they stay above ground one day the longer for their pains? Not a bit of it. It'll all be just the same in the end. First they dash this way, then that. And what I says is: if you stay where you are you'll be just as far forward in the long run.'

Cisco's father nodded without attempting to understand. As a poacher, he had little sympathy for representatives of the law, but he was quite ready to call any man his friend who stood him a drink.

'Take your case, for instance,' went on François. 'You think yourself pretty smart when you go setting your snares up there, Perdigane way. But d'you think I couldn't catch you any day I wanted? Of course I could. Easily. And you'd be fined I don't know what – several thousand francs.'

'*Hombre! Qué mala bestia!*'

'Take note of what I said. *I could.* But what good would it do? Can you answer me that? None. No good at all. Neither to me nor to the municipality. For, since you've no money, you couldn't pay. And you'd start all over again the next day, and I'd have to go chasing after you. And the only result would be we couldn't any longer sit down to a drink together, as we're doing now. So you see …'

Guartorella held his head on one side, pensively. This at least was up his street. Still, it was all rather subtle, and it's doubtful whether he really caught on.

'All the same,' began François again, feeling his way very cautiously, 'as far as this honey business is concerned, if it was you that robbed the hive, or one of your kids, you went a bit too far. The whole town's turned upside down. And it won't do you any good, either, if they make you build a scaffolding that'd make even an archangel go dizzy.'

They both turned to look at the Bastide, over which the red flag still fluttered gaily.

'I tell you it wasn't me who did it. Nor Cisco. Couldn't have been, for at that time we were …'

He stopped abruptly, suddenly aware of what he was saying. There are some alibis that can get you in a worse mess than the one you want to get out of.

In the little town, the mothers hurried hither and thither, stirring up in their passage a tremor of curiosity. The 'lark', as M. Belaigue called it, seemed to have abolished for the time being all social distinctions. People greeted each other and eagerly exchanged gossip who normally would have passed merely with a nod.

Unlike the men who were still in conclave in the Town Hall, discussing the most effective means of forcing an entry into the Bastide, the women plumped for more peaceful methods, vying with each other in indulgence.

They all found excuses for their erring offspring.

'It's all the fault of that schoolmaster.'

'What business had he to threaten to keep them in? They're laid down by law, the holidays, and he'd no right to stop them.'

'Drove them too far, he did. What's more, he knows it. Doesn't dare show his face in the street.'

'He's too proud – that's what the trouble is.'

'I always said he was as stupid as he was tall.'

'He's about as suited for his job as I'd be to say Mass.'

'If you ask me, his poor wife's no cause to complain being where she is. She's much happier there than ever he could make her. It was an act of mercy, it was, taking her.'

'It's his being so stiff-necked – that's what I put it down to. Why, if he made so much as a move ...'

'Perhaps he didn't think of it,' said Mme Daranluz, struck by the idea. 'He's a good man, I can vouch, only he's got his head in the clouds.'

'There you go, Mme Fine. You always stand up for everybody.'

'It's not that. I'm trying to understand. What I find hard to bear is that my Pierrot shouldn't have said a word to me about it.'

Indignant as ever, Mme Grosbelhomme refrained from defending M. Grillon.

'A good man or no, it isn't talking about him that's going to bring me back my Tatave. To think of him spending the whole night in that place. I'd like to get hold of the one who led them into this.'

She was really suffering agonies of apprehension, and Mme Muche tried to comfort her.

'You mustn't lose heart, Mme Grosbelhomme. We've seen smoke, so we know they've managed to light a fire. I heard my husband say there was any amount of wood there. He's trying to work out a plan with the other councillors. He's sure to find a way.'

'He'll find nothing at all, your husband. All he's good for is shouting other people down. You heard what he said when he saw the letter Tatave wrote out. Snatched the megaphone from M. le Curé and started swearing at them for all he was worth. Is that the way to make those boys see reason?'

In her heart of hearts Mme Muche thought just the same, but she deemed it her duty to affect an air of wounded dignity. Once again she reproached herself for having been too friendly with people whose natural vulgarity always came out sooner or later.

'For my part,' asserted Mme Daranluz, 'I'm sure everything would come right if M. Grillon spoke to them in person, telling them the theft of his honey was forgiven and forgotten and would never be mentioned again. They like him really, I know they do, and I'm certain they'd listen to him.'

The suggestion was hailed as excellent. Why had no one thought of it before? The five mothers hurried off towards the school.

At the end of his chain, Ranavalo barked furiously, trying hard to pass for a redoubtable watch-dog.

Déodat appeared in the doorway in his straw hat and mauve braces. At the sight of the deputation coming ceremoniously across the playground, he hastily disappeared to put on his jacket.

In spite of appearances, he was profoundly affected by Georget's running away and joining in the revolt. Abandoned by his son, insulted by the mayor, and made painfully conscious of the town's displeasure, he had spent the night tossing and turning in his bed, going over one by one every incident of that eventful day and examining his conscience to make sure he had done his duty. More than anything, he brooded over the words and attitude of Mme Fabienne. He hadn't slept at all. And in the morning, when he had sought to regain his serenity by visiting his cherished bees, he had been overtaken by a feeling of disgust for all humanity.

Now he was in for another ordeal.

He glanced at himself in the mirror, threw out his chest, and walked out to meet his visitors, composing his features into the benevolent expression he put on for inspections and prize-givings.

It didn't help matters. On the contrary; his artificial cordiality froze the mothers and made them more ceremonious than ever. When he invited them in, no one wanted to enter first, and there was a lot of deferential fuss as each made way for the other.

A little later he was addressing the deputation with the inward determination that he was not going to allow himself to be put upon.

'Our children,' he was saying – 'and observe that I say "our" children; for I am speaking to you not only as their teacher but as a parent like yourselves – our children, having violated my premises and desspoiled one of my hives – as is proved incontestably by the facts I have put before you – have now set themselves up in open rebellion, an act which only aggravates the case against them.'

The schoolmaster wished to make his point of view very clear indeed, which induced him to use so many words that he merely clouded it. It didn't seem to occur to him that the women he had before him, who were listening open-mouthed, were quite incapable of threading their way through his long though no doubt faultlessly constructed sentences.

'Placed under the painful obligation of taking punitive measures, I thought the matter over very carefully, taking in fact two days and nights to arrive at my conclusion, which was that a collective fault could only be dealt with by a collective punishment. Before taking any action, however, I was resolved to exhaust every possibility of an appeal to their better nature. And it was only after repeated and most indulgently worded appeals had failed, that finally ...'

Mme Muche kept nodding, to prove to herself that she was following his reasoning. The other mothers followed her example.

'I would like to point out to you that the punishment I finally imposed deprived me of my holiday no less than the delinquents. And I would like to ask which among you is ready to accuse me of having acted without due consideration or of having exceeded my rights?'

Following the best principles of oratory, he paused for a reply.

Naturally, no one spoke.

Then, raising his voice a tone and a half, he went on:

'And now, ladies, having examined my conduct and admitted its reasonableness, you want me to don a shirt of penitence, to stand up before all the world and tell my own pupils that I have acted wrongly, to declaim through a megaphone an apology which would not only be wholly insincere and unjustifiable, but which would give our children a poor idea of authority. In other words, you want me – both as father and as schoolmaster – to grovel in public at the risk of undermining for ever not only my own position but the honour of the profession to which I belong.'

Another silence. It was impossible to argue about it.

All the same ...

'But, M. Grillon, we're not asking you to eat humble pie *really*. Only to pretend.'

'We've got to get them out of there somehow,' said Mme Muche. 'That's all that matters. Afterwards you can punish them to your heart's content.'

'And I can assure you it's not my Tatave who'll give you any more trouble. I'll see to that. From now on he won't be going out alone, to be at the mercy of bad influences.'

The somewhat insulting nature of this remark passed unnoticed, since each mother was thinking of her own boy in exactly the same terms.

Déodat took his head in his hands.

'Mesdames, Mesdames,' he groaned, 'what is it that you are suggesting now? Not only are you prepared to undermine my authority

175

as a schoolmaster, but you even go so far as to incite me to break my word. Just think what you're saying. Supposing I was weak enough – and, let me add, stupid enough – to take back all I've said, what could anyone think of the deplorable example I should set by cynically punishing the boys after the conclusion of a truce? No, ladies, what you are proposing is nothing less than moral fraud.'

He was rather pleased with himself. Fixing his eyes tenderly on the pleasant features of Mme Grosbelhomme, he said to himself:

'She cannot fail to understand me now.'

But she merely sighed, discouraged.

'That won't bring my boy back, will it?'

And for the first time she wondered how she could ever have thought seriously of linking her life with that of this pompous ass.

Old Mother Broc was eating junket in the kitchen behind her shop when she heard a great flutter and flurry over by the moat. Putting down her bowl, she rushed out, spoon in hand.

An extraordinary agitation seemed to have taken hold of the geese at the foot of the castle. One of them in particular was going round and round with its beak in the air, beating the water with its wings and screaming for all it was worth, while the others looked on, providing a chorus of indignation.

Suddenly it left the surface of the water and, as though attracted by some invisible magnet, flapped its way upwards.

'Good heavens!' exclaimed Mme Broc, 'here are my geese flying off like swallows.'

She suffered from cataract and couldn't see very far. Before long all she could make out of her goose was a fluttering white mass hugging he wall of the Bastide, still proceeding on its upward course until finally it disappeared over the battlements.

'Help!' she cried, waving her spoon. 'Help! Help!'

FIVE

THE goose-feathers were not to be wasted. They were used to convert the cavaliers' head-gear into plumed helmets. If this adornment in fact added nothing to their martial aspect, the failure was not apparent to imagination run riot, and the boys were firmly convinced they looked more imposing than ever.

Pierrot himself looked complacently at the fantastic and barbaric shadow of his head, enormously enlarged, which the firelight threw on the castle wall.

Victorin was ordered to light the candles and bring in the prisoner.

The court-martial was about to start.

'How do you do a trial?' someone had asked.

'Nothing simpler,' was Pierrot's answer. 'First of all you need a judge, and that'll have to be me, as I'm in command. Then there must be a chap to write down the sentence.'

'Clerk of the court,' explained Tatave.

'Exactly. And it'll be you.'

The chronicler promptly got out his note-book and a suitably wide choice of fountain-pens.

'Then there's the prosecutor, and that's got to be me too, as I'm the only one to know what he's done wrong. Then prisoner's friend. Perhaps I'd better do that as well, seeing as how we are old friends, Fébo and me.'

'Then what do the rest of us do?'

'You'll be the jury.'

At the fire, the goose was roasting on a spit. It was a complicated affair, that spit, and it was its discovery that had inspired the resourceful Cisco to go goose-fishing on the moat. With a beautiful spit like that at their disposal, it seemed a shame not to use it.

It was smelling good already as the skin of the ill-plucked creature began to sizzle. Now and again the long-disused mechanism – overhauled by Riquet, of course – gave a kick. The fat that oozed out dropped into a rusty tray. In their haste, the young cooks had forgotten to draw the bird, but what difference would that make?

'Pity we've got no salt,' sighed the Chevalier Guartorella, who had been initiated by his father into the art of camp-fire cookery by the time he was ten.

It was thus a smell of cooking that first greeted Fébo when he was led into court at the end of a string. The string was really there only for form's sake – just to show he was a prisoner.

At once the boys were grave. It was no light responsibility to sit in judgement on an old man, particularly when you didn't know what he'd done.

On the improvised table lay the axe, its blade glittering in the fire-light. It was impressive, to Pierrot at all events, so much so that for a moment he lost his nerve.

He leant over towards the clerk of the court.

'What do we begin with?' he muttered to gain time.

'First of all you must ask him his name and age.'

'But we know that already.'

'That makes no difference. You have to ask. Otherwise I can't write down what he answers.'

'D'you think he could sit down?'

'I don't know. That's up to you. Only he'll have to stand up to take the oath.'

'Right, Victorin, pull the pump over here so that he can sit on it. Then cast off his chains.'

'Don't cut it,' begged Cisco. 'We haven't got any string to waste.'

'M. Fébo, what is your name?'

The poor old man's brain was in a state of utter confusion. So much had happened to him since the previous morning. How could he tell whether he was on his head or his heels? He seemed to have been translated to a topsy-turvy world where children ruled: such serious children, so convinced of their importance that he felt quite intimidated by them. How could he know that his white beard produced precisely the same effect on them?

'Well? You're called Fébo, aren't you?'

'Yes.'

'How old are you?'

'Seventy-two.'

Tatave hesitated, then decided he must write down what the prisoner said, whether it was true or not.

Pierrot stood up, saying:

'Now I'm the prosecutor. And I want you all to listen without interrupting. Afterwards you'll say whether you agree or not.

'Knights, my first accusation is against myself. I put too much trust in M. Fébo, the man we now have before us. This is what happened – and you'll see that I was the first to go wrong.'

The jury listened open-mouthed to this unusual prosecution, and the clerk of the court forgot to take notes.

'It's like this: I was counting on Fébo to show us the way through the mountains. As an old friend of mine, I felt sure he'd want to help us in our struggle against injustice. As you know, everything was ready and our provisions were waiting for us in old Féroulet's hut. From there we were to make our dash for the frontier, and with Fébo knowing the country, everything would have been all right. And now, instead of being free and far away, we're stuck here, besieged by our enemies. It's not so good, is it? But it's my fault. For trusting a grown-up. I'll never do it again; I've learnt my lesson. For Fébo, here present, not only didn't want to come, but he couldn't keep his tongue still. He talked. To M. Grillon, of all people. So the cat was out of the bag.'

'*Ma qué! Nos es verdad,*' protested the old man, suddenly coming to life and showing signs of extreme agitation. 'I only wanted to warn him that his *punicion* ...'

'Silence!' growled the prosecutor.

Victorin approached the prisoner threateningly, but Pierrot ordered him back to his place.

'Let him be, Victorin. We don't want any rough stuff ... To go on with what I was saying – when I realized we'd been betrayed I said to myself, "If we don't go, we're rotters; and if we do, we shan't get many miles before our parents catch up with us and drag us back." Then I thought of locking up Fébo, so that he shouldn't spill the beans, in case he hadn't done so already. Only how could I be sure he hadn't?

'So, even with Fébo in the dungeon, it seemed better to change the plan altogether at the last minute. I got the Chevalier Henri du Martel to examine the drawbridge, and when he promised he could work it ...'

All eyes were turned to Riquet.

'D'you mean you were in on this all the time?' asked Cisco, with just a touch of jealousy.

'Of c … c … course I knew. Why not? Since I had to d … do the job.'

'Come on! We're not going to argue about that,' went on Pierrot. 'What I was saying was just to show you that M. Fébo, here present, is very guilty indeed. For even if he didn't give us away, it was because of him that we had to scrap our first plan.'

'Why because of him?' asked the slow-witted Victorin.

'Silly ass!' answered Georget. 'Do you think our chief could have gone off and left the old chap to starve in that hole?'

'We could have written them a postcard to say he was there,' suggested Tatave. '*The informer is in the dungeon in the Bastide. Get him out quick. Warning: This is the fate of our enemies.*'

'Shut up!' snapped Pierrot, annoyed at not having thought of that himself. 'Letters take a long time to come from abroad. They might have found Fébo already dead. Sometimes they get lost altogether.'

'Go on!' said Tatave. 'Only the other day I read of a man going twenty-five days without food and being none the worse for it.'

'Drop it! I'm the prosecutor, and I'm the only one allowed to speak without permission. When I've finished, I'll do the defence.'

But Riquet wanted to say something and he held up his hand.

'All right. What is it?'

'What I w … want to know is what the p … poor old man's charged with …'

'What do you think?' retorted the clerk of the court. 'With high treason, of course.'

Then, turning to Fébo, he went on:

'Accused, stand up. Hold up your right hand. Say after me: I swear …'

With a puzzled frown on his face Pierrot asked:

'Why are you doing that?'

'They always do it,' Tatave answered, quite sure of himself.

'All right. Swear him in. And now I'm going to be prisoner's friend.'

He took off his plumed helmet to mark his change of role.

'First of all I want to tell you that Fébo's a good chap, a jolly good chap. And he never had a father or a mother. And he's old. What's more, he didn't mean to do us any harm – did you, Fébo? And the jury should take into account that he taught us to make pea-shooters out of reeds.'

The jury seemed to be quite ready to admit these extenuating circumstances.

'He cut us all catapult forks,' added Georget.

'And the p ... padlock f ... for our t ... treasure-chest. He got it for us.'

'Besides,' said Pierrot, winding up the defence, 'you mustn't forget he's a grown-up, though less than the others. And you can't expect grown-ups to understand anything. And if they don't understand, they can't be guilty, can they?'

The boys nodded gravely. That was unanswerable. Grown-ups were grown-ups, parents were parents, and there was nothing that could be done about it. Not for the present. Later on, when they were parents themselves, everything would be different; but until that golden age arrived you had to admit the imperfections of existence. Things were looking much brighter for the man in the dock.

And then, he'd already been twenty-four hours in prison. Wasn't that punishment enough?

'Do any of the jurymen wish to ask the accused any questions?'

Certainly. Henri du Martel did.

'Fébo, c ... can you make b ... bread?'

The judge, prosecutor, and prisoner's friend shrugged his shoulders.

'Really, this isn't the moment to bother about that. Of course Fébo can make bread. He can do anything.'

'Oh!' said Riquet.

For him the matter was as good as settled. A man as useful as that must obviously be acquitted.

'What I'd like to know is how you knew Fébo'd talked to my father?'

'You can't ask that, Georget,' said Tatave acidly. 'You can't ask the judge questions.'

But Pierrot was more accommodating.

'I don't mind answering. There's no reason why you shouldn't know. Maria told me.'

'Did she hear what he said?'

'Not exactly. But as they never speak to each other as a rule, and as Piquet looked very angry, it was obvious ...'

'Why not ask him?'

Tatave at once turned to the prisoner.

'Stand up, M. Fébo. Raise your right hand and say after me ...'

The old man was sworn in all over again. He looked so pitiful that Pierrot couldn't help changing his tone.

'Look here, Fébo. Try and remember what happened on Friday. You spoke to M. Grillon by the pump in the yard, didn't you?'

'Yes.'

'What did you say to him?'

'I told him not to punish you, as you didn't take the honey.'

That started Georget thinking.

'How did he know we didn't take it? Unless he took it himself.'

Fébo understood and protested vigorously, clenching his fists and waving his arms, but he spoke in such a jumble of French and Spanish that no one could follow.

'He'd better speak Spanish,' said someone. 'Then Cisco could tell us what he means.'

'Chevalier de Guartorella, the court orders you to act as interpreter. Will you please interrogate the prisoner?'

For a minute or two questions and answers followed each other in that beautiful Catalan dialect which sounds rather like a sunburnt French idiom, more mellow than the Provençal.

Meanwhile the young chief had slipped his hand into his cartridge pouch. His relations with Mascha were a little strained now that the latter no longer got his ration of milk.

That was another worry. As if he hadn't got enough on his shoulders already, without Mascha's going into a sulk.

And Pierrot sighed.

'It's like this,' explained Cisco. 'The prisoner says he knew we didn't take the honey because Pierrot told him so, and he always tells the truth.'

An approving silence. No one could say anything against that. A real court of justice might have hesitated, but these boys went straight to the point.

'He knew we were planning to run away and wanted to stop us getting into trouble. So he tackled Piquet and tried to get him to change his mind about keeping us in. But he didn't tell him anything – at least he says he didn't.'

This time the old man raised his hand without being told.

'I swear,' he said.

And in the most dignified way he spat on the ground.

The case looked very different now. The knights had been completely won over, though there was still one point which Tatave wished to get cleared up. Pointing at the prisoner, he said:

'I want to know if the accused knows who did steal the honey, or if he has any suspicions.'

'Yes. That's a good question,' said Pierrot, now beaming with something like tenderness. 'Fébo, answer the Chevalier de Grosbel.'

Another flow of protestations in the old man's peculiar jargon. No, he didn't know who had taken the schoolmaster's honey, and, what's more, he didn't care. All he wanted was that the punishment should be lifted so that they wouldn't go off into the mountains, November being a bad month up there.

That finally settled things. Changing his part once again, Pierrot was now the judge. He put on his helmet.

'The court will now pass judgement.'

It was a solemn moment for all except the blacksmith's apprentice, who jumped from his seat and knelt down at the fire.

'Chevalier Henri du Martel, I call you to order. What are you doing?'

'Can't you see? The g ... goose is getting d ... dry. I'm only b ... basting it.'

The judge repressed a smile. Poor Riquet! it wasn't his fault. He was made that way. His mind would never rise above material things.

'I told you just now Fébo was a jolly good chap, and he's that more than ever now. I pronounce him not guilty, and to make up for his having been put in prison unjustly I hereby appoint him Quartermaster-General of the Garrison. Are we all agreed? Hold up your hands.'

Swept along in the tide, Fébo raised his too, saying once again: 'I swear.'

'Good. Now go and fetch him a helmet, someone. And see if there are any feathers left.'

It was decided to drop the night watch. It didn't seem to serve any purpose, a night attack being judged impracticable.

They all lay down on the sacks of corn. These were too hard at first, but when the string was cut and the corn loosened a little there was sufficient give in them to make them most comfortable.

The feeling of security was absolute, yet Pierrot couldn't get to sleep. All the others did, and little by little being the only one awake induced in him a feeling of loneliness which in turn made him acutely anxious. Gently stroking Mascha, he reviewed all the problems before him and one by one went through the various questions on which he'd have to make a decision in the morning.

First of all, there was the food. They'd done pretty well for themselves that day, thanks to the goose, though it hadn't been very good. That was Riquet's fault. He'd had the bright idea of putting a couple of red herrings into the fat, so that he would salt the bird in basting it. It had given it at the same time a strong taste of fish. They ought to have used the remains of the ham. That would have been salt enough. But no one had thought of it.

Then they'd made a sort of gruel by boiling up some corn. Flavoured with chocolate it hadn't been bad at all, but what would it be like when they'd nothing left to flavour it with?

The little chief was learning a lesson many have had to learn before – that food plays a very big part in warfare.

Cisco had promised to catch some rooks and had assured them he could make an excellent soup with them. That was problematic, however. There was no hope of another goose, as Mme Broc had withdrawn her flock into the safety of her garden.

Then there was the question of morale. It wasn't as good as Pierrot would have liked. There was always the hefty lout Victorin, who never missed an opportunity of airing defeatist sentiment. He was now snoring like a pig. Lucky fellow!

He must find ways of keeping them occupied. That was most important ... Means must be devised for grinding the corn so that Fébo could make bread ... The oven would need a thorough clean out, not having been used for ages, for centuries perhaps.

There were some musical instruments belonging to the town band. They had provided considerable amusement on their discovery. Then they could play marbles, and even organize a tournament. Playing at bull-fights – that was a good game too.

If only there had been some milk for Mascha. That was a worry for which he could find no solution. Still worse were the moral worries. It was all right when he was on the go, but, lying inactive, it was impossible to banish the thought that he must have grieved his father and mother, and also that Viette must miss him terribly. And then, how would they get on at the inn without Fébo to lend a hand?

He knew perfectly well that nothing was to be gained from this adventure. Still, that didn't make him waver. Never for one minute did he toy with the idea of throwing up the sponge.

How could he? His followers believed in him. And, after all, they were in the right – that was the most important thing of all. And to prove one was a man!

In this way he was talking himself round and whipping up his courage, when a strange sound suddenly caught his ear. His body stiffened and all his senses were strung up to the keenest pitch.

Somebody was moving in the castle. It wasn't the scampering of rats, such as had scared them on the first night. No, this was something quite different. A slow, hesitating, shuffling sound. It came from the vaults below, where the dungeons were. Yes, somebody seemed to be there, moving slowly, dragging his feet.

Pierrot listened. If only Victorin wouldn't snore so loudly. And there was Tatave, suddenly bursting into a fit of coughing, for he had indeed caught a cold during his early morning watch.

Pierrot held his breath. The blood was throbbing at his temples. With all the strength of his will he tried to banish the ghost stories from his mind, the stories which three days ago he would have laughed at without a moment's misgiving.

But, try as he would, they came back to him now. Particularly the one about the beautiful Éléonore who appeared at regular intervals to bewail the three barons who, for love of her, had met their death.

The noble Chevalier Pierre d'Aranluz would have liked to stop up his ears and put his head under the bed-clothes. Only there weren't any bed-clothes, and in any case he'd never have forgiven himself if he'd lost his nerve. No, the only thing was to keep quite calm and reason it out. There weren't such things as ghosts. There couldn't be. Nobody believed in them. At least nobody but superstitious old people like Fébo. It was all very well for them.

But what was he to do? Raise the alarm? Call his troops to arms so that they could face the unknown thing together? It was tempting. And if they found nothing he could always say he had raised the alarm for exercise, to keep them on their toes.

What decided him against that solution was his awareness that it was prompted by cowardice. He was afraid, was he? Very well, he must face the thing alone.

Clenching his teeth, he got up, threw another log on the dying fire, and picked up the axe, for moral support rather than for any use it might be. He'd need both hands to swing it, and with one busy holding the torch ...

With beating heart, but firm in purpose, Pierrot made his way down the tortuous passage which led to the nether regions. His torch gave only a faint glow, but when he turned a corner he found the passage was lighter. Another glow of light seemed to emanate from somewhere in front of him. And, louder now, those hesitant, shuffling steps were still approaching.

Not to betray his presence, Pierrot switched off his torch. Stuffing it in his pocket, he gripped the axe with both hands. A cry for help was ready on his lips. He'd make it: *Blood and Freedom!* That would be more dignified than *Help!* and would bring his troops rushing to him in a moment.

The steps came nearer and the boy raised the axe. Then round a bend in the corridor a flickering candle came into view and behind it a female form.

'Who goes there?' he called.

He couldn't recognize his own voice. But the beautiful Éléonore, far more frightened still, emitted a piercing scream and dropped her candle, which immediately went out.

SIX

WHEN you intend to leave your mark upon the world of letters, it is a misfortune to be called by so ordinary a name as Durand.

True, he might have written under a pseudonym, but that idea wasn't in the least attractive to the editor of the *Éclair Perpignanais*, who was as a matter of fact also the founder of the paper and practically its sole contributor. Writing under any other name would make it only the more easy for his family to ignore his activities, and he wanted their recognition quite as much as the world's, perhaps more.

For the fact was that the Durand brothers disapproved strongly when their only son and nephew announced his intention of turning his back on the old-established and honourable family business – Messrs Durand Frères of Agen, manufacturers of crystallized fruits – to try his hand at journalism. They had done all they could to thwart his aim, and it was an essential part of his ambition to make them realize their mistake.

Any lack of lustre on the part of a surname can, however, be redeemed to a large extent by a correspondingly high-sounding Christian name.

Balthazar, for instance.

Yes. That would do very well. Balthazar Durand. That had weight. It had style. The sort of name you couldn't forget once you'd heard it.

So Balthazar was adopted. It had failed, however, to impress any of the Paris editors to whom he had in the first place applied for work. There was nothing for it, therefore, but to start a paper of his own, on the strength of which he had recently been appointed special correspondent for the region to a Paris evening paper. There was no salary, of course. He was just paid for anything they took, and at a very low rate at that.

With the enthusiasm of a novice he started off in a big way, bombarding *Paris-Cinq-Heures* with a series of long and most carefully written articles, none of which had so far found its way into print, the truth being that nothing ever happened at Perpignan which seemed of interest to the world at large.

If only something really sensational would happen! Balthazar sometimes dreamt of a new Spanish war. That would be just the thing.

It was his father's buyer, just returned from the nut market at Casteilcorbon, who gave him the tip.

'You ought to run over there yourself. There are some surprising things going on in that little town. Just the thing for you.'

First thing next morning the journalist was on his motor-cycle making for Casteilcorbon.

The fine weather held, the slanting rays of the sun threw the shadows of the poplars across the road in front of him. The engine purred. And when he finally came in sight of the Bastide silhouetted against a pale blue sky he congratulated himself. Even if nothing sensational came of it, he was going to enjoy a pleasant trip on a perfect autumn day.

He thought it would be tactful to call on the mayor first, and he asked for his house.

A man in a képi told him the way, and he streaked along the Grande Rue Noble, narrowly missing Grisouille, who was loitering in the middle of the road.

He knocked on the door that had been indicated, and a moment later an angry man in his braces was calling him a damned fool and a nitwit and much else besides.

Balthazar beat a retreat, vowing vengeance for this inhospitable reception.

'You, my friend,' he muttered under his breath, 'don't yet seem to have learnt the power of the Press. Wait till you see what I say about you in *Paris-Cinq-Heures*.'

He next called at the presbytery.

M. le Curé wasn't there, being engaged in celebrating the High Mass of All Saints' Day. But he managed to secure an interview with his servant, Valérie, who was the ideal person for a journalist in search of information to fall on. With a grey-green complexion and a tart way of speaking, she seemed to have been conserved for many years in a jar of vinegar.

Her tongue never flagged as she pottered round her kitchen stove, and Balthazar had only to listen to obtain a detailed and even somewhat magnified version of the recent events in Casteilcorbon, and he was soon patting himself on the back for his journalistic flair in having known at once where to go for first-hand information.

He was already composing his first article in his head, and from time to time he jotted down some particularly colourful phrase of the local idiom. He was grateful – not least for the cup of coffee she gave him – and made a note to remind him to send Valérie some complimentary copies of the *Éclair Perpignanais*.

The flow would never have stopped of its own accord, and he had some difficulty in extricating himself so as to reach the church just as the Mass was finishing.

Outside the big double doors, which were wide open, some men were standing. They were the cautious ones who sat on the fence, neither caring to slam the door on salvation nor to range themselves overtly in the camp of the faithful.

François Tistounet was one of them, and no one, not even Valérie, could have been more ready to be interviewed by a journalist than he. And what person could be more fitted to provide the desired information than the man who had first discovered where the boys had gone?

'Just look at them!' he exclaimed, pointing at the Bastide, on whose battlements three brass helmets gleamed in the sun. 'Just look at them! They're having a fine time, the little devils, I don't doubt it. But you'll see. We'll get them in the long run. Tire them out, we will. Then, won't they catch it!'

Balthazar would have gone to see the schoolmaster, but he was itching to begin his article, so he put the visit off till later.

Entering the Auberge Daranluz, he chose a table in the café and settled down to write. Dragging her slippers over the sawdust on the floor, a tall, unkempt girl slouched up.

'What can I get you?'

'Some coffee and a roll and butter.'

'There's no coffee left. And the mistress always locks the butter up when she goes out.'

Balthazar was not in the least offended by her sulky, hostile tone. On the contrary, he was interested. He studied her red lips, her bold and rather crafty eyes, the dirty dress she had already outgrown, but what intrigued him most in this young person was her distant and contemptuous manner. Her mind seemed elsewhere.

He smiled at her.

At that, she began to be interested herself, and she smiled back. He wasn't the usual sort in those parts and he wore tweeds of a cut she had rarely seen outside the cinema.

'Where is your mistress?'

'At Mass.'

'And you?'

'Oh, me ...'

She said it with such bitterness that he was more interested than ever, and he looked again at this girl who seemed to have no illusions about life.

'What's your name?'

'What's that to you?'

A peasant at the other end of the room rapped on his table and called out:

'Maria!'

Balthazar laughed.

'You needn't bother to tell me.'

Maria shrugged her shoulders.

'You see what it's like,' she muttered, then called out: 'I'm coming.'

A minute later she was back.

'Have you made up your mind what you want?'

'Look here, Maria. Bring something to eat and something to drink. I don't care what. Choose something you like yourself. Then you'll sit down beside me and we'll have a little chat.'

Maria opened her eyes wide.

'You don't waste much time, do you?'

It was said with a touch of admiration, and Balthazar went on blandly:

'I've come specially from Paris. I'm a journalist and I've been sent to cover this story of the boys who've shut themselves up in your castle. I've already asked one or two people, but they all said the same thing: "Go and see Maria at the inn. She can tell you about it better than anyone."'

'Go on! You didn't even know my name.'

All the same she was flattered and came nearer. He noticed her finger-nails bitten down to the quick, her dirty ears, the smell of her breath – for she was chewing a clove of garlic.

'You do know all about these boys, don't you?'

'I dare say so. In fact ...'

190

'What?'

'Nothing.'

'Listen – I'm hungry and thirsty. Bring a couple of glasses. You're not afraid of me, are you?'

'Afraid? Of you? But if the master came in, or the mistress …'

'Are they nasty to you? Do they beat you?'

At that idea she couldn't help smiling.

'Heavens, no! He's much too decent for that. So's she – underneath. Only, they've got plenty to say. And they don't like it if I'm familiar with the customers.'

'But if I invite you?'

Maria weighed the pros and cons. After all, why not?

'Just wait a minute. I'll toast some bread and we'll have *chouacholles*. It's a treat – you'll see.'

Balthazar Durand bent once more over his reporter's note-book, a brand new one for the occasion. His first headline he crossed out as not sufficiently striking. He wanted something sensational that couldn't fail to catch the blasé Parisian eye.

Finally he wrote:

A NEW EUROPEAN CONFLICT

And under it, in smaller characters:

Behind age-old ramparts a handful of children
defy a Radical-Socialist Mayor

Casteilcorbon. 1 Nov.
(From our Special Correspondent)

No one can foresee the end of the conflict which has suddenly flared up in a charming little town in the Roussillon, from which our special correspondent, Balthazar Durand, has telegraphed the following details, which are as picturesque as they are unprecedented …

At that point Maria returned with two large glasses of *rancio*. Sitting down at his table, she at once began greedily dipping fingers of warm toast in the golden wine.

'So you write for the papers!' she observed amiably.

'Yes, Beautiful.'

'And you're going to talk about us?'

'Of course. That's what I've come for.'

'Does it bring you in any money?'

'It ought to. If it's interesting enough. That's why you've got to help me.'

Obviously it brought in money. She glanced at his apple-green tie and the silk handkerchief of the same colour which peeped out of his breast pocket, his signet ring, and gold-mounted fountain-pen.

'All the same,' she said, 'you've got to have some guts for that job, I suppose.'

The young man looked at his notes.

'Come on, Maria. I'm ready for you. Tell me the names of these kids.'

'They're not kids. They're knights.'

'Knights?'

'Yes, and they've got an axe to defend themselves with. And they're doing themselves pretty well, I don't mind telling you. What with old Mother Broc's goose and the baker's *fouaces* … I think it's just wonderful.'

The girl's eyes lit up.

'Yes, they're fine eyes,' thought Balthazar. 'It's a pity she snuffles all the time and can't stop scratching her head. But I'd better forget about that, as I shall no doubt have to make up to her a bit if I'm going to get anything out of her.'

'And, you know, they won't stop at anything,' she went on. 'Why, they even put Fébo in prison.'

'Who's Fébo?'

'Just a silly old buffer, if it comes to that. He's the official guide to the Bastide. Works here too – at the inn, I mean – though he's not good for much except the washing-up.'

'What do you mean by saying they put him in prison?'

'Chucked him into a dungeon, they did. Just like that. Then they tried him. But you mustn't say anything about that, as nobody else knows.'

Decidedly this was a windfall for any journalist.

'Tell me, Maria … How do you know all this?'

The girl bit her lip. She had been indiscreet. And, like any woman, feeling at fault, she promptly took vengeance on him.

'What the hell are you getting at? You've got some cheek. Wasting my time like this. What goes on here's no business of yours … That'll be thirty francs. For my share. You can settle up with Mme Daranluz for the rest … Did you ever hear of such a thing? …'

She was so indignant that Balthazar meekly produced his money.

'Listen, Maria,' he pleaded. 'Don't be angry. You know you're not half so pretty with a frown on your face. I didn't mean any harm. I'm just very interested in what you've been telling me. And I quite agree with you. I think they're wonderful too, those young knights. By the way, they tell me the biggest of them is the mayor's own son.'

Maria glanced out of the window.

'Hell! Here they are. Coming back from church.'

Quickly she snatched up her empty glass and made for the kitchen, Balthazar running after her.

'Maria, Maria, you mustn't slip off like that just as we're getting started. Look here, I've got an idea. What'd you say to a run on my motor-bike? We could pop down to the sea ...'

The girl considered the proposal. She wiped her glass on the corner of her apron and then put it back on the shelf behind the bar. That was a wise precaution. Sometimes Mme Fine checked the drinks paid for against the number of dirty glasses.

A ride on a motor-bike! A trip to the sea!

'The thing is, it's a holiday, so the place will be full all day ... All the same ... I'll slip off somehow. Wait for me in the lane behind the cemetery at three o'clock.'

'You promise to come?'

'Yes.'

'Honestly?'

'Honest.'

As they say, opportunity is everything. Certainly our young journalist seized his with both hands. Telephoned to Paris at his own expense, his article appeared next day in the one o'clock edition, between a picture of the Chrysanthemum Show at the Grande Palais and one of the President of the Republic laying a wreath on the tomb of the Unknown Soldier.

From there, the story was picked up by several provincial dailies, who reprinted it with embellishments of their own. Naturally Balthazar Durand's own *Éclair* made the most of it.

He was on the threshold of fame.

He had been as good as his word, and in the *Éclair*'s version there

were several digs at M. Guillaume Muche, who had so unceremoniously slammed the door in his face.

The mayor, when he read the article, was in such a towering rage
that the whole distillery trembled.

Mme Broc, who also sold newspapers, had to order five times the
usual number.

Balthazar had taken a room at the Auberge Daranluz, and the place,
at all times the centre of gossip, served excellently as an observation
post. Every time he passed the mayor's windows, Mme Muche hastily
got out the digitalis tablets and gave one to her husband. He always
needed it.

'If I don't wring his neck before I've done with him …'

But the articles went on, and the mayor of Casteilcorbon, raging in
impotence, wasn't spared by Balthazar's pen.

And finally the mayor took action. Tarasse was ordered to call out
the Fire Brigade, requisition all the ladders in the town, and work out
a plan for taking the Bastide by storm.

The blacksmith was consulted about the possibility of sawing
through some iron bars and also about constructing a platform of
some sort on which the ladders could be lodged.

Every suggestion was promptly reported, but *Paris-Cinq-Heures*
sent a telegram clamouring for further details. It was all most gratify-
ing; particularly as all the local reporters were forced to look up to
Balthazar. His prestige as representing a Paris paper combined with
his uncanny possession of inside information gave him a unique
position.

'If only those boys can hold out!' he said to himself.

In the morning of 3 November the weather broke. A west wind
drove ragged clouds down towards the sea, and it was so cold that
keeping watch on the upper platform had to be abandoned altogether.

In any case, the town seemed quiet. The siege had already lost its
novelty and people went about their business with no more than an
occasional cursory glance at the Bastide.

To keep out the damp, a blazing fire was kept up all day long in the
guardroom. Riquet saw to that, and so lavish was he with the fuel that
it looked as if their stock would only last for another fortnight.

The boys were now suffering from a certain amount of boredom, particularly Victorin, who had never been capable of a sustained interest in anything. The marbles tournament had proved a failure, for the tiled floor was so uneven that every shot was a fluke.

The band's instruments had had more success, but the fun of making an infernal din couldn't last for ever. On Tatave's advice, Pierrot had had the bombardon taken up to the roof, to be used as a siren in case of an alert. The big drum had been propped up to serve as a table at meal-times and also as a desk at which Tatave could sit to do the paper work.

With the utmost good will, Fébo had set to work unasked. He composed a strange dish of corn flavoured with the brine from the barrel of herrings.

To please him, the knights pronounced it excellent.

'If only we had some bread,' sighed Victorin.

'And some bars of chocolate.'

'Or a pot of jam.'

Pierrot slipped his hand into his cartridge pouch, thinking:

'And some milk for Mascha.'

Out loud he reproved them.

'Come on, now! No complaints. As knights I don't think much of you. We'll try and make some bread tomorrow. For the time being, don't forget that this is a siege.'

'How are you g ... going to g ... grind the corn?'

'I don't know yet. As a matter of fact I'm counting on you to think up a way.'

Riquet was pleased.

'But that's not all,' objected Tatave. 'You can't make bread without yeast.'

'We'll have some,' answered Pierrot serenely.

His confidence was infectious and they all brightened up, except Riquet, who was deep in thought. He bitterly regretted not having brought his mother's coffee-mill which stood on the kitchen mantelpiece, and wondered whether corn could be ground between helmets. In the end he decided not. What you needed was a stone.

Suddenly he burst out:

'Who'll c ... come with me to f ... fetch the c ... cover of the w ... well? Victorin – you're the strongest.'

Pierrot watch them go with an anxious furrow on his forehead, as there was something he didn't want them to find out.

On the pretext of going the rounds at nightfall, Pierrot led Cisco and Tatave down towards the dungeons. The wind had veered to the north now and whistled through every cranny.

'Look here,' said the chief when he had them alone, 'what would you say if I told you we could clear out tonight and make a dash for the frontier?'

The Chevalier de Grosbel snuffled twice and fidgeted with his Balaclava helmet.

'I'll consider it,' he answered cautiously at last, thinking uneasily of the weather. 'But first of all how should we get out?'

Authoritatively, Pierrot parried the question.

'I was asking you. What would you say?'

'We could lower the hose-pipe down from the battlements,' suggested Cisco, 'and slide down it.'

But it was more than doubtful whether he relished the idea. As for Tatave, his face was a picture of dismay, but he adroitly brushed the suggestion aside with:

'Think of Fébo. He'd never manage it.'

Pierrot grinned.

'I didn't ask you *how* we'd get out, but whether you'd like to. What's the answer?'

'Yes. Every time,' said Cisco promptly.

'Not me.'

Tatave's natural instinct was to say the opposite. Besides, he feared the unknown.

Pierrot sighed, discouraged by the split vote.

'You said yourself we could hold out for six months,' explained Tatave. 'And if you said it I take your word for it. That'd take us to the spring and make all the difference. Explorers always wait for the right season to start off.'

Cisco didn't agree.

'I'd say: clear out when you can. Afterwards, you never know. We might funk it.'

'Funk it!'

Tatave was outraged.

'Well, put it this way – we'll have worn out the soles of our shoes. Mine are pretty far gone already. Not that that matters – to me. But you softies ...'

Pierrot cut him short:

'That'll do.'

'What about putting it to the vote?' suggested Tatave. 'If I cut up bits of paper we could have a secret ballot.'

'No,' growled Pierrot, 'we won't have a vote. You'll do as I tell you.'

To which Cisco couldn't help answering:

'Then why did you ask our advice.'

'Because ...'

'You're a funny chap, Pierrot. You ask us our opinion and then bite our heads off when we give it.'

Pierrot had to admit there was some justice in that. He tried to explain.

'It was just to see if you thought the same as I did.'

'What did you think?'

'That's my business.'

'Just as you like! But you're being very mysterious about it all. We've got to answer questions we don't understand. Like the catechism.'

'I can understand, if you don't,' affirmed Tatave.

'That's right! Side with Pierrot.'

With a melancholy look on his face, Pierrot gently stroked Mascha's fur.

Fébo was the first up, as usual. The crow of the cock always started his catarrh going, and, like many other old men, he began the day with a series of coughs and drastic throat-clearings which woke up all the others.

They listened intently, waiting to hear him spit. Finally Georget sniggered.

'He won't. Nothing's ever wasted with him.'

They had got used to having the old man around. He pottered about doing much the same as he would have done at the Auberge Daranluz – sweeping, clearing away the ashes, chopping wood, going about it all so slowly that he seemed to be idling, yet with such proficiency that work disappeared under his hands.

He went his own way. Nobody ordered him about. The boys, in fact, still a little intimidated by the presence of a grown-up, were all out to be nice to him in every way. For his part, he was as accommodating as they were, and raised no objection to being made a knight or having his name changed to Phoebus.

The only thing he missed was his tobacco. Victorin's cigarettes had gone long ago. What was his surprise then this morning to find a packet of tobacco waiting for him on the big drum?

'*Maravilloso!*' he exclaimed.

It wasn't the only marvel. Beside it were two boxes of sugar, an enormous sausage, several pots of jam, a veritable stack of slabs of chocolate, some candles – in fact everything Balthazar Durand had been able to think of buying.

Roused by his exclamations, the others gathered round to share his wonderment.

Only Pierrot slept, worn out by the excitements of a sleepless night.

SEVEN

WITH becoming ceremony, Pierrot unfolded the copy of *Paris-Cinq-Heures*.

'Who's best at reading aloud?' he asked, scanning the circle of knights.

'Riquet,' suggested Georget mischievously.

The wretched stutterer reddened, but without anger. Nobody could really take offence at Georget because he had such a sense of fun. Also because, for all his teasing, there wasn't a grain of malice in him.

'You are,' said Cisco. 'Fire away. We're all ready.'

But Pierrot refused.

'No. Not me. Here, take it, Cisco. It's the first column on the left-hand page.'

Indeed the headline caught Cisco's eye at once.

CASTEILCORBON
The Bastide Still Holds Out
Thirteen-year-old in Command
Pierrot the Gallant Knight

To see his own name in the newspaper! What a thrill it had given the young leader.

He had hardly been able to believe his eyes when Maria had handed him the paper in the middle of the night.

His heart had thumped in his breast. With pride. With fear too.

Even now his pulse quickened as he watched for the reaction of the others. What would they think of it? For that matter what did he think of it himself? They had become famous, certainly; but what would be the outcome? What were they heading for?

From our Special Correspondent, Balthazar Durand.

It may have occurred to some people that the events I have been relating have been nothing but a publicity stunt, cunningly contrived to bring visitors to an out-of-the-way spot. If so, I can assure them that this charming and picturesque little town, with its beetling fortress, has no need to descend to such dubious methods to attract tourists, who come regularly to stand and wonder at the noble keep, which, in a remarkable state of preservation, rises high above the roofs of the town, apparently oblivious of the march of progress around it.

For four days now the drawbridge has been up, the entrance obstinately closed, and, as to the troops of Louis XI, Francis I, and Richelieu, the fortress opposes its stern and obdurate refusal.

Who are they, the doughty warriors behind the walls? A handful of boys not yet out of school, driven no doubt by the romantic yearnings of their tender years to resuscitate the age of chivalry.

'That's beautiful,' said Georget, his eyes shining.
'Yes, but it isn't true,' objected Victorin.
Cisco went on reading:

The instigator of this rebellion and commander of the stronghold is a boy of thirteen, Pierre Daranluz, son of the worthy innkeeper of this little town. Indeed, the defenders spring from the most respectable families of Casteilcorbon, and the fact that one of them is the mayor's own son adds a piquant touch to this remarkable adventure.

Is that why the mayor has so far taken no steps to put an end to this escapade? Or is the reason to be sought in the fact that this worthy, despite the rude energy of his tongue, is not a man of action at all?

'What does he mean by that?' asked Victorin anxiously.
'He's just handing your father a bouquet,' answered Georget.
'Wait a minute,' said Cisco. 'There's something about yours too.'

Much as we may admire the courage of these impetuous youths, we cannot end without a word of sympathy for their worried parents, in particular for the devoted schoolmaster, M. Déodat Grillon, who has been bereaved, not only of a whole class, but of his own son. At the foot of the fortress the poor teacher stands, a woeful figure, meditating on the vagaries of youth and on the hard lot of those whose task it is to educate it.

With that peroration Balthazar had laid down his pen with a look of self-satisfaction on his face. But when Cisco put the paper down, having read the article with great gusto, his audience, though unquestionably flattered, were a prey to mixed feelings.

'Whew!' muttered Victorin, shaking his head.

He seemed crushed by the weight of his own heroism, besides being daunted by the vision of his father reading the article. Riquet, ever practical, was totting up what his celebrity was going to cost him in clouts over the head and kicks up the backside.

On the other hand, although his name hadn't been mentioned by Special Correspondent Balthazar Durand, the Chevalier de Grosbel was pervaded by intense jubilation. He kept his eye on the paper, intending to get hold of it as soon as possible. He would cut out the article and paste it into a new exercise book which henceforth would be consecrated to Press cuttings. It was the opening of a new chapter in his life. Never again would Mme Grosbelhomme dare to say to him in public:

'Tatave, blow your nose and pull up your socks.'

Georget and Cisco were no less elated, though without the particular satisfaction of wreaking vengeance. And in Georget's case the elation was mixed with a touch of melancholy on account of the final paragraph.

Pierrot didn't dare ask them what they thought. A matter of delicacy. He felt as though a medal had been pinned on his breast before the whole regiment.

As though astonished by the silence, Mascha crept out of the cartridge pouch, ran down Pierrot's leg and squatted on the big drum, lineal descendant of the Round Table, where he looked first this way, then that, critically surveying the assembled knights.

But a simple snuffle from Tatave was enough to make him run for cover up his master's sleeve.

At last the chief spoke.

'You don't ask me who wrote the article?'

'Who w ... was it?'

'The same person who sent the tobacco and the other things.'

'Jolly decent chap.'

'Cisco told you his name, Balthazar Durand.'

'But how ...'

'The thing is – he wants to visit us here. Do you agree?'

'But how ...'

'Don't bother about that now. I'll tell you later. The first thing is to vote. Those who agree to his coming here hold up their hands.'

Every hand went up.

'Right. That settles it. Blood and Freedom!'

He raised his hand to recapture Mascha, who was now perched on the top of his head. Then he went on:

'We must get everything ready to receive him properly. And ... there's another thing. There'll be someone else with him, a ... a lady ... a girl, if you like. And I needn't ask you to behave to her with the manners of ...What I mean is, you've got to be nice to her.'

Wonders followed on wonders, but the boys were no longer surprised at anything.

'How do the visitors get in, as we can't very well open the front door?' asked Georget. 'Is Victorin going to hoick them up on a string like old Mother Broc's goose?'

'Chevalier de Grillon, for the last time, will you please not turn everything into a joke? After what Cisco's been reading to us, I should have thought you'd have more sense of dignity.'

Pierrot was dying to get the whole story off his chest, but something still held him back: a fear of divulging information that had best be kept secret. Finally he made up his mind.

'First of all swear you won't try and find out more than I tell you.'

Fingers were crossed.

'Well, chums – I mean knights – the old story of underground passages to the Bastide isn't rot after all. Not by a long chalk. They're there – real underground passages. At least there's one. And it's been left to us to discover it.'

Tatave's face was absolutely radiant. It was almost too good to be true.

'A secret underground passage!' he echoed.

And his voice seemed to come from far away, out of a world of dreams.

'An underground passage!' said Balthazar Durand to himself as he crept down the stairs of the inn with his shoes in his hand. 'An underground passage! It's almost too good to be true. And that I should be let into the secret!'

He started and clutched at the carved ball of wood that surmounted the newel-post.

How silly of him! He cursed himself for being so jumpy. It was only the two dogs, who had long since made friends with him, and who now came up and thrust their wet muzzles against his hands.

The doors and windows giving on to the street were always carefully locked and bolted at night. So were the big double doors which closed the courtyard to the outer world. But the back door, which opened on to the yard, could be opened from either inside or out by merely lifting a latch. Maria, for instance, was able – on the rare occasions when she was up first – to enter the kitchen without disturbing anyone.

Cautiously Balthazar lifted the latch and stepped out into the darkness. He almost cried out, for, forgetting Maria's instructions, he walked straight into a puddle.

One of his socks was sopping wet.

'Boulou! ... Barbette! ... Get back,' he called to them as loudly as he dared.

They had followed him out.

To put his shoes on, he sat down on a stone step. There was a puddle on that too.

'Boulou! ... Barbette! ...'

But the dogs hadn't the slightest intention of obeying him, and he could hear their steps following, pitter-patter, behind him as he made his way across the yard to the ruined tower in the corner.

Riquet raised his torch and peered into the blackness.

'It's only an ... another c ... cellar.'

Tatave bristled.

'You musn't call our underground passage a cellar.'

Ever since Pierrot had told them about it, the knights had been itching to see it. He had been inflexible, however.

'Not now. You'll see it tonight. In the meantime you can chop some dry wood for torches.'

Time had hung heavy on their hands. Then at last Pierrot led them down towards the place where two nights ago he had scared the wits out of La Belle Éléonore.

Suddenly Victorin had a revelation.

'If he can get in, we can get out. So we can go to Spain, after all.'

'Oh no, we can't,' said Pierrot. 'First of all because we're not running away from anybody – not now. Secondly because the passage only leads to my place, to the ruined tower in the courtyard. That's as far as we'd get. To break out from there, we'd have to start unlocking doors, and we'd be heard in no time.'

'Who discovered the passage?'

'Maria. She heard you playing on the trombone.'

That was quite true. A few days previously she had uncovered the entrance to it in moving some rabbit-hutches which were kept on the ground floor of the tower, just below her room. What she had disclosed was merely a half-blocked-up hole in the ground, to which she paid no attention at the time. It was two or three days later, when she was clearing out the hutches, which had begun to smell, that she heard a distant droning sound followed by a faint shout of laughter. Puzzled at first, it was not long before her imagination had got to work.

Presently Pierrot called a halt.

'You stay here. I'm going on alone, to fetch him.'

'Once he knows the way, how d'you know he won't tell?'

Tatave had a prompt answer to that:

'You've got to blindfold him, then turn him round six times. They always did that.'

'Quite true. I hadn't thought of that. But what shall I blindfold him with?'

That was a difficult question. The handkerchiefs carried by the knights were much too dirty. They'd have done for a boy, no doubt, but not for the Special Correspondent of *Paris-Cinq-Heures*.

Once again it was the Chevalier de Grosbel who came up to scratch.

'Here! Take this,' he cried, unbuttoning his trousers. 'My belly-band.'

They were face to face, the one as shy as the other.

'Good evening, Monsieur,' said Pierrot very politely.

And Balthazar could find nothing better to answer than:

'Good evening, my little friend.'

Boulou and Barbette pranced with joy and licked the hands of the young master they had lost.

Maria, holding the lamp, smiled awkwardly, not knowing how to introduce people to each other. She had merely slipped a coat on over her nightgown, and, with her hair full of cobwebs, she looked more of a slut than ever.

Pierrot had something to say which caused him considerable embarrassment, and it was only after some hesitation that he came out with it.

'I'm awfully sorry, Monsieur ... But the thing is ... If you want to come and see us in the Bastide, I'm afraid I've got to blindfold you ... Of course I know you're all right – after all the things you sent us and what you wrote about us in the newspaper – but I've got to think of the others ... You understand?'

Balthazar understood perfectly.

'Sure you don't mind?'

On the contrary he was enjoying every moment of it, and was only too ready to fall in with their game.

Pierrot wound the strip of flannel round his head, talking all the time, in the end producing something rather like a turban.

'It won't interfere with your breathing ... We thought of using our handkerchiefs, but they were all too grubby. This is quite clean. You needn't be afraid. It's Tatave's belly-band – I mean Chevalier de Grosbel's ... And by the way, it was awfully decent of you to call me your little friend. But it wouldn't go down at all well there. In the Bastide you'd better call me Chevalier d'Aranluz. Or just Chevalier.'

'Quite right, Chevalier, quite right ... Steady there! Not too tight ... And while we're talking as man to man would you mind explaining to me just why you've shut yourselves up in that place?'

That phrase 'man to man' went straight to Pierrot's heart. Here at last was a grown-up who seemed to catch on. You could deal with a chap like that. The boy was at once ready to open up, but Maria butted in unceremoniously.

'That's no business of yours,' she snapped. 'Besides, you promised me to ask no questions. Now put your hands on my shoulders and follow me. I'll warn you when we come to a step.'

She spoke in a tone of such familiarity that Pierrot thought for a moment that she was speaking to him. She turned down the wick of her lamp, which was smoking a little, then started off, feeling her way cautiously, the journalist following.

In spite of what Pierrot had said he had some difficulty in breathing through his nose, and the belly-band smelt of stale sweat.

Perhaps he wasn't enjoying himself quite so much after all, and he almost jumped out of his skin when a sentry suddenly challenged them with:

'Abracadabra! Blood and Freedom!'

What embarrassing creatures grown-ups are!

From the moment Balthazar Durand came among them, the boys were no longer quite so sure of being knights.

They didn't mind Maria. She, after all, was more or less one of themselves, even if she was a girl. Indeed Victorin seemed delighted by her presence. He couldn't take his eyes off her.

But this gentleman with thinning hair and a bow tie ...

Admittedly he behaved very well. He offered Fébo a cigar, stroked Mascha, though he held mice in abhorrence, and did his utmost to throw himself into the game. To tell the truth, perhaps he overdid it a bit, even asking for a fireman's helmet for himself.

But that didn't alter the fact that their visitor was proving himself a good ally, and presently he was addressing the knights, assembled now in council of war, while the chronicler took copious notes, putting his tongue between his teeth in the effort to keep up.

'I beg you not to think, Knights, that I have come in a spirit of mere curiosity. I am your friend, and I come to warn you that grave danger is impending. The powers that be have decided to make an end of this episode, taking your stronghold by storm this very morning, striking before dawn, when you may be expected to be asleep.'

'Yes, my poor boys, it's quite true,' put in Maria. 'M. Tarasse has scrounged round for every ladder in the place, and the blacksmith's just finished building a raft.'

'My father?' burst out Riquet, very interested. 'Oh hell! But how do they think they'll get in?'

Balthazar explained what he believed to be the plan of attack. Naturally he didn't know every detail, for it had been worked out in secret session of the Municipal Council. But secrets entrusted to François Tistounet, M. Tarasse, and M. Belaigue – who were to be the chief executives – were not secrets for very long, particularly as many of their difficulties were thrashed out in discussions over a glass of wine at the Auberge Daranluz, with the result that by this time there were few people in the town who did not know pretty well what was afoot.

'Well, there you are!' he said at last. 'Forewarned is forearmed. And if you keep a sharp look out ...'

'Looks to me as though we're in a pretty pickle,' groaned Victorin, who had been very impressed by the thoroughness of the preparations.

'What are we to d ... do?' asked Riquet.

Georget had an idea.

'Let's clear out. Through the passage. Then we'd climb up the church tower and watch the whole show and cheer them when they got in. It'd be a wonderful joke.'

In the desperate straits the knights were in, this idea was not altogether unattractive, even to their leader.

Not to Tatave, however.

'Are you mad? It might be funny, but that wouldn't alter the fact that we'd thrown up the sponge.'

To everyone's surprise, he leant over towards the schoolmaster's son and whispered something in his ear.

Georget reddened at once, and the next moment he'd changed his mind.

'Tatave's right. We mustn't give in.'

'But what else can we do?'

'Resist,' replied Tatave sententiously. 'Fight to the bitter end, to the death if need be. Wasn't that what we swore?'

'Fine!' said Balthazar. 'I must say you're wonderful chaps.'

That tipped the scale. Such a handsome compliment had to be lived up to. Pierrot was ashamed of having inwardly faltered for a second. His instinct told him the hard way was invariably the right one.

All he said was:

'Blood and Freedom!'

At what followed, Balthazar gazed in increasing wonderment. In one of his articles he had already described the cavaliers' young chief, but more or less at Maria's dictation, and not without his tongue in his cheek. Now that he saw him on the job, he soon realized that Maria had not exaggerated, for the boy went about it with a thoroughness, determination, and power of command which bore witness to a quite exceptional character.

'First of all we must rig up the hand pump, with the suction pipe led down to the moat. Chevalier du Martel, you'll take the nozzle, at the postern, and stop anybody getting at the drawbridge. They couldn't do much, if they did. But you never know. Chevalier Phoebus and Victorin – you'll man the pump. The rest of us will man the battlements. We'll want all the ammunition we can collect. Marbles for our catapults and logs to throw. Lots of logs, and as big as we can handle ...'

'Pity we've no boiling oil,' sighed Tatave.

Maria listened, fascinated, picking her nose.

'And what can I do?' she asked.

'You?'

Pierrot hesitated. In principle, women took no part in warfare. Still, there was Joan of Arc, of course …

'I tell you what – you'll be liaison officer.'

'What's that?'

'Between the chaps down here and the rest of us up top. You'll keep us informed of what's going on, and you'll help to keep up our morale.'

Maria pursed her lips.

'I'd sooner chuck logs,' she said.

A reply which raised her greatly in the esteem of the cavaliers, who so far had been inclined to look askance at her presence.

All that was left now was to find a job for their visitor, who naturally was unwilling to retrace his steps when so momentous a struggle was impending. On the other hand, Balthazar was reluctant to take an active part in the resistance even though he was largely responsible for it. Rather obsequiously he made a suggestion.

'As far as I'm concerned, Knights, if your leader agrees to it, I'll be the war correspondent, the historian of your great exploits. And to begin with, I've got my camera here, so if you'll stand in a group I'll take a flash-light photo of you.'

He gave them a sugary smile, not noticing the black look he got from the official historian, Gustave de Grosbel.

Soon after midnight all was ready. The pump was in place, the hoses rigged, the catapults tested and found in working order, and at least a hundred logs stacked behind the battlements.

A hunk of bread and a bar of chocolate were doled out to each. Then Pierrot ordered his troops to rest.

'I'll keep watch myself,' he said. 'I can't leave that to anyone. And the moment I give a shout, everyone to action stations.'

The others were only too glad to get a bit of sleep. For the last hour, Boulou and Barbette had been sleeping in front of the fire, their muzzles tucked under their tails.

Only Tatave stayed up, busy with the manufacture of a strange concoction. In an empty condensed-milk tin he put some of M. Muche's alcohol and was trying to dissolve in it one of those sulphur candles used to disinfect casks, of which there was a considerable provision in the Bastide. To complete his mixture he added a handful of the green powder used for spraying vines.

'Why don't you turn in, instead of making that filthy stink?'

'It's important. I'm trying to discover the formula.'

'What of?'

'Greek fire.'

Pierrot left him to it. Putting on his helmet he climbed up the spiral staircase which led to the upper platform.

The air up there was so keen that, when he breathed, his chest seemed twice its usual size.

Everything seemed quiet in the town. Only the windows of the Town Hall were still lit up.

The thirteen-year-old watchman shivered with cold. And with apprehension.

EIGHT

LES CHEVALIERS DE CASTEILCORBON
Chronique historique
par
Le Sieur Gustave de Grosbel

Tatave was so proud of his title and so pleased to write his high-sounding name beneath it that he put it at the head of each chapter, only varying the colour of the ink.

The urge to write had been fomented by competition, for he now had a rival in the person of Balthazar Durand, and he wasn't going to let the grass grow under his feet.

So, before his impressions had time to fade, he settled down to record them for future generations.

The so-called war correspondent had returned to the inn by the way he had come, accompanied by Maria. Georget was on the watch above, to give warning of any signs of the attack being renewed. The others, tired out by the night's work and the excitement with which it finished, had fallen asleep as soon as their heads had touched the corn sacks.

Tatave was no less tired than they, and it was with no little self-esteem that he fought back the encroachments of sleep for the sake of posterity.

For a minute or two he groped for a suitably telling chapter heading, then he wrote.

Drama at Dawn

After weeks and weeks of unrelenting siege, during which the knights had to live on dead rats and boiled crows &c, &c, their courage was still undiminished, knowing as they did that Heaven was on their side.

One night Marie-Éléonore, niece of the Comte de Roussillon, who fortunately knew of the secret underground passage to the keep, moved by the heroism of the defenders, came to them on a secret and mysterious visit, bringing a basket of victuals and the comfort of her gracious presence.

Accompanying her, his eyes bandaged because of the secret, was the Count's Counsellor.

This man, enchanted by the beauty of the Count's niece, did not hesitate, to please her, to reveal the plan of the assault which his master was preparing. In fact he was a traitor, and there can be no other word for him.

'Knights,' he said, 'before the first crow of the cock this day, you will be undone. If you don't watch out.'

'Woe betide us!' cried Pierre d'Aranluz, crushing a crystal goblet in his mailed fist.

Carried away by his narrative, Tatave raised his fist, but, before he could bring it down upon his desk, he remembered just in time that the latter was the big drum.

'Prepare for battle,' roared Pierre d'Aranluz, in a voice that shook the walls.

Then, lifting Marie-Éléonore's hand to his lips, we went on:

'As for you, gracious lady, I beg you to retire the way you came. Sad should we be were you to meet your death among us in the dire struggle which lies ahead.'

'Never,' she answered nobly.

When all was ready, there was nothing to do but wait, and we did it.

Suddenly a clarion call roused the cavaliers from their slumber. Sounded on a trumpet by Pierre d'Aranluz himself, it echoed under the vaults and reached even to the ranks of the besieging army, bringing dismay to their hearts.

The drama had begun. The defences were manned. Fortunately among the knights was one whose name modesty forbids me to mention whose fragile frame was more than redeemed by his indomitable courage and resourcefulness in battle. The first to join his leader on the battlements, he drew from his pocket a box of matches and lit the wick of a Roman candle he had had the foresight to bring with him.

By its light, the knights were able to measure the extent of their peril.

Tatave jumped and stopped writing. A faint sound had reached him from the corner where Pierrot was lying. It sounded like a sob.

'What's come over him?' thought the scribe. 'Perhaps he's having a nightmare.'

Satisfied with that observation, he returned to the assault.

Around the stronghold a vast array was gathered in silence, their helmets gleaming in the light of the Roman candle, their spirits dark with fear.

There were women among them who screamed at the stars of fire, thinking they would fall on their heads.

'Light another,' cried the chief.

Again the invading host was lit up, and this time it could be seen that they were trying to put up a ladder on a shelf of rock that in one place jutted out at the foot of the Bastide.

It was really two ladders tied together. Even then it was too short to reach to the top. All the same, one of the warriors climbed up it, looking back all the time to see if the others were holding it steady.

Soon his intentions came to light. Reaching one of the lower loopholes, he started chipping the stonework with a mace, as though to force a passage through the narrow opening.

So far the defenders had only used their catapults, with what ravages in the enemy ranks it was difficult to judge. Now, at the order of their chief, they started hurling all sorts of things, as planned, which caused great havoc and confusion among the attackers. So much so that the chap on the ladder sang out:

'For the Love of God don't let go.'

Still he went on chipping just the same.

So Pierre d'Aranluz, who had so far held us back from chucking any of the logs, now cried:

'Logs, boys. Let him have it.'

Fortunately the defences below had not been neglected either. For, having launched an assault craft on the moat, the attackers attempted to approach the lower postern, which, as all know, is just below the main entrance, now closed by the drawbridge.

Our artillery was waiting for them. Through the iron grill of the postern a nozzle was trained on them, and as they came near they were drenched with water, and it was icy cold, that water, believe me.

Seizing the psychological moment to clench the victory, Pierre d'Aranluz now gave the order:

'Release the Greek Fire.'

That was formidable. There was a whole demi-john full of the stuff all ready, and when it was poured out and lit with a match, a mysterious blaze spread all over the walls of the stronghold, dripped down upon the enemy in trickles of fire, whose intense heat melted breastplates like butter, and spread over the moat, which became a lake of flames. At the same time red and green Bengal lights were shot from the battlements, by whose light a terrible disorder could be seen in the ranks of the routed besiegers. Their defeat was complete.

Tatave read through what he had written and found it a very beautiful piece of prose. Admittedly he had tampered with the truth here and there, particularly when he came to the Greek fire. M. Muche's alcohol, had, it is true, caught fire at once, having been previously heated up by Fébo, but it had gone out no less quickly, and Tatave had to confess to himself that his invention was not yet perfected.

He would have been very surprised to learn that his precious Greek fire had in fact been the principal reason why the mayor had suddenly given the order to abandon the assault.

'Whew! It's pretty nippy up there,' said Georget, rubbing his hands. 'And now it's started to drizzle. You'd better put some more clothes on before you go up.'

'I haven't got anything to put on,' said Tatave.

'Take a sack. That'd be something. You can wear it like a coal-man.'

'Anything doing?'

'I should think not! They won't start that again in a hurry.'

Tatave closed his note-book and carefully screwed the caps on his fountain-pens.

'Pretty good show, wasn't it? I bet my mother was there. And Piquet too. That'll stir up some trouble between them.'

Methodically he got ready to go on watch. First the Balaclava helmet, then the fireman's. Over that his hooded cape and finally the sack over the lot.

In the end he had added nearly a foot to his stature.

Less certain than his friend of the result of their escapade, Georget deliberately changed the subject.

'Everybody asleep?'

'Yes ... At least' (Tatave lowered his voice) 'I'm not sure about Pierrot. Sounded as if he was crying just now. But that's impossible. Anyhow, keep an eye on him.'

He moved off towards the spiral staircase, looking like a little gnome hawking carpets.

Georget sat warming his hands at the fire, stunned by what he had just been told.

Pierrot crying! Unthinkable! How could he be, after what had happened? A victory like that! It had been wonderful to see him giving orders. He had seemed to be defending the Bastide single-handed.

He had thought of everything and prevented them using up their ammunition too soon.

The fireworks had been stupendous. Fired in all directions they had scared the women and kept them running this way and that.

Pierrot crying! Pierrot who had made short work of the hefty lout Victorin when he had spoken of surrender. Pierrot who had forced the journalist fellow to relieve Fébo on the pump. And all the time keeping everybody's spirits up by telling them they were winning and that the Bastide would never fall.

Pierrot crying! Georget couldn't bear to leave the matter in doubt any longer, and, before turning in, he went over to the corner where the chief was lying.

There was little light from the fire and he couldn't see much of Pierrot's face, but when he touched it he knew at once.

'What's the matter, old chap?'

Pierrot didn't answer. His whole body was shaken by sobs. The despair of a child is complete and absolute, for he has no experience by which to measure it.

Nothing is more touching than the grief of one we have regarded as immune from human weaknesses, and Georget Grillon was profoundly moved at finding in his leader a boy as vulnerable as himself, though it may be added that Georget was pretty good at hiding his feelings behind a joke.

He groped for some consoling words, but could only stammer:

'Come on, what is it? ... You mustn't ... Hush, think of the others ... What would they say?'

The others! Magic words.

Abruptly Pierrot stopped sobbing and pulled himself together.

He sat up, and, opening his hand, said:

'Look.'

Lying on the palm of his hand, Mascha lay dead.

This was the most heart-rending moment of Pierrot's young life. This was the first object of his love he had seen die. It might be only a white mouse: that didn't make any difference. He had loved it. A belated sob shook him again.

'And the awful thing is, I killed him myself.'

'You?'

'Yes. It must have been when I leant over the battlements to throw a log. I crushed him. I didn't know anything about it at the time. It was only afterwards when I took him out to say good night to him – I found him quite cold with a little drop of blood on his nose. You see, it's the punishment of God.'

Georget couldn't help shrugging his shoulders.

'God? Do you really think he bothers about things like that?'

Pierrot frowned.

'Besides,' went on Georget, 'if there was a God there wouldn't be all this trouble in the world. Unless he made the trouble too, and then you couldn't call him good.'

'Shut up. You don't know what you're talking about. Of course God's good, or I'd never have had Mascha at all. And Mascha loved me. I know he did ... And now I've gone and killed him ... Of course it was only an accident, but that doesn't alter the fact that I did it, that he was killed by his own friend ... I thought what we were doing was right, but now I don't know, since it's killed Mascha ... It wasn't God that killed him. It was me, I tell you, me ...'

Georget found it difficult to understand. Death was presented to his mind in such a very different guise. His mother, with a white face, lying still on a bed. A mother! After all there's a difference between a mother and a white mouse! Supposing Pierrot's mother died? What would he think then?

He almost asked the question, but thought better of it. It was hardly the way to comfort a chap. Instead, he said:

'Fortunately you've got the dogs. They love you too ... I must get some sleep now. Good night.'

'Good night.'

Dogs? Yes, there were the dogs. Boulou and Barbette were nice. He was fond of them, of course. But you didn't have to protect dogs; they could look after themselves, and that made all the difference. And then ... Well, they couldn't run up your sleeve and wriggle in your hair ... No. A dog was just a dog. While Mascha ...

And it seemed to Pierrot as though life had lost its meaning.

'This is too much!' muttered M. Grillon as he stood disconsolately contemplating the scene.

'Too much!'

Ranavalo capered round him, then crouched at his feet, wagging her tail, looking up at him expectantly. But today her master could make no response to her morning exuberance.

'And she didn't bark this time either,' said the schoolmaster to himself, his mind in a turmoil.

He glanced at the Bastide, where there was nothing to see but a flapping flag and a rising wisp of smoke.

'In that case ...'

He would have liked to give Ranavalo a hearty kick, but was too much under the sway of principles to give way to any such outburst.

Crushed by his discovery, he didn't even think of repairing this new disaster, and, leaving the pillaged hive just as it was, he turned back to the house, a downcast man with shuffling gait, as though suddenly grown old.

After breakfast, he sat on at the kitchen table with his head in his hands until the boys of the lower form arrived. He forgot all about shaving.

A tug-of-war was going on between his self-esteem and his scruples. He was a scrupulous man, exceptionally so, but he also had a decidedly good opinion of himself. It was going to cost him a lot to admit he had made a mistake, still more to say so before all the world. Yet that was exactly what he ought to do. He was no longer interested in finding out who had robbed him. What mattered was the rehabilitation of those he had wrongly accused. His duty lay before him, clear, straight, inescapable.

And yet ... Well, he needed a little time to think it over. So, giving his pupils an exercise to do, he plunged back into his own reflections, taking no notice whatever of paper missiles and other classroom sports, which went on unchecked.

Yes, his duty was clear – that was settled. What occupied him now was to determine how he should set about it and to foresee the consequences.

He had hardly been seen in the town since his row with M. Muche. The only dignified course had seemed to him to withdraw and meditate on the folly of human passions. His reappearance now would certainly give rise to eager comment, particularly if, as seemed likely, he felt obliged to call on all the parents of the boys concerned.

'And once again,' he repeated, 'I shall find myself up against vulgar incomprehension. But Fabienne, at any rate, ought to appreciate the nobility of my motives, and if she does, that will repay me for all the rest.'

Fortified by that hope, he dismissed the class a full three minutes early and set out for the mayor's house, striding along with a vigour that was so infectious that Grisouille, who had nothing better to do at the moment, gaily trotted after him.

The Allée des Trois Tourelles was still strewn with logs which no one had been adventurous enough to pick up. Déodat forced himself not to look up at the battlements, having little doubt he had been noticed and was now being talked about. To feign indifference seemed the best way of preserving his dignity in front of his pupils.

Suddenly he thought of the donkey following him. That was just the sort of thing children pounced on with their scurrilous minds, and he grew more and more self-conscious.

All at once he swung round, waved his arms, and shouted at the animal:

'Shoo! Be off!'

Grisouille stopped dead and studied him closely.

'Be off!' he shouted again, not angrily, but with great firmness.

Then he resumed his walk. Grisouille pondered for a moment, then fell in behind him again, though this time at a more respectful distance.

Mme Muche opened the door. She had hardly stopped crying for the last two days, and her eyelids looked as though they had been boiled in tears.

Recognizing the schoolmaster, she recoiled imperceptibly.

'Here we are again!' she said to herself. 'More complications, and no doubt another row.'

But she forced a smile to her lips.

'My husband isn't back yet, Monsieur.'

'In that case I'll wait for him, if you don't mind.'

The distillery siren blew. He couldn't have long to wait.

'If you'll come this way ...'

She took him into the drawing-room, feeling in her apron pocket to make sure the tablets were there. They'd be needed.

M. Grillon refused to sit down. To add solemnity to the occasion, he was wearing gloves.

Guillaume Muche came in with his belly thrust out before him and his thumbs hooked in the sleeve-holes of his waistcoat, a favourite attitude of his when he sent some importunate traveller about his business.

'Monsieur,' he began at once, 'if it's the mayor you want to see, I'm available every evening between six and seven. If it's on business, my secretary can arrange an appointment at my office. In my home I'm not at anyone's disposal, least of all at a time when reasonable people take their midday meal.'

Disconcerted by this frontal attack, Déodat took a deep breath which sounded too much like a sigh.

'Monsieur,' he managed to reply, 'it's not as mayor that you are receiving this visit, nor yet as … industrialist, but as the father of a boy whose care has been confided to me.'

'In which capacity you have acquitted yourself in the worst possible manner, M. l'Instituteur, which indeed I intend to report to the proper authorities at the first suitable moment.'

For a second, M. Grillon closed his eyes. Then, sustained by the promptings of his conscience, he began again, speaking very gently:

'I have come, M. le Maire, to give you a piece of information which I am afraid can only strengthen your unfavourable opinion of me, so you can believe me when I say that I have not undertaken this mission lightheartedly. To come straight to the point, my garden was broken into again last night and another hive was pillaged – I might say destroyed, in view of the fact that there was a sharp frost this morning – a new hive which was giving unusual promise … There, M. Muche! That's what I've come to tell you.'

With a rather touching gesture, he opened his gloved hands, as though placing himself at the other's mercy.

Guillaume Muche opened his keen, coal-black eyes.

'What earthly interest is that to me?'

At this gross lack of understanding, M. Grillon bristled, but he forced himself to remain outwardly calm.

'Of no direct interest to you, no doubt, but to our children of very great interest indeed. I accused them of theft, misled by appearances, which were in fact very much against them.'

Indulging in his favourite form of repartee, the mayor hurled the word back at his visitor.

'You can go to blazes with your appearances.'

'I'm taking my leave of you now, in fact I would not wish to stay under your roof a moment longer. I have accomplished my task. You now know the truth. Our children are guiltless. Indeed I would go as far as to say that their action in rebelling against the injustice with which I was treating them – in good faith, mark you – has even a certain merit.'

'Merit be damned!'

'Well, there you are! You know. They say that only fools are incapable of changing their mind, and I might add in my own defence that the man who never made a mistake never did anything else.'

In a trice the distiller's face turned scarlet.

'So that's what you've come to tell me, is it? At a moment like this …'

He whipped a newspaper out of his pocket and brought it down with all his strength on the mantelpiece.

'At a moment when these damn-fool whipper-snappers are causing us the utmost annoyance, because of you, M. l'Instituteur, because of you … at a moment when we are being held up to ridicule in the newspapers and when the whole district, indeed the whole of France, is laughing at us … at a moment when I have on my hands two men injured by logs and a wife who never stops crying over our nitwit of a Victorin, dragged into this escapade because he's too stupid to know better … at a moment like this you come here to tell me that your pupils were quite right to take you for what I think you are but which I won't give a name to. The newspapers are doing their best to make me look a fool, but let me tell you this, M. l'Instituteur – if there's any fool, idiot, or imbecile among us he's standing where you're standing now, or my name's not Guillaume Muche.'

Déodat took another deep breath. Even now he kept himself in hand.

'I had hoped my frankness would meet with a different reception,' he said. 'But no matter. Nothing will stop me proclaiming the innocence of my pupils. As was my duty, I have come in the first place to you, but as that is of no avail I must publish the truth elsewhere, if necessary in the columns of the newspapers, whose representatives are not far to seek.'

At the mention of the newspapers, the mayor's face went still darker in colour.

'You'll do no such thing,' he roared. 'You'll go straight home and keep your damn-fool mouth shut. If not you'll regret it – I'll cook your goose for you if it's the last thing I do on earth.'

'But …'

'There's no "but" about it. There's just one damn-fool silly thing left for you to do in this sorry business – that's to go blabbing to those pestilential newspaper men.'

The mayor opened the *Éclair Perpignanais* with a flourish.

'Listen to this:

'We are in full agreement with those of our readers who have written to us expressing their astonishment at the continuance of this ridiculous siege, which a minimum of skilful handling and psychological insight would have avoided. We have before us the spectacle of a bunch of children playing knights in armour, but, instead of their being treated as such, they are taken seriously, and against them has been launched a major offensive which anybody could have seen was doomed to ignominious failure, and which in fact resulted only in minor injuries to two men and the beginnings of a fire. For that we may be thankful, as there might well have been fatal casualties. It is difficult to find words sufficiently strong to characterize the ineptitude of the authorities concerned.

'There you are, M. l'Instituteur! That's the sort of thing he's writing, this Balthazar Durand. And that's the sort of man you're now going to pour out your heart to, beating your breast and telling him it's all your fault … All right! Go and tell him that silly rigmarole about your honey – and see what use he makes of it. And while you're about it you can tell him I'm resigning. I'm not going to be mayor of this town, if any upstart journalist can come and teach me my own business. Go on, hurry up. Go and make friends with Balthazar Durand if you like, but in any case clear out of my house, you and your gloves and your absurd solemnity. Get out before I kick you out.'

M. Grillon found himself in the street without having any clear idea of how he'd got there. He blew his nose, took yet another breath, then set out for the herbalist's.

When Mme Fabienne heard the bell ring, she thought it must be some emergency call. Otherwise people rarely disturbed her at meal-times.

Throwing off her apron, she went into the shop, but stopped dead, horror-stricken at the sight of the schoolmaster.

For him to visit her, openly, in the middle of the day could only mean one thing – that something had happened to Tatave.

'Is he injured?' she stammered. 'Don't conceal anything. Let me know the worst.'

M. Grillon thought her very beautiful in her distress. He took his hat off with a sweep.

'Let me reassure you at once, my dear lady. I've not come about your dear boy. At least, not about him especially. I come with good news.'

Noticing his gloves and the solemnity of his manner, another idea darted through her mind – he had come to ask her hand in marriage.

Torn between embarrassment and pleasure, she asked him to come in. He refused a chair and remained standing as he talked.

He talked on and on, but to tell the truth Mme Fabienne was soon bored by the story of his hives. Though outwardly attentive, her mind was occupied in taking stock of him. She noticed he hadn't shaved, and took rather a poor view of that omission. She noticed that the stubble on his chin was grey. It made him look a bit older. As for the innocence of those boys, what was the point of hammering away at that? As though anyone couldn't see that her Tatave wasn't a thief!

'I felt I must come and tell you the whole story at once, so that this false accusation shouldn't rest a moment longer on the heads of our poor children.'

'My poor Tatave!' she was saying to herself. 'To think I was considering giving you this old windbag for a stepfather!'

'Not for a moment do I regret the loss of this second hive,' he went on, 'for it has restored to us something far more precious, our confidence in the younger generation. That is why I have taken the liberty ...'

'That's all very well, my friend, but it doesn't make any difference to the situation. My Tatave is still shut up in that Bastide, and every minute of the day I'm wondering what sort of state he'll be in when he comes back to me.'

'Excuse me, but it makes all the difference in the world. Since I acknowledge their innocence, there's no longer any question of my punishing them. In other words, there's no longer any reason for them to hold out against us.'

'But how are you to let them know?'

'I admit there's that difficulty.'

His voice had changed slightly. His optimism was evaporating.

'Look here,' said Mme Fabienne, 'let's go and talk it over with M. le Curé. Perhaps he'll have an idea.'

'With the curé?'

The suggestion was disconcerting. It hurt his pride to seek the advice of the Church, which he regarded as an obscurantist institution. But after all this wasn't the moment to think of his pride. Besides, if it would please Fabienne ...

'Splendid!' said the Abbé Escoutou.

There was a trace of yolk of egg at the corner of his mouth, for they had caught him just as he was starting his lunch. He hated anything which jolted him out of the ordinary routine of his life, but, since annoyance was unchristian, he did his utmost to hide it.

'Look here, M. le Curé, things can't be allowed to go on like this. My Tatave, who's the best boy in the world, has been dragged into this disreputable adventure and ...'

'That's not quite what we've come to discuss,' interrupted M. Grillon. 'The thing is that my pupils were the victims of injustice. Call it a judicial error, if you like.'

'Splendid ...'

'I have no idea who robbed my hives, but I do know for certain that it wasn't them. And since an unmerited punishment was imposed on them, I am bound to admit that they were justified in rebelling against it.'

'Wait a moment, my dear M. Grillon. You're taking indulgence too far. The first duty of those boys was to obey. Remember what they taught you when you did your military service. Carry out your punishment first and complain afterwards.'

'I could never accept that, M. le Curé. It strikes at the very root of human dignity.'

'All the same, I consider your pupils acted very wrongly in revolting against their parents and their teacher. To say nothing of the fact that they put themselves in a position in which they were unable to perform their religious duties, at all events not properly ... No. We cannot approve what they've done, though naturally we shall receive them with open arms at the first sign of repentance.'

'How are you going to get them to repent?' asked Mme Grosbelhomme.

'I don't know exactly. But there's a new element in the situation now which you may not be aware of. You haven't seen *Paris-Cinq-Heures* today, have you? I don't read the papers myself as a rule, but under the present circumstances ... Now, where did I put it? Valérie! Valérie! Where's the paper got to?'

The housekeeper had been making as much clatter with her saucepans as she decently could as a hint to the visitors that their arrival was untimely. She now came bustling in with a fork in her hand and a hostile look in her eye.

'The joint's ready,' she announced, deciding that, since hints were of no avail, she must make it quite plain to the visitors that they were intruding.

'Splendid ... But that wasn't what I called you for. Where's the paper?'

'How should I know? Unless it's in your overcoat pocket. That's where you usually put it.'

'Oh, yes. Of course. Thank you. And now my glasses ... It's not fun growing old. Ah! Here they are. That's better ...'

With regard to the events in Casteilcorbon, this newspaper is fortunate in having secured the services of its special correspondent Balthazar Durand. For not only was he the first on the spot, but he has throughout been supplying our readers with news that was well in advance of that published by our rivals. Never was the expression 'inside information' more apposite. For while the mayor with all the municipal services at his command was trying vainly to reduce the stronghold by a frontal assault, M. Balthazar Durand was in the heart of the citadel itself, interviewing its defenders and watching them repel the attack.

I have seen the defenders of the Bastide, he writes, and have even photographed them. I cannot reveal how. A reporter is not a policeman, and however desirous I may be to see the termination of an episode that brings nothing but dishonour and ridicule on the authorities of this little town, I must not say a word which could betray the one weak spot in the defences.

And who are these defenders I interviewed? A bunch of mere

children. The son of the mayor is the only one old enough to be in long trousers, though not old enough, it must be added, to exert a sobering influence on his comrades, whose heads are full of romantic nonsense. Nothing could be more comic than the solemn tone in which they address each other by ancient titles of nobility.

Your reporter too was awarded a title – that of Official War Correspondent – which carries with it the right to wear, like the knights themselves, a fireman's helmet adorned with goose-feathers …

'You see, Mme Grosbelhomme … That makes things look different, doesn't it?'

'In what way?'

'It's like this … Here's M. Grillon telling us that the boys never stole his honey, and he no longer wants to punish them. So there's really no point in their holding out any longer … On the other hand, here's a journalist who, if he's speaking the truth, has means of getting in touch with them. A go-between, sent to us by Providence.

'He's staying at the Auberge Daranluz I believe. Try and get hold of him. See if he'll act as a …'

Mme Fabienne was already on her feet.

'Oh, but you must come with us, M. le Curé. Please. It'll make all the difference.'

The Abbé Escoutou threw a wistful glance in the direction of the kitchen. But wasn't the hardest course always the right one?

Meekly he fetched his hat and followed the others out of the house. That evening Maria joined the knights earlier than usual. She was quite at ease among them now. Putting down on the big drum the things she had brought – a four-pound loaf and a shapeless packet badly tied up – she started chattering at once, giving the news, of which she had plenty.

'I slipped away as soon as the meal was over, and to hell with the washing-up. I told Mme Fine I'd a splitting headache … Now look here, you chaps, you'd better watch out. I don't like the way things are shaping.'

From inside her dress she produced two crumpled newspapers.

'But first of all you ought to see what he says about you, and I expect you'll like it no better than I do. Here's *Paris-Cinq-Heures* and the *Éclair*. He told me I wasn't to show them to you.'

'Who?'

'That newspaper man of ours. If he'd known me a bit better, it's the last thing he'd have said, for telling me not to do something is the best way of getting me to do it. I nipped into his room before coming. Here, Cisco, read it out to them.'

He opened the papers and started reading. The story, flattering enough in itself, was completely marred by the sneering comments, each one of which damped their spirits like a bucketful of cold water.

... Children playing at knights in armour ...

... A bunch of mere children ...

... Nothing could be more comic than the solemn tone in which they address each other by ancient titles of nobility ...

'That's enough,' cried Pierrot at last, bringing his fist down with a thump on the big drum.

Thoughts and feelings were in a turmoil. Only Tatave was able to speak calmly.

'I knew he was a traitor from the start. You can see. I've got it written down. But I couldn't say anything at the time, as he'd managed to throw dust in your eyes.'

'He's worse than a traitor. He's a criminal.'

'A dirty crook ...'

They each had to have their word for him, and they'd have gone on a long time if Maria hadn't intervened.

'Listen. That's not what matters. Who cares what they say in the papers? It's all rot, anyway ... What I've come to tell you is much worse than all that, and I'm all hot and bothered about it. Before lunch was over the curé came with Tatave's mother and Georget's father – Piquet as we call him. They made a bee-line for Balthazar's table and in a moment they were all huddled round it, putting their heads together. After a bit, the mistress joined them, and Balthazar stood them each a coffee and a glass of liqueur. "That stinks," I said to myself. But there was no way of finding out what they were saying. You know what your mother's like, Pierrot. Kept on sending me on useless errands to the kitchen, to keep me out of hearing.'

'You can leave my mother out of this,' said the gallant knight.

'Oh, I didn't mean anything. It was just to show you they were saying things that they didn't want me to hear. Finally, I did manage to get near them as I cleared the tables. They were talking about the disappearance of the dogs. Balthazar grinned and smirked and they fired questions at him which I couldn't catch. But in the end the curé said: "Splendid. God will bless you, my son." '

'You see,' said Tatave. 'He's given us away. He's told them about the underground passage.'

Maria shrugged her shoulders.

'Perhaps he has. Perhaps he hasn't. I couldn't hear any more, as I was sent off to the kitchen again.'

The knights were profoundly shocked. Balthazar's perfidy went beyond all bounds. After all the things he had given them and the encouragement ... After revealing the enemy's plans and even helping to work the pump during the attack ... And then to go over to the other side ...

Once again Pierrot reproached himself bitterly for being too trustful. The expression on his face had changed since Mascha's death. He had done a lot of thinking. And the more he had thought about his responsibility as chief the less clear his duty appeared. To make up for inward doubts, he became outwardly more and more dictatorial. This was just as well, as the enthusiasm of his followers was waning. The flush of adventure had faded. What with the cold and Fébo's boiled corn, the game was beginning to pall.

For a moment Pierrot's courage flagged too, and he would have liked to be one of the rank and file.

'Am I any less of a boy than the others?' he thought. 'Why should I have to take everything on my shoulders?'

But he pulled himself together, asking:

'Is your chap coming back here again tonight, Maria?'

Maria bristled.

'Don't call him that. He's not "my chap". I've no use for him at all. Quite apart from what he's done to you, he's running after all the little girls in the place. Even Nièves. Yes, Cisco, your sister. A little girl like that! It seems they've been seen out in the country together ... As for whether he's coming tonight, I think he is. He said he wanted to show you the photos he took ... Of course that's just eyewash. He wants to get hold of some more stuff to put in his articles. That's all he thinks about. That's why he made up to me. But I can see through him now, the little skunk.'

'Knights! Knights!' cried Balthazar from the depth of the dungeon. 'Listen to me, please. What you're doing is absurd.'

His voice became more and more supplicating as he lost little by little the human dignity which M. Grillon was wont to speak of.

Blinded by Tatave's belly-band, he had only been able to offer a haphazard resistance when the hefty Victorin had fallen upon him. Seized by many hands, his bottom pinched by Tatave, he had finally been deposited triumphantly, all trussed up with string, in front of the fire, like an explorer about to be roasted by cannibals.

'We mustn't hurt him,' said Pierrot.

But that didn't stop Maria from sitting down on the prisoner, pinching his nose and shaking his head from one side to the other.

It hadn't been easy to get him down the ladder into the dungeon.

No chance of his escaping now. Nevertheless Tatave eagerly volunteered for the post of janitor, and from the floor above he looked down contemptuously on his literary rival, at the same time fondling the axe.

'Knights! Knights!' whined the war correspondent. 'You must listen to me. It's serious. I was bringing you an offer of peace. I'm your friend, and I can promise you won't be punished … You must believe me … I've got a cold as it is, and in this place …'

When he had had enough of the journalist's lamentations, the incorruptible janitor put his head down into the hole.

'Shut up, traitor, or I'll spit on you.'

'To work,' cried the chief. 'Flood the passage.'

Naturally the idea was Riquet's, whose training at the forge seemed to have given him a sound grasp of military engineering. At any rate he understood the principle of a siphon.

Once again the pump was rigged up. The suction hose was lowered into the moat, the other led down into the passage. A few strokes of the pump, and the rest could be left to natural forces.

'Wonderful!' shouted Victorin from below. 'It's coming out thick as my arm.'

Astonished themselves at their success, the knights were jubilant. For a while they sat in ecstatic silence listening to the sound of running water. Admittedly the stagnant water didn't smell any too good, but the dogs were the only ones to mind. They stood up, sniffing uneasily. Finally, as another scent reached their nostrils, they dashed off on a wild chase after the rats which the flood was dislodging. The boys joined in, armed with anything they could lay their hands on, and a grand hunt ensued. Only Georget kept out of it. Rats gave him the shivers. But, feeling he must do something, he got up on the big drum with a trumpet by way of huntsman's horn.

Echoes of the din reached the prisoner's ears, and he considered them far from reassuring.

The happiest of all was Maria. Her retreat was now cut off.

'*Dios mio!* What are we going to do with her?' asked Cisco, speaking in the disgusted tone he always adopted when girls were under discussion.

'We'll keep her.'

'I suppose we'll have to give her a title.'

There was a good deal of discussion on that point, till Pierrot said finally:

'We must leave that to the Chevalier de Grosbel.'

'She certainly deserves one.'

'If it hadn't been for her, we'd have had the whole crowd trooping along that passage first thing tomorrow morning. We'd have been properly caught.'

'And think of all the things she b ... brought us to eat.'

It was near midnight. The water was still running. A feeling of security and of having gained another victory filled the boys' hearts. And, with that, they were suddenly hungry.

Riquet was eyeing some gingerbread brought by the unhappy war correspondent.

'Don't touch them,' ordered Pierrot, intercepting his glance.

'They might be poisoned.'

'Perhaps. But even if they were all right we wouldn't lower ourselves by eating them.'

That left the big loaf and the mysterious packet Maria had brought. Proudly she pulled it over towards her and began to undo it.

'Here's something to put on your bread,' she announced.

Necks were craned.

'Honey! Ugh,' exclaimed Fébo disgustedly.

There they were – three sections of honeycomb still in their wooden frames, just as they had been taken from the hive.

Maria licked her fingers.

'Nice of me, wasn't it? You've got to look out, you know, with those nasty things … Take care there aren't still some crawling about … You think they're asleep, and the next thing you know they're all over you, in your hair and all. The first time, I got so badly stung, I was limping for days … If it hadn't been for your sake, I'd never have had a second shot.'

NINE

Ten days had been enough to strip the poplars of their last yellowing leaves, and the trees now stood up gaunt and motionless along the main road. Nothing moved in their branches except the rooks, which perched in them when they were tired of the battlements of the Bastide.

Ten days ...

From the Auberge Daranluz it was now possible, as always during winter months, to tell the time by the clock in the church tower between the fourth and the fifth plane tree along the Allée des Trois Tourelles.

At about eight o'clock on the morning of the eleventh day, that is to say on Wednesday, 9 November, Georget, who was on watch, saw something which gave him a nasty jolt. Along the main road, between the bare poplars, a red object had come into sight and was rapidly getting bigger. Already he could distinguish the wheels, the row of silvery helmets, and the brass fittings glittering in the sun.

The fire-escape from Perpignan.

'That's torn it,' said the look-out, with a mixture of despair and relief that the inevitable end had come at last.

He blew a blast on the bombardon to raise the alarm.

The scarlet vehicle swept into Casteilcorbon and drew up in front of the Town Hall. Lazily, the firemen got down from their perches. There were thirteen of them, including the driver. An unlucky number, that.

Georget watched them through the telescope, studying every detail – their leather jerkins, their parti-coloured belts, their top-boots. They looked calmly up at the Bastide, then stood around in little groups. It wasn't long before some of them went into the inn.

All the small boys of the town were gathered round in no time, staring at the gleaming vehicle.

Pierrot was watching from above. Gravely, but it seemed reluctantly, he gave the order:

'Bring up the rest of the logs.'

Tatave hastily scribbled it down for future use, but he regretted that at so historic a moment their chief had spoken in such simple words.

The life-and-death struggle had come.

The knights prepared themselves for death.

It wasn't until ten that the other car arrived. A black, luxurious one. It, too, stopped in front of the Town Hall, where the whole Council was waiting, hastily summoned by François Tistounet, to greet the 'unexpected' arrival of the Prefect of the Department.

They had been obliged to come just as they were, in their working clothes, Guillaume Muche being the only one in a collar and tie.

He had had a good deal to say as he struggled with the over-starched collar.

'What the hell's he want to come barging in here for?' he kept repeating, though what was really bothering him was whether he ought to call the Prefect Monsieur or Your Excellency.

When the moment came, all doubts were instantly dispelled, and he opted for the second form of address.

Indeed, M. Arnold Laprade de la Chaize was the very incarnation of provincial aristocracy. His name had certainly served him well. For it cannot be denied that quarterings of nobility stand a man in good stead in the service of La République. His hair, his clothes, and his opinions blended perfectly. It seemed as if this young prefect – and he was the youngest in the whole of France – found each morning, as he looked in the glass, the smile which suited him best, and he succeeded in keeping it there for the rest of the day. Nor was the picture in any way spoiled by a slightly impish wit and a contempt for red tape.

He enjoyed puzzling his subordinates. When he said yes to a question, he would sometimes add: 'But you'd better be quick about it, as tomorrow the answer might be no.' And he would laugh in so strange a fashion that they would hurry away wondering whether it was still yes or already almost no.

How could a Laprade de la Chaize fail to be captivated by the knights' escapade, each new development of which he had followed with gusto in the newspapers?

'M. le Maire,' he began with his usual disarming urbanity, 'M. le Maire, let me first of all assure you that I have come here quite un-officially.'

With easy grace he shook hands with the councillors and even with François Tistounet, who has never quite recovered from the surprise.

'You were quite right to refer the matter to the Département, and, as you see, our loyal Fire Brigade has promptly hastened to your aid. We are of course in complete agreement – this ... this joke – shall we say this ill-considered joke – cannot be allowed to continue much longer. So I thought I would call on you in person to tell you how much I appreciate the restraint with which you have so far acted and to give you my best wishes for a speedy conclusion of this affair.'

Muche could hardly believe his ears. He stood with his forefinger hooked into his collar, thinking to himself:

'Really, he's not such a bad chap after all, this Prefect.'

Opening his elegant hands, Arnold Laprade de la Chaize seemed to be asking his hearers a favour as he went on:

'Supposing we all put our heads together. First of all perhaps you'd put me in the picture, starting from the beginning. And, by the way, as a matter of curiosity, I'd like to see the schoolmaster and the parents of the boys concerned.'

'Tistounet! Tistounet!' shouted the mayor, now full of zeal. 'You heard what His Excellency said. Bring them here at once, at the double.'

What the Prefect kept to himself was the fact that he had intervened at the express request of Messrs Durand Frères of Agen, anxious about the fate of their son and nephew respectively, and, still more, under pressure from *Paris-Cinq-Heures*, which in its latest edition had announced the mysterious disappearance of their special correspondent, and had launched out into a scurrilous tirade, not only against the Mayor of Casteilcorbon, but against the Departmental authorities as well.

After the children, it was now the grown-ups who were gathered round the fire-escape. The Place de la République was almost as lively as on a market day, but the goods dealt in this time were only rumours. Mme Broc was one of the first on the scene, leaving her shop to take care of itself, dealing out, right and left, every idea which came into her mind.

'Lord help us! It's as bad as in '83, when all those people disappeared. You know – from that haunted house at Estagel. It was the devil's work, believe me. And so's this. It's prayer that's wanted. That's what the Reverend Mother says. Prayer's the only thing to cast out the devil.'

'Go on!' sneered Pépé Combasil. 'The fire-escape'll be much more useful.'

'It's all very well to laugh. But what's been going on's not natural. First of all it's Fébo, vanishing without a trace. Then it's the boys shutting themselves up in the Bastide. And don't forget my goose. Then the dogs. And now half the water's gone from the moat. No, it's not natural.'

'And that's not all,' put in Sébastien. 'It seems the chap with the motor-bike's missing too, and the gendarmes are hunting for him everywhere. That's right, isn't it, Mme Fine?'

Pierrot's mother had just come up, followed by Viette, capering about like a young lamb.

'Yes, indeed,' sighed Mme Fine. 'There doesn't seem to be any end to our troubles.'

'You're hardly the one to complain, Mme Fine. With your place full of people all day long and doing a roaring trade.'

That was Pépé again. Mme Fine gave him a black look, for there was some truth in what he said. With all the journalists hanging about, takings had indeed soared, though the good woman would have swapped them without a second's hesitation for her missing boy.

Guste, the baker, joined them, then the Abbé Escoutou, who hadn't been able to resist for long the temptation to glean a little news.

'Yes, M. le Curé, it's the firemen from Perpignan with that there ladder. They'll pick those boys off the battlements like birds out of a nest. There's forty of them at least – that's what Tistounet said just now as he went off to fetch M. Grillon. Only he did say the ladder wasn't long enough. Said we'd only get them by tiring them out.'

'Oh, Tistounet! He's been saying that for the last week and more.'

'What's going on?' asked Mme Grosbelhomme, in more of a flutter than ever. 'More bad news, I suppose. And what do they want the schoolmaster for?'

'To congratulate him.'

'Congratulate him? What for?'

'It's the Prefect. Seems he's been congratulating everybody. My Benoît too. There's an important meeting going on now.'

'So long as they find a way of getting Tatave back.'

'They seem to be chiefly worried about the journalist.'

'What's so odd is his motor-bike being there. It's still in the garage. And the doors to the yard were bolted inside ...'

'Do you think it's him what's carried off Maria?'

'She's not gone far,' affirmed the baker's wife. 'I saw her yesterday up on the roof of the Bastide. I'm sure I did.'

'So did I,' said Guste. 'And with her skirt blowing out in the wind we saw her ...'

'That'll do, Guste. No need to tell us what you saw. And with M. le Curé standing here.'

The Abbé Escoutou made a gesture with his hand, brushing the subject aside indulgently.

'I don't care to think of my Tatave being locked up with the likes of her. If the mayor had only acted with a bit more drive.'

Mme Fine turned on her impatiently.

'Drive! Drive! It's easily said, but you need quite a bit of it to climb up a hundred-foot wall.'

Viette listened intently.

'Are they going to fetch Pierrot?' she asked at last. 'They won't hurt him, will they?'

Which expressed what was at the back of all the mothers' minds.

Arnold Laprade de la Chaize was enjoying himself enormously. Never, since he had been the Government's representative in the Department of the Pyrénées-Orientales, had he come upon a bit of official business that was anything like so amusing.

As the story was unfolded, and M. Muche painted the villainy of the schoolboys in darker and darker colours, he regretted more and more keenly that he was too old by thirty years to join the ranks of the insurgents.

Thirty years too late! Alas! Yet, as the mayor stormed on, he could pass the time agreeably enough picturing himself strutting along the battlements, brandishing his prefect's sword, which had a mother-of-pearl handle.

'Nitwits, Your Excellency, damn-fool nitwits – that's what I always thought of them. But then, when they sent me that letter ... Where is it, now? ... Here ... Just read it, Your Excellency ... Unheard-of impertinence ...'

But if M. le Préfet was enjoying every moment of it, and if at the back of his mind he kept framing the words: *blustering old fool*, he kept such a perfect control of his features that no one had any suspicion of what was going on in his mind.

Calmly he read the letter the mayor had handed him.

'So it comes to this,' he said firmly. 'These little rascals have been protesting their innocence from the start, and, from what M. Grillon has been telling us, they weren't altogether unjustified. And I must add in passing that the scruple which has prompted their master to admit his mistake does him the utmost credit.'

M. Grillon's breast heaved. Here at last was someone who understood him.

But Guillaume Muche gave him a look which condemned him to damn-fool nitwitry in perpetuity.

'All things considered,' went on the Prefect, 'we should be well advised to regard this affair as a simple misunderstanding, magnified out of all proportion by the romantic imaginations of these extraordinary boys. Don't forget that thirteen to fourteen is the golden age of unreason. So, if you agree, we'll forget our years and our experience and render homage to the determined resistance of these knights. With that, we can talk to them as equals and come to terms over an honourable armistice.'

Guillaume Muche was aghast. As equals! An honourable armistice! Then this Prefect must be as much of a damn-fool nitwit as those who were causing all this trouble!

'What I would advise you to do, M. le Maire, is to hoist a white flag over the Town Hall. You could do the same over the school, M. Grillon. And all the boys' parents over their houses. They don't need to be real flags, of course. Table-napkins will do perfectly. The important thing is for it to be made quite clear to those young sparks – absolutely clear – that we ... that we call off hostilities.'

'But, Your Excellency! You can't really mean that.'

'It's not an order,' answered the Prefect, raising his eyebrows. 'It's merely my advice. But before you turn it down there's one thing I would like to point out to you. Theoretically, the fire-escape reaches higher than the battlements of the fortress. Theoretically, it would if it could get close enough to the base. But from the other side of the moat it would have to be lowered to an angle which would bring the end some ten feet short of the requisite height. The captain of the Fire Brigade has worked it out carefully, and that is his verdict.'

Dropping all pretence, M. Arnold Laprade de la Chaize smiled blandly at the assembly, obviously delighted by the captain's report.

'You see, gentlemen, our ancestors knew what they were about when they built these strongholds. And when we see them standing up to modern mechanical contrivances, we cannot but be proud of belonging to the race which created them.'

His enthusiasm was so infectious that it fired the Council with a sudden patriotism which found vent in a burst of applause, even the mayor joining in.

Maria never worked so hard nor with such goodwill. She was stacking the logs that were brought up from below, a stack at each corner of the keep, so that they would be at hand from whichever direction the attack was delivered.

Each log in turn she pictured crashing on to the head of one of the worthy citizens of Casteilcorbon, and the thought warmed her heart. For she hated her townsfolk, though she would have been at a loss to say why. Just the little daily pricks and humiliations, no doubt, that are the lot of a little slavey who is an orphan into the bargain. And now all her pent-up resentments were materialized in the shape of good, hard, heavy logs. It seemed to her that she would be happy for the rest of her life if she could just go on heaving logs over the battlements on to the heads of the people below.

Since she had been shut up in the Bastide, she had enjoyed every minute of her liberty. For here she was a queen. At any rate she was treated as such by a group of gallant knights. Even Fébo – who seemed to be getting a little crazier each day – even Fébo fell into line, waiting on her almost deferentially, always helping her first when he doled out the boiled corn with chocolate sauce.

Only the day before she had had the pleasant experience of repulsing Victorin, telling him out loud that he was not only a lout but a dirty swine as well. And then Tatave had put her up to his own particular diversion, that of spitting on the prisoner, a sport in which she displayed both keenness and skill.

Pierrot, of course, knew nothing about it. He would never have stood for such a thing. Maria judged his character pretty shrewdly, at any rate to the extent of knowing that he would never understand the joy that can be derived from being thoroughly beastly to someone. And, funnily enough, that was just why she adored him.

At the moment he was looking through the telescope, surveying the steadily growing crowd around the fire-escape.

He was grave.

Ten days of responsibility had left their mark on his face. Maria would have liked to reassure and encourage him, to make him laugh as he used to when they washed-up together in the scullery. But ever since she had brought that honey – and she had meant so well – he had hardly spoken to her. Sometimes she caught him looking at her reproachfully. She would have liked to explain to him … Just what did she want to explain? And how was she to go about it? She knew it was hopeless and held her peace.

Suddenly she started at the sound of his voice.

'Maria! Quick! Come here!'

She came over and leant over his shoulder.

'Look. Do you see?'

'Looks to me as if the whole place was crawling with maggots.'

'No, over there, to the right of the fire-escape … Do you see that black splodge? That's the curé. Then there's a lighter splodge at his side, and then a tiny one – that's Viette.'

Maria borrowed the telescope, but could see nothing but a misty disc peopled by phantoms.

'I don't see anything. Looks slimy – more like white of egg than anything else.'

What she was really thinking she kept to herself – that she didn't care who was there. What she would have liked was to heave a log right into the middle of them for the fun of seeing them scatter in all directions.

But at that moment she saw a tear glisten on the boy's cheek, and her hatred of humanity was obliterated by a great tenderness. She wanted to throw her arms round him and press him to her. She wanted to nurse and comfort him.

It was the first time her maternal instinct had peeped through the hard tomboy shell. But she made no move. After all, he was the son of the house in which she was a servant. He was her superior, and she couldn't forget it. Perhaps also an obscure delicacy prompted her to ignore this moment of weakness.

She went back to her logs, groping nevertheless for some helpful word to say to him. All she could find was:

'They must feel pretty small down there when they look up at us.'

Meanwhile in the lower regions of the Bastide a dark conspiracy was being hatched.

Panting and swearing, the Chevalier Henri du Martel was just starting up the spiral staircase with another load of logs when his name was called.

'Here! Riquet!'

Cisco and Victorin were standing by the store of wood, their job having been to select the logs that made the most suitable projectiles. Riquet noticed at once that there was something funny in their attitude. They seemed embarrassed. They had something to say to him, but didn't know quite how to begin.

Finally Cisco asked:

'Are you still keen on this silly game?'

Victorin mumbled something, looking down at his toes.

Riquet was so taken aback by the question that he merely stared.

No. He wasn't keen at all. He never had been. His imagination was not strongly developed, and all this chivalry and romance, with its blood oaths and passwords and fancy titles, left him stone cold. The food was awful. And it required no imagination to visualize the clouts and kicks in the pants which were to be the inevitable outcome.

But he had never complained. He had never thought of complaining. Pierrot wanted things that way: that was enough for him. He had sworn obedience and he obeyed, making himself as useful as he could. What more was there to say?

'We've had enough of it,' went on Cisco. 'We can't go on like this for ever. It's all very well playing up the old folks, but you can go too far. You think so too, don't you, Victorin?'

The hefty lout shifted his weight from one leg to the other, keeping an eye open for the sudden irruption of their leader or the inflexible Tatave.

'Sure, we've had enough of it,' he growled.

'And you know, Riquet, a fight with real firemen's hopeless from the start. We've done pretty well as it is. There's no point in burning

238

our boats. After all, if we give in now, our parents can't do much. We'll tell them it was Maria who took the honey.'

Henri du Martel went crimson to the roots of his hair.

'You mean you'll g ... go and sneak?'

'Don't be silly.'

'I d ... don't see what's silly about it?'

'You don't understand the first thing about it,' explained Cisco. 'You can't sneak on a girl, because girls don't count. Least of all Maria. She isn't one of us at all. She's only a little slavey. Besides, she'd no business to go taking that honey at all.'

'If you side with us, we'll be three against three, and as we're older that ought to count as a majority ... Look here. This is what we'll do. I'll go up with those logs and talk to Pierrot to keep him busy, while you go below and get the drawbridge down, since you're the only one who knows how ... And I bet you anything you like your dad'll be so glad to see you he'll forget all about kicking your backside ...'

'If you don't like the idea,' put in Victorin, 'you can always say the thing came down by accident. He wouldn't know any different. At least ...'

He didn't say any more, for Riquet had dropped all his logs except two which he poised menacingly. Stammering worse than ever, he snarled:

'D ... d ... do you w ... want m ... me to b ... bash your faces in?'

It was at that very moment that a long blast on the bombardon came echoing down the spiral staircase. Still holding his two logs, Riquet dashed up to the top as fast as his legs could carry him. The others followed at a more leisurely pace, drawn more by curiosity than by the call of duty.

On the upper platform, Georget and Tatave, hugging each other, were dancing frantically round the flag of the Friendly Society. Maria was uttering strange savage cries. Boulou and Barbette, thinking this was some new game, barked furiously, driving off the rooks that nested under the battlements.

With a log in each hand, Riquet stood and gaped. He even lost his stammer for a moment when he asked:

'What's up?'

Behind him, the other two appeared. They were greeted by Georget.

'Knights, this is the greatest moment in our lives.'

'Amen to that!' cried Tatave. 'Abracadabra! We've won. The only thing is now to celebrate the victory.'

'Not yet,' said Pierrot. 'It may be only a truce. Come and look.'

The new-comers came to the edge and looked over. Above the Town Hall a large white flag flapped heavily.

'Whew! A white flag!' muttered Cisco. 'They've hoisted the white flag.'

'Which means they're lifting the siege.'

'More than that,' said Tatave. 'They've capitulated.'

'Will they send emissaries?'

'How'll they send them, you great lout? And what for?'

'To discuss terms.'

'Victorin's right for once. There'll have to be terms. And, as we've won, it's for us to dictate them.'

'Terms? What d … do you m … mean?'

'Don't be an ass, Riquet. You know what a peace treaty is. You have to have it all down in black and white.'

'Particularly with Victorin's old man. It may be only a trick.'

'I say!' protested Victorin feebly.

Maria called out:

'Look! There's another.'

A second white flag had been hoisted over the school entrance. After that, they kept popping up all over the place – over the inn, over the presbytery, and again at the convent. The Reverend Mother was not to be outdone, and had got out all her Joan of Arc banners and streamers in Papal colours, white and yellow.

Tatave snuffled, even in the hour of victory.

'They're surrendering all along the line.'

'After all, it's about the only thing they could do,' put in Cisco, more cynically than ever, 'seeing we were going to fight it out to a finish.'

Riquet reddened again.

'Fight it out t … to a w … what?'

'You be careful, or you'll be stuttering again,' retorted the other with complete self-assurance.

'Come on. We're wasting time,' said Pierrot. 'Let's get down to

240

business. We'll send them another message setting out our conditions. Tatave will write it.'

Tatave got ready.

'*All prisoners to be returned,*' began the leader. 'They always put that in treaties. Though of course we're the only ones to have any.'

There was naturally a lot of argument about the terms, and it was finally decided that each of the knights should choose one for himself—anything he liked, provided it satisfied a legitimate aspiration.

Even that entailed a good deal of discussion. Riquet's first choice had been central heating for the school. Not that he had ever felt cold there. It was just that he would have liked to watch it being installed.

That was turned down, however. It wasn't a legitimate aspiration. When it came to Tatave's turn he announced gravely that he and the Chevalier de Grillon had a secret clause to insert.

'What about Maria? She hasn't said anything yet.'

'I'll choose for her,' said Pierrot. 'She's to have some bread and honey every time she goes to sweep out the classroom.'

'And what about you, Pierrot?'

'I don't want anything for myself.'

'Oh, come on! Be a sport. We've all chosen something. You must come into it too.'

'Very well. We're to be received with military honours as we march out of the Bastide.'

Not only were all the members of the Council present, but, as an exceptional measure, certain others had been invited too: the schoolmaster, Mme Grosbelhomme, M. Martelot, and the mason, Guartorella.

Reading out loud, the Prefect was coming to the end of the latest note from the occupants of the Bastide.

Those are our conditions. If you accept them, the *garde champêtre* can let us know by sounding the retreat on his bugle by four o'clock this afternoon. If he does not, it means hostilities continue.

Whereunto we have this day set our seals …

Gravely the Prefect read out the sonorous names and titles, and then the final:

Abracadabra. Blood and Freedom.

'What wonderful boys!' thought Arnold Laprade de la Chaize. 'Here was I doing my best to find an honourable way out for them, but it seems I have got to grovel in the dust. Never mind! My ancestors won't turn in their graves at seeing me licked by such noblemen as these.'

He smiled. He looked round the table at the councillors.

'Gentlemen,' he said sweetly, 'I'm going to ask you to give me a free hand to get this business settled as speedily as possible. You will agree with me, I feel sure, when I say that these young people are guilty of nothing beyond being rather too big for their boots. Their terms are quite in keeping with the chivalry that has gone to their heads, and, if you make allowances, not altogether unreasonable. I speak of course only of the published clauses. There remains the secret clause which was personally addressed to two people here present.'

All heads were turned towards M. Grillon and Mme Grosbelhomme. The former blushed like a boy whose first love-letter has been discovered. The latter, not in the least disconcerted, chuckled good-naturedly.

The Prefect would have loved to know what the joke was, but he was much too well bred to ask indiscreet questions, least of all in public and of a lady.

'Then may I take it that the secret clause is agreed to? ... Excellent. In that case I don't think I need detain you any longer. Your devoted mayor and I will work out the details of our ... our capitulation, and decide how to bring these children back into our humdrum world without jolting them too painfully out of their dreams of grandeur. Before this meeting breaks up, however, I would like to say one thing more. The way in which these boys have stood up for what they believed to be their rights is a testimonial both to their upbringing at home and to their education at school, and so long as we can produce boys with a sense of honour like theirs we need have no fears for the future of our beloved country.'

Guillaume Muche led the applause. Guartorella, who had been fidgeting nervously with his cap, dropped it hastily to join in the clapping. Déodat was still red in the face, but now it was from pride.

Everybody seemed pleased. As the meeting broke up, M. Laprade de la Chaize buttonholed the innkeeper.

'You can take my word for it, your astonishing boy will be with you before the day's out. Will you tell Mme Daranluz that with my compliments? And, by the way, I've heard great things of her cooking. I shall give myself the pleasure of sampling it presently, and I shall be glad if you would join me, M. Muche – that is if it won't damage your career to be seen lunching with a reactionary. M. Grillon has already promised me his company.'

At three o'clock Tistounet blew a flourish on his trumpet. It was not the retreat, in fact it wasn't a bugle-call at all, but the tune of an old and more than improper song, of which fortunately nobody knew the words.

M. le Préfet emptied his glass of Jurançon and smacked his lips.

'He certainly plays well, that *garde champêtre* of yours.'

Mme Fine arrived hugging four bottles to her bosom.

'Indeed he ought to,' she answered, perfectly at her ease, 'seeing as how he was a trumpeter in the Spahis. And now for the liqueurs. What's it to be? We've Cognac Muche, Armagnac Muche, Crème Basque Muche …'

With a neatly turned compliment to the distiller, M. de la Chaize managed nevertheless to avoid sampling his products. What he called for was some *anisette*, smuggled in from Spain, which was quite unprocurable in Perpignan. He had got the idea from Balthazar Durand, who had broadly hinted at its existence in one of his articles.

Mme Fine went red in the face, but she none the less went and fetched a bottle marked Menthe Verte from under the counter.

'Much as I dislike uniforms,' said the Prefect, changing the subject, 'I'm inclined to regret not having put on my own to greet our young heroes. We need a little ceremony, and if you would like to do me a great favour, my dear Muche, you'll go and put on your official sash.'

The mayor almost choked over his liqueur.

A quarter of an hour later a rocket shot up into the air from the roof of the Bastide and burst into a shower of stars.

It was the reply of the victors.

At the same time the people clustered in the Allée des Trois Tourelles saw the flag of the Friendly Society reverently hauled down.

Under orders of the Prefect, twelve of the Perpignan firemen had fallen in in front of the entrance to the Bastide. The mayor was there with his red-white-and-blue sash, looking sourly at the reporters and still more at the Press photographers, who were out to make the most of their opportunities.

Jokes were bandied about, but as minute after minute passed without developments the nerves of the crowd began to be affected, as though in sympathy with the almost unbearable feeling of suspense in the breasts of Mme Grosbelhomme and the other mothers.

More like a shrew-mouse than ever, Mme Martelot wept copiously into her handkerchief. Mme Muche hid behind her husband, holding herself in readiness for all eventualities. The baby Raphael in his mother's arms shrieked exasperatingly, until finally Mme Guartorella sat down unceremoniously on the road to pacify him.

At exactly four o'clock a creaking sound was heard, and the old drawbridge quivered. A stream of dirty water was flowing out through the postern grill into the moat.

Dead silence.

It was as though the inhabitants of Casteilcorbon suddenly realized the exceptional character of the moment they were living through. A sort of pride, vague and irrational, filled the breasts of the innkeeper, the schoolmaster, and even the rough blacksmith; above all, perhaps, of the poacher Guartorella.

Naturally, the presence of the Prefect, the firemen standing to attention, and the mayor's sash counted for a good deal, but, whatever it was, nobody felt like laughing.

Slowly the heavy bridge began to move with the clanking of chains that had ten days previously put the fear of God into the *garde champêtre*.

Water continued to pour out into the moat, and so tense was the silence of the crowd that the splash of it could be heard by everyone. Arnold Laprade's thoughts had skipped back a few centuries to the fortress of Rochebaron, perched high above Bas-en-Basset, in which his ancestors had been beleaguered, and which made the command of a Prefecture seem very small beer indeed.

Soon, to almost everyone's surprise, the portcullis came into view, for few had been aware of its existence.

When the bridge had only one foot more to go, a sudden clamour burst out. It came from the church bells, rung by the Abbé Escoutou, who felt that, since the arrival of the Prefect, civil authority was tending to eclipse his own, and who was determined that the Church should play its part, too, in the re-establishment of peace.

Viette, sitting on her father's shoulders, was the first to spot Pierrot, and she shouted and waved her hands.

'And there's Boulou and Barbette.'

The dogs barked furiously behind the portcullis. Their reappearance added to the general stupefaction.

'Can anybody see my Tatave?' asked Mme Grosbelhomme anxiously, standing on tiptoe and craning her neck.

But with the pealing of the bells nobody heard her.

It wasn't surprising if she had difficulty in recognizing her boy, as his face was half concealed by his helmet.

'Good heavens! How tiny they look,' thought the Prefect. 'Like little birds in a cage.'

Guillaume Muche was the first to venture on to the bridge. Striding up to the boys, who were holding on to the bars of the portcullis, he roared:

'Why the hell don't you come out?'

Thoroughly intimidated, the boys could find nothing to answer.

'Come out of there, will you?'

Come out? Easier said than done. With all their strength combined they wouldn't have been able to lift one tenth of the weight of that portcullis.

'So it comes to this,' thought the mayor; 'they've been having us on. If they've held out so long, it was merely because they didn't know how to get out.'

With that, the flood-gates of his wrath were suddenly opened wide and he poured out on the unhappy boys all the spleen which, hitherto, the presence of the Prefect had kept in check. And his abuse was richly interlarded with threats.

Pierrot stood still, listening gravely.

'There you are!' he said to himself. 'That's grown-ups all over!'

In vain did Tatave urge him to give the order for the drawbridge to be raised again. Pierrot was at the end of his courage. What was the good of prolonging the struggle against so unscrupulous an enemy?

Perhaps it was just as well that Tatave's advice was ignored. M. Guillaume Muche might well have been crushed between the drawbridge and the portcullis. If not, he would have had to jump into the moat.

The firemen had to take charge, jacking up the portcullis inch by inch. With an air of great dignity, the mayor walked back to the bank of the moat, prompted in part by the presence of the two yapping dogs who would in a minute or two be released. He rejoined the Prefect, who was graciously allowing a group of journalists to interview him; he was not the man to miss an opportunity of increasing his popularity.

The portcullis was now high enough for the boys to get out without crawling ignominiously. The dogs, of course, had been out long since, but then dogs have no dignity to preserve.

It was Cisco who thought of the journalist.

'Hey! What about our prisoner?'

'Gosh! We've forgotten all about him. He's still in that stinking hole.'

'What a pity!' said Tatave. 'We could have led him out in triumph. But perhaps it's not too late.'

But Pierrot shook his head.

'No. Let him be. He's had enough. We don't want to rub it in. It wouldn't add anything to our victory.'

Riquet had caught sight of the surly blacksmith in the crowd and was already trembling. Cisco, on the contrary, was quite unmoved by the mayor's threats.

'Don't take any notice of what he says. We all know him. When he flies into a rage he doesn't know what he's saying.'

'Come on, chaps. We'll go now,' said Pierrot. 'Victorin, you'd better carry the flag.'

'Oughtn't we to sing something?' asked Georget.

'No. Just fall in behind me. Blood and Freedom!'

Holding his head high, the little chief marched boldly forward. The red-and-green flag, somewhat discoloured by ten days' weather, floated out in the breeze displaying its motto: *All for one. One for all.*

Fébo brought up the rear, limping slightly, as the damp air of the Bastide had awakened his rheumatism.

The slanting rays of the sun shone on the knights' helmets, which had been specially polished for the occasion. The church bells pealed.

The firemen were brought to attention. M. Arnold Laprade de la Chaize took his hat off with a sweep. Carried away by his example, François Tistounet drew himself up stiffly and saluted.

Everyone stood stock still.

Did the grown-ups really understand for once? Did they understand these children and respect their high ideals?

At all events there was one who did – the aristocratic Prefect from Perpignan.

But alas! ...

Instinctively Mme Fine rushed forward to meet her son. And it was only then that she suddenly came to realize that he was the leader, the culprit, the one responsible.

It was too much for her. Swept off her feet by an irresistible impulse, the result of ten days and ten nights of anxiety, she raised her hand.

She didn't think. With all the fierceness of her maternal instinct ... Smack! Smack! ... she slapped the triumphant Pierrot on both cheeks ...

The following morning, on Thursday, 10 November, the boys sat in class.

The schoolmaster had taken somewhat longer than usual over blowing his nose, as though at grips with some inward emotion.

That was all. No reproaches. No allusions even, at least nothing direct.

Only a gentle and somewhat rambling homily on the virtues of patience and industry, with special reference to the life of *Apis mellifica*, the honey-bee.

Grown-ups? Yes, indeed! A strange race! But if in some of the households of Casteilcorbon the provisions of the armistice convention were already a dead letter it is all the more pleasant to dwell on the fact that, whenever she came to sweep out the classroom, Maria duly received a slice of bread lavishly spread with the produce of the said *Apis mellifica*, from which observance two of our ex-knights were able to deduce that the secret clause of the treaty would be no less scrupulously honoured.

During break the six boys gathered by common accord on the far side of the playground, over by the Tour de la Reine.

'I tell you what,' said Cisco, 'I've got an idea. Being knights is a wash-out. But there's no reason why we shouldn't be pirates. During the holidays, I mean. We'd go over to the sea, near where my Uncle Ricardo lives. We'd take a boat …'

'We don't know anything about boats.'

'I do. I'd be the pilot. Riquet could see to the motor. Victorin could row when we ran out of petrol. Tatave would keep the log. We might even take Fébo as chief steward.'

'What about me?' asked Georget.

'You could be master-at-arms.'

François Tistounet was standing outside the school gate. The mayor had told him to keep a discreet eye on the boys when they went back to school. Grisouille, inquisitive as ever and always on the roam, came and put his head familiarly on the *garde champêtre*'s shoulder.

'Well? What do you think of them now?' asked François, having no one else to talk to. 'You see? Good as gold. I always said we'd get them in the end.'

So far Pierrot had said nothing. He was still chewing the cud of his humiliation.

'Not a bad idea,' he said at last, 'but I don't see that there's anything for me in it.'

The others looked at him with dismay.

'Nothing for you? Why, you'd be the Chief Pirate and captain of the ship. We couldn't do without you.'

At those words, Pierrot smiled again, revealing the dimple he had kept ever since he was a baby.

'All right,' he said, 'you can count me in. We'd go off to the Islands and tame strange animals. We'd start a new country where there'd be no more grown-ups …'

'You see,' said Tistounet again. 'Good as gold, I tell you. Good as gold.'

Some other Penguin fiction
is described on the
remaining pages

JOHN BUCHAN

New writers of adventure stories are constantly being compared
with John Buchan, but the standard he sets is difficult to match
with its brisk narrative and ingenious imagination. He has the
knack of leading his characters into the most difficult and confus-
ing situations, and yet resolving their problems satisfactorily,
leaving none of the ends untied. His novels are almost all set in
periods of international crisis, but he keeps his sense of proportion
– a very Scottish characteristic – for big events and his feeling of
wonder for little things.

The Three Hostages was the first of his novels to be published as
a Penguin in April 1953. In 1956, ten of his books were published
simultaneously, a compliment first paid to G. B. Shaw and H. G.
Wells. Those now available are

THE THIRTY-NINE STEPS

THE ISLAND OF SHEEP

GREENMANTLE

MR STANDFAST

THE THREE HOSTAGES

which tell of the adventures of Richard Hannay, a South African
mining engineer who has a successful career in the British Army
as a spy-catcher, and

HUNTINGTOWER

in which the Gorbals band of Diehards protects a princess.

ELEPHANT BILL

J. H. WILLIAMS

1120

'Elephant Bill' is the name by which Lt-Col. J. H. Williams was known throughout Burma, where he spent over twenty years in the jungle, living with elephants and their riders, working with them in the vast teak-forests. His life's work was the training, management, and well-being of elephants. He has stories to tell of elephants in every aspect of their lives: of the wild herds and the lonely tuskers, of elephants in love and anger, of mother elephants and their calves, of rogue elephants, tigers and ghost-tigers, of elephants hauling great teak-trunks down from the mountains to the river.

The thrilling stories on almost every page are the more impressive for the quiet modesty of the writing, which is full of the author's humour and of the gentleness and charm which won him the confidence of the remarkable animals under his care.

During the war, when the Japanese overran Burma, Elephant Bill became 'Elephant Adviser' to the Fourteenth Army. In that capacity he organized the recruiting of elephants and their riders from behind the Japanese lines, and their employment in the jungle country on bridge-building and other military tasks. During the big Japanese advance on India he brought out as many elephants as possible by a new route over precipitous mountain-tracks and through pathless jungle. This fact surpassed Hannibal's crossing of the Alps, and is the climax of a book full of interest and excitement.

GERALD DURRELL

THE OVERLOADED ARK

The story of a six months' collecting trip made by Gerald Durrell and John Yealland to the great rain forests of the Cameroons in West Africa to bring back alive some of the fascinating animals, birds, and reptiles of the region and to see one of the few parts of Africa that remained as it had been when the continent was first discovered.

'. . . a book of immense charm. The author handles English prose with the same firmness and discretion that he used to dispense towards the pangolins and lemuroids that fell to his snares and huntsmen in the Cameroons. How seldom it is that books of this kind are written by those who can write . . . a genuinely amusing writer.' – *Time and Tide* (1228)

THE BAFUT BEAGLES

The Bafut Beagles was the name which Gerald Durrell gave to the pack of African and mongrel dogs with which he hunted and captured many of the oddest and most elusive creatures in the Cameroons. His adventures in pursuit of such fauna as flying mice and booming squirrels were often as strange as the animals themselves. (1266)

NOT FOR SALE IN THE U.S.A.

ONE OF OUR SUBMARINES

EDWARD YOUNG

1000

Commander Young joined up as a Sub-Lieutenant in the Royal Naval Volunteer Reserve in April 1940, and four months later entered the submarine service, the first R.N.V.R. officer ever to do so. After three years of almost continuous war patrols in all weathers, from Norway to the Mediterranean, and after escaping from a sunken submarine, he became the first 'wavy-striper' to command an operational submarine. This is his story. It was placed by the *Sunday Times* 'in the very highest rank of books about the war'.

The main part of the narrative describes the author's time in command; and besides being an account of H.M. Submarine *Storm*'s wartime operations, it is at the same time the story of a very amateur sailor learning an unusual job.

'Here, in unaffected terms, so openly written that at the end of the book it seems that the author has barely passed muster as a submarine captain, is as near the whole truth about conditions in a British submarine as one is likely to get.' – *The Times Literary Supplement*

NOT FOR SALE IN THE U.S.A.

C. S. FORESTER

'One of the best storytellers alive'. – Edwin Muir in the *Listener*

Ten books by this author were published
simultaneously as Penguins.

MIDSHIPMAN HORNBLOWER

A SHIP OF THE LINE

FLYING COLOURS

THE COMMODORE

belong to his famous 'Hornblower' series, while

DEATH TO THE FRENCH

THE GUN

BROWN ON RESOLUTION

THE AFRICAN QUEEN

THE GENERAL

THE SHIP

are stories of the Army or Navy.

PAYMENT DEFERRED

'A striking study in suspense and terror. There is force and horror
amazingly well rendered.' – *Daily News*

NOT FOR SALE IN THE U.S.A.

JOHN WYNDHAM

THE DAY OF THE TRIFFIDS

The Day of the Triffids and *The Kraken Wakes* are among the very few books of their kind that can stand comparison with *The War of the Worlds*, *The Time Machine*, and the other astonishing science-novels of H. G. Wells. This book is fantastic, frightening, but entirely plausible; for John Wyndham combines an extraordinarily inventive imagination with the technical skill of a first-class writer. Not only does he make his story seem scientifically possible, but the characters he creates are living people.† (993)

THE KRAKEN WAKES

The almost imperceptible beginnings of the awakening and rise to power of forces from beneath the surface of the sea, and the terrifying consequences of this new threat to the world, are seen through the eyes of a radio script writer and his wife.* (1075)

THE CHRYSALIDS

This is the story of life in a frightening world, where all development is unpredictable and stability is upset by uncontrollable genetic mutations.* (1308)

*NOT FOR SALE IN THE U.S.A.
†NOT FOR SALE IN THE U.S.A. OR CANADA